A KISS IN THE WIND

Jennifer Bray-Weber

ISBN-10: 1514307111
ISBN-13: 978-1514307113

ACKNOWLEDGMENTS

It's true. Writing is a solitary venture. But a novel doesn't get from a budding story idea to the hands of readers without an enormous amount of support. With that, I am fortunate to have the following people in my life.

My deepest gratitude to…

…first and foremost, my husband Mark for his love and patience as I shoot for the moon.

Stacey Purcell, Melissa Ohnoutka and William Simon, aka The Usual Suspects, who have been my moral support through enough trials and tribulations to send any sane person running in the other direction. Either that or they find me entertaining enough to keep around.

…Northwest Houston RWA and the Ruby-Slippered Sisterhood for their generous encouragement and invaluable friendships.

…John Roundtree, Rhonda Morrow, Cheri Jetton, Candi Wall, Tess Grillo and Marie-Claude Bourque, all who have read my pages and survived.

…my parents and daughters whom I continuously strive to make proud.

…the incredible team at Carina Press, particularly my editor, Denise Nielsen, for believing in this adventure and the sexy pirates and spirited women who inhabit my world.

CHAPTER 1

Puerto Plata, Hispaniola, 1726

"Crazy wench. Let go!"

Marisol tightened her grip on the coarse barrel of the pistol poised a mere inch from her face. Death's diseased aroma wafted over her with the depraved wretch's breath. A frenzy of alarm pumped through her veins, fueling new untapped strength. "Bloody hell, I will!"

She struggled with him, unwilling to release his gun and reach for her own weapon. She pushed and pulled with the ruffian in a gruesome dance of sorts, a ballet amid the squalid dregs and wet filth of the dark alley. Their curses and grunts chased the shrouded silence back up the stone walls. No passerby would take notice, no more than they would a cheap strumpet and her jack.

Marisol slipped on the slick cobblestones and, losing her balance, brought the vile man down with her.

The pistol went off. An unforgiving percussion echoed down the alley.

He landed on top of her, knocking the wind from her lungs. Sharp pain sliced through her back with the force of the fall. A moment passed, then another.

The man's weight crushed against her. She gulped shallow,

tainted breaths in the pocket of air between his shirt collar and sweaty neck. *I must get free.* Marisol thrashed beneath the cur. Fear urging her on, she pressed against his chest and shoved him off, rolling him to his back. She scuttled to her knees. But he didn't move, didn't get up to finish her off.

What have I done?

Marisol dropped the gun. Blood on her hands trickled down between shaky fingers. She stared at them, turning her hands over to see the crooked red pathways on her skin. Even in the shadows, the deep color glistened. Slowly, she curled her fingers into fists, resting them on her knees, and looked down at the dead man before her. The blood from his chest wound filtered through his tunic, spreading down his side. Spent gunpowder still singed her nose.

Numb emotions lingered beneath her breastbone. She willed herself not to think of him as a man who might be mourned by someone who loved him, a mother, or a wife with children. Would they be waiting for him? Wondering when he would return home?

No. No pity would be spared for the likes of him, a paltry criminal. Had Alain taught her nothing about survival? *Warm your rum with the blood of another, for if the bastard gets the chance, your course will be run and the devil will have you.*

She would not let the compassion seize her heart.

Leave that for the weak-minded.

Marisol took one quick glance around the darkened back street. She wiped the blood against her lap then reached into the dead man's coat, searching his pockets. She pulled out a pouch containing silver coins, three of them. Marisol forced a smile. How fortunate. Something for her troubles. She stuffed the pouch into the folds of her dress.

Continuing her search, her hand grazed across paper in another pocket. She smiled again as she picked up and read the letter for which she'd been searching. The missive was cryptic but given more time she would be able to decipher it. With any luck, it would reveal the information she so desperately sought, information that could lead her to her missing brother. She would do anything to find Monte. Marisol glanced down at the corpse. Perhaps she had become too desperate. *Foolish man. You really should've been more careful.*

Urgent voices carried down the mud brick walls. She inhaled sharply, her heart hammering inside her chest. Spanish soldiers. She needed to find a way to escape undetected. Her options were limited. She could not go back down into the alley, to be sure, not with the soldiers coming.

She scrambled to her feet and fled to the obscure darkness of a shadowy wall, feeling her way along until she came to a door. Over her shoulder, she chanced one last look at the dead man. She wished it hadn't happened that way, but it had. *'Twas his blood or mine.*

Gripping the letter tight, Marisol sent up a silent prayer that the door wouldn't be locked. She pushed open the entry, relieved by her good fortune, and scurried inside. Pressing her back against the door, she reached down to latch it securely. She took a deep breath before looking at the letter in her dirty hand, catching sight of her dress as she did so. The smear of blood had already begun to darken, no longer red with life, as it stained the coarse wool fabric. She groaned in frustration. A change of clothing would be in order lest she be caught. Alain would be furious with her if he had to rescue her again.

A single candle sconce lit the narrow hallway. Spirited music and voices drifted from the end of the passage. Silence lay beyond the two doors on her right. She tried the first door, locked. With the second, she had better luck.

Scanning the small room to ensure she found no one inside, she crossed over to the oil lamp and turned up the flame. Perfumed oils clung thick to the air. Beads and stockings hung from a dirty mirror. Two rumpled beds leaned against a wall along with several open trunks. A public house. And a seamy one, at that.

Colorful dresses with gaudy embellishments lay draped askew on the trunk lids. Marisol rummaged through the clothes, picking out what she hoped would be an inconspicuous dress. She changed quickly, selecting a blue one trimmed with a pink tucker that fitted too snug against her breasts. No time to fuss over it. She stuffed the pouch of coins and the letter into the pocket of the skirt and rolled her soiled dress up, tossing it into a corner.

She had to get out of there. Marisol couldn't go back into the alley. Leaving through a crowded tavern was not the best idea, but what choice did she have?

She passed a laughing couple in the hall.

"Better get in there." The woman, her arm draped across her companion's shoulder, tilted her head back toward the noise. "The men are getting restless for company."

"Aye, we are." Her fellow grabbed her bottom tightly.

She laughed again, pushing past Marisol into the room behind her. "Must be the new girl."

Marisol groaned again. This might get tricky. She stepped into the front room of the tavern. It was early evening and already rowdy men, rumming and gaming, filled the brightly lit place. Any one of them could be the potential recipient of the letter she had safely tucked away. She couldn't rule out the few women about, sitting on laps or serving the drink either. Even the trio of musicians who played a lively tune was suspect. Heavy tobacco smoke filled her lungs and stung her eyes as she looked for the exit.

She skirted her way around the tables. Halfway through the room, a rough hand grabbed her wrist.

"Dance." The man swayed in his seat but his hard stare was even.

"No. I don't—"

"Dance!" The man's drunken shout attracted the notice of several other patrons in the tavern, including that of an attractive man at a nearby table. The striking fellow eyed her with roguish intent. His eyes fixed on Marisol, he said something to the pretty woman who sat to his left, her arms spooled around his muscular biceps, and she threw her head back in a peal of laughter. Leaning forward, he placed an arm across the tabletop. He was handsome indeed, with golden hair that hung freely past the shoulders of his dark brown waistcoat, and Marisol found herself straightening her spine beneath his scrutiny.

She cursed under her breath. She did not need this sort of attention. Surely someone would recognize her.

The drunk yanked her down to level with his face. His breath fouled with the stench of alcohol and sickness. "Dance fer me, or I'll gut ye." He pulled back his fearnought jacket, flashing a rusted gully knife tucked under his belt.

Marisol raised her eyebrows. Had the room not been so crowded, she would have felt obliged to deal with the bilge rat, and without much effort. But she couldn't. Not with so many watching. She didn't know which was worse, facing Alain's wrath for stirring up a den of soused men or humiliating herself by dancing. Oh decisions, decisions.

"Dance, whore."

That did it. Her mind made up, Marisol grabbed the vermin's wrist, readying to flip him out of his chair. Alain's wrath be damned. Instead, she became distracted by a young seaman who rushed through the door and moved swiftly to the side of the blond man she had noticed watching her, bending low and whispering in his ear. *Damn.* Marisol's gut coiled with instinct as her admirer's countenance sharpened. *The message must be about the dead man in the alley.* If he was the one the letter was intended for…she needed to find out more about him. And now. Before he finished his ale and left.

Out of the corner of her eye she watched as he dismissed the seaman and turned to the woman, dismissing her, too. She wore a pout of disappointment as she left the table.

Marisol loosened her grip on the drunken sailor's wrist. "If you would like for me to dance, sir, you must release me."

He smiled, his teeth jagged and stained. "Aye, dance." He released her wrist and sat back in his chair for the show.

Marisol snatched a glass of rum off his table, downing it in one gulp. The liquor burned a trail down her throat and she savored the smooth taste. If she had to dance, then a little jolt to her senses would help her get through the horror of it. She moved her hips, first slowly in little circles, then quicker with the beat of the music. Lifting her arms above her head, she clapped to the rhythm, twirling away from the grinning man grabbing for her. She twisted her torso and swung her elbows around. The tavern came alive with whoops and vulgar raillery. Those not inclined to watch their hands of cards clapped along.

If she could drink a couple more half pints of the liquor, well, she might be able to get through it. She reminded herself that these sots didn't care that she couldn't dance. She could have wallowed in pig slop and they still would want her entertainment. The damn bastards.

The drunkard stood, reaching for her again, and again she twirled away. The whirl of the room and the rowdy crowd smeared in her vision as she spun. With each intermittent glimpse of the blond rogue, she slowed. He was finishing off his cup. Closer and closer she moved to him. She pushed off with her foot to make another turn, but her right toe caught on her left heel. Just as she tripped forward, he rose from his chair. She crashed into his chest and the momentum knocked him backward to the floor. They both landed with a thump, Marisol sprawled on top of him. An eruption of laughter exploded in the room, and the scoundrels returned to their own vices.

Her heart stopped as she lifted herself on her palms. His eyes met with hers and they were the most beautiful shade of green she had ever seen. She struggled not to fall into them, under their hypnotic pull. Her gaze lowered to his lips that curved into a wicked grin. She swallowed hard and bit her lower lip. Dimples appeared in his whiskered cheeks.

He cleared his throat. “Excuse me.”

Shaking her head, she dragged her eyes back to his. “Begging your pardon.” Could those dimples get any deeper? His firm grasp tightened around her waist as he rolled her off him and onto her bottom.

“Graceful.” He laughed. “You’re not well seasoned to dance, are you?”

She tamped down the mild agitation building against him. “I was tripped,” she said flatly.

“I can see that.” He took her ankle, lifting it. Teasing her, he smirked. “Hazardous little imps.” He rubbed her ankle above her boot gently with the pad of his thumb. “Are you hurt?”

His calloused skin scratched a rough circle that sent a pleasurable sensation through her, agitating her further. She shook her head.

“Good,” he said. “Name’s Blade. Blade Tyburn.” He smiled, but did not release her ankle.

Why did that name sound familiar? A rapid search through her mind for some recognition came up empty. She returned his smile while plucking her leg from his grip. “Marisol Castellan.” Curse it. She told him her name. Her bloody real name. Damn his bedeviling dazzle.

"'Ey." The drunkard teetered over to them. "Git yer hands offin' 'er." He reached down and grabbed Blade Tyburn by his shoulder. "She wit' me."

Tyburn's smile faded as he turned his head only a fraction, his stare cutting down to the man's grasp. "You'd best remove your hand, friend." He paused to leer up at the lout. "Before you lose it." The deadly tone of his voice left little doubt of his seriousness.

"You threatenin' me, boy?"

"Threats are wasted on your ilk."

"Mind yerself, Porter," someone called out. "That's Capt'n Tyburn of the *Rissa* yer rallyin' ta."

The drunkard's eyes rounded with clarity and he snatched his arm away. "M' pardon, Capt'n Tyburn." He averted his gaze to the floor in a submissive nod.

The *Rissa.* The *Rissa.* She was certain she'd heard of the ship before. But she couldn't remember where.

The captain rose to his feet. "Be gone, then." He turned back to Marisol, extending his hand to help her up.

She gazed upon his strong hand and questioned if it was wise to touch him again. His allure distracted her from her intentions. She shrugged. No one had ever accused her of being wise. She let him pull her up. The space between them was far too scarce for her liking. Marisol felt small before him, standing both in the shadow of his brawny breadth and his very agreeable good looks. "Um, I give you my thanks."

"Capt'n Tyburn."

The captain turned back to Porter, frowning that the drunk still staggered behind him.

Porter pointed at Marisol. "Reckon I'll take 'er back, now."

Marisol planted her hands on her hips. "And I reckon you won't." She didn't fancy herself as a man's property, not even Alain's. Nothing boiled her pot like a man staking claim where it didn't belong.

"I came 'ere ta get me a woman." Porter's brow furrowed. "Thadda be you."

She tilted her head. "Pity. You're going to be disappointed, then."

Porter took a step forward. Captain Tyburn stopped him with a solid hand to his chest. "You're a bold one in a clam. I believe I told you to be gone. Not only have you ignored me, you are harassing a lady. This, I don't accept."

"She ain't no lady."

Marisol gave a chuckle. Something else she had never been accused of.

The captain smiled curiously at her. He gave Porter a shove backward. "Take your leave before you get yourself killed."

The drunkard stumbled back, bracing himself on a chair to avoid tumbling. He grabbed a liquor bottle off a table and swung high at Captain Tyburn. Deflecting the swing with his left forearm, Tyburn delivered a crunching blow squarely to Porter's nose. His head jerked back, blood spilling from his nostrils, and the poor fellow collapsed to the floor out cold.

No one in the room cared enough to take notice of the incident. In a common place like this, brawls must happen regularly. All the better for her. But if she didn't get out of there soon, Alain would string her up.

He despised rescuing her from bad situations. He said it made him look heroic, a trait he didn't want to be saddled with.

"I suppose I should thank you for defending me." Marisol hoped she didn't sound too dismissive.

"Nonsense." He bent to remove the bottle from Porter's hand and set it on the table. "Any fool can see you don't belong in this tavern."

A gentleman, blast it. Well, this should be easy. But when he turned back to her with his crooked smile, Marisol thought she might melt. It had been a long while since she felt that way.

"Why are you here?" he said. "This is a dangerous place for an unescorted lady."

Dangerous? Tsk. 'Twas nothing where she was concerned. "I had a bit of business." She smiled, satisfied with her answer. "And you? Can I assume you come here often?"

"Occasionally." He nodded to someone behind her. She peered over her shoulder to a group of men in the corner. "Tonight, however, I had some business of my own." The men got up from their table, not bothering to finish their drinks, and left the tavern.

"Would you mind seeing my way outside?" She turned to face him but avoided his eyes for fear she would forget what brought her to him. "I would hate to have another ruffian pressure me to dance for him."

"As would I." Captain Tyburn held out his elbow for her. "Someone could get hurt."

She scowled at him but he laughed heartily. It was a rich, bold laugh. An infectious laugh. She couldn't help herself and joined in with his good humor. She took his arm and let him lead her to the doors.

It was quieter outside, but the din of the night's debauchery carried out into the street. The salty air hung heavy from the lack of the sea breeze, leaving Marisol's skin clammy. The moonless sky held a dark court despite the many stars.

"So, you are a ship's captain?" she asked, scanning their surroundings. Not many people out this night. Though she was not from Puerto Plata, Marisol found it odd there wasn't more activity about. They were only a few blocks from the port and she would have expected more bustling than a few wayward pub dwellers.

"Aye. Are you expecting someone?"

Marisol was startled by the captain staring down at her. "No."

Wavy locks of his hair cast shadows across his angular face in the flickering light of the lamp torches. The effect heightened her awareness of him as a dangerous man. Probably more dangerous than she cared to know. She swallowed back her nerves. "Will your business have you staying in port long?" His response may either justify or rule out her suspicion he was the recipient of the letter.

He let down his elbow, releasing his accompaniment of her. "That depends upon the discretion of another."

She frowned. What did he mean by that?

Three men sprinted across the street, disappearing in the darkness. Behind her, Marisol heard voices in the alley. Damn. Time to go.

"Some friendly advice, Miss Castellan. Find yourself a safe place tonight, away from the port." He glanced past her. "I sense there will be trouble this night." Looking back at her, his eyes settled on her mouth. "A good deal of trouble." He reached up to caress her cheek then cupped her chin in his large hand. "You are so lovely. I should wish to meet with you upon my next visit to Puerto Plata."

Another ripple of desire spread through her. He rubbed his thumb across her lips and, for a moment, she thought her legs might liquefy from under her. She parted her lips and closed her eyes. In the inviting fog of his erotic gesture, she slipped, letting the tip of her tongue lightly wet his thumb. He smiled and nodded once. "Yes, you would be a most pleasing attraction to hasten my return."

Marisol stepped back, narrowing her eyes. She had nearly let him seduce her. It would take more than a gentle touch and a few well-placed words for her to succumb to a man's charm. "Unfortunately, Captain Tyburn, I, myself, am just passing through."

"Oh?" He appeared too relaxed and dropped his hand to rest upon the sword hanging from his hip. "What ship are you sailing with?"

"The *Egeria.*"

His smile thinned.

"Bound for Havana," she added.

"Would you like me to see your way to the ship?"

"Thank you. You are very kind, Captain Tyburn. But I believe I've played upon your kindness too long."

He took a step forward. "I'm certain you wouldn't mind the company."

She stepped farther back. "Another time, perhaps."

He raised his hands in deference. "I'll be a perfect gentleman."

Marisol had her doubts. "I'm sure you would be. But no."

"A lady shouldn't be out on the streets alone at this hour. 'Tis unsafe."

"The *Egeria* is the first ship at the dock. I'll be fine."

"It wouldn't be a bother."

"No, no." Why was he being so persistent? Agitation crept back in and she folded then unfolded her arms. "I appreciate the offer. Really. I should go now." Before Alain came looking for her.

"Of course." Captain Tyburn bowed. "It has been a pleasure

to meet you, Miss Marisol Castellan."

"And you, as well. I bid thee a fair good-night." She made a quick curtsy and walked away from the captain. Her steps were brisk, but not because of any lurking danger. And not because of the upbraiding she was sure to receive from Alain for being gone so long. No, it was Captain Blade Tyburn. She needed distance from him and his enticing eyes.

Marisol threw a glance over her shoulder for a last look at the magnificent captain. The light in which he stood seemed to not come from the street lamps, but rather from him, radiating from him like the rising sun. Turning back toward the quay, she ran her hand over the five objects in her skirt and grinned.

* * *

Blade admired Marisol Castellan before she disappeared down the street toward the docks. Though he couldn't see her anymore, the image of her swaying hips as she hurried away burned into his mind. He shifted to relieve the pressure in his trousers still throbbing from her sensual response to him touching her lips. She was something to behold, an exquisite beauty. Her long black hair shone with a promise of silky softness and her creamy brown eyes reminded him of tea stains on the whitest of lace. He smirked as he remembered the smooth feel of her ankle and the curvature of her firm calf. And that body, that ample, luscious body. Oh, the things he would like to do to that bonny lass.

He found it charming how she tugged on her ear each time she had lied to him. Blade was certain she hadn't even realized she had done it. She wasn't sailing on the *Egeria.* That merchantman ship had just arrived from Havana and would be heading to Puerto Rico. He didn't know why she was in the tavern, but it wasn't for business. A woman in The Laughing Dog conducted only one kind of trade and clearly that was not the case with Marisol. So why had she lied? He wondered if it had anything to do with the dried blood under her fingernails.

"Capt'n."

The last remnants of her sweet image faded with the sound of his first mate's voice. Willie came up from behind to stand next to him.

"What do you have for me?"

Willie spat on the ground. "Well, Spanish soldiers found a fella with a hole in his chest back there in the alley." He thumbed toward the corner of the drinking house. "Probably your go-b'tween."

The news did not come as a surprise to Blade. One of his crewmen had already informed him there had been a commotion outside involving soldiers. He suspected then his meeting with the messenger had been postponed indefinitely and it was time to move out.

"And what does our Spanish rat have to say?" His tone sounded more sardonic than he intended. Traitors turned Blade's stomach. He despised men who would not claim loyalty to any one faction, no matter for whose betterment. It was cowardice. For that reason, Blade preferred not to know the name of any man willing to talk against their countrymen so as not to cloud his judgment. At times, however, he had to admit that for a few coins it was in his best interest to listen to gossip from an anonymous miscreant. "Did the soldiers find anything?"

Willie shook his head. "Nothin' but a pistol lying beside him."

Blade frowned. "That explains why they didn't storm the tavern looking for a killer."

"Aye, that it does." Willie spat again.

With the murder weapon beside the body, the soldiers would have nothing to search for. They would just assume the wound to be self-inflicted rather than waste time on another commoner's death. Pity.

Nodding his head slowly in contemplation, Blade frowned. His mission had become more difficult. Without the information intended for him, he would have to rely on his instincts to see him through this. And his instinct right now was to ready the men.

"Who's anchored since our arrival?"

"The *Sugar Lady.*" Willie pulled out a small pouch from his belt. Opening it, he grinned. "Got me some fine tobacco from one of the *Sugar Lady*'s hands." He stuck his nose inside and inhaled deep. "Mighty good, I'd say."

Willie held out the pouch to Blade. Blade ignored the offer.

"And?"

"Port's busy tonight." Willie tied the tobacco back on his belt. "B'sides the two merchantmen." Willie tugged on the sack to cinch it tight, adding, "The *Tigris* and *Sablewing* have dropped anchor."

"*Sablewing.* Isn't that Carrion's ship?" That was all Blade needed. Carrion. That bastard had always been trouble. Real trouble. His bloody acts of piracy had been responsible for muddling up so many of the *Rissa*'s own questionable affairs and negotiations. Blade's mood darkened by the minute.

"Aye. It's Carrion, all right." Willie looked toward the docks. "What do ya suppose he's doin' here? Do ya think he's here for the same reason we are?"

Blade followed his mate's gaze, hoping for a glimpse of a raven-haired beauty returning to him for a night of pleasure. No such luck. The night held something more sinister ahead for this part of the island.

"Can't be sure," Blade replied. "I doubt a man as business-minded as Charles Windham would be stupid enough to commission too many in his endeavor. His illicit good standing with the *audiencia* is not nearly secure enough to keep him from a chopping block." But then, a rich man paying favors to the Spanish high courts didn't always mean a shrewd man.

As much as he loathed doing it, Blade had to meet with Carrion and find out what the captain was doing in Puerto Plata. And soon. Carrion must be behind the unease creeping into the town. The evening was still relatively young, too early for a raid. Yet the signs were there. He had to find out what the pirate was up to. Crossing paths with the desperado during this commission from Windham didn't settle well with Blade. Carrion wouldn't hesitate to impinge on Blade if it meant lining his coffer. Particularly if that meant denying Blade of his fee for safely delivering Windham's precious cargo.

Several men darted between the shadows and Willie reached for his pistol. Blade stayed Willie's draw. "Go round up the men. Prepare arms." Blade checked his own pistol. "And have Sam meet me back inside. I'm going to pay Carrion a visit."

Adjusting the green sash and sword tied at his waist, Blade had a sudden moment of paralyzing realization. "Shit!"

"Capt'n?" Willie watched him as he patted his coat, digging into his pockets.

"Son of a bitch. It's gone." Rage burned up Blade's neck as he felt its heat redden his face. "It's gone," he repeated. His cameo, his most prized possession, was gone. "That little tramp," he snarled.

Marisol Castellan had proven she was a hell of a lot more than some pretty chit. And now she had much more to worry about than a tavern full of lewd drunks. The awful little thief better hope he didn't find her, because when he did, he was going to kill her.

CHAPTER 2

Black bay water lapped at the fat pilings slick with slime along the quay. The smell of rotten wood and decaying bait choked the sea air. From the edge of the docks, Marisol stared at the *Rissa.* The ship loomed silent against the still backdrop of the night. Captain Tyburn. The *Rissa.* There was something familiar about them, but she couldn't decide what. She let her eyes follow a rat as it scurried up a taut rope securing the boat dockside. The rodent stopped to gnaw for a moment on the line's fibers before crawling out of sight. The nagging feeling she should know more about the captain and his ship chewed at her mind.

"Where've you been?"

Without looking away from Tyburn's brigantine, Marisol waited for Luc to join her. "In my quarters," she said.

"That's not what I meant, and you know it."

She glanced at her older brother. He stood scrutinizing the ship before them, slowly taking in each detail. He had a handsome profile, though his dark curls drove her crazy when they covered his eyes.

"I suppose."

Luc huffed and turned to glare at her. "You took off on your own, didn't you?"

His eyes. He had their mother's eyes. Marisol saw nothing but love in those beautiful brown eyes. Even when he swore he would string her up by her toes, Luc's eyes always gave away how he really felt for her.

She shrugged in response.

"Damn it, Marisol." Luc slapped his hat on his thigh. "Alain is going to skin you alive when he finds out. He is not the forgiving sort."

"Who's going to tell him?" She tipped her head. "Are you going to tell him, Luc?"

He dropped his gaze in frustration. "You know I won't."

No, of course he wouldn't. Although it would have been easier on him than to always cover up her misadventures and messes. She certainly was a trial for her poor brother.

The particulars of this evening she would keep to herself, especially that of the dead man. Luc would be better off not knowing. Her actions only served to cause him suffering, and he'd suffered enough. The burden of that death was hers and hers alone. But Marisol knew if she let it, guilt would eat at her dreams, torturing her with visions of his soul fleeing from eyes that dulled. She must not let that happen. Her only recourse was to push her remorse to the deepest corner of her mind.

"Here now." She smiled. "Do you want to know what I found?"

Luc laughed. "Found? Is that what you call it? Did you *find* this new dress?" He picked at the pink ruffle on her sleeve.

"Never mind that." She dug in her skirt, pulling out the letter she had taken earlier from the dead knave. "Do you know what this is?"

Luc watched Marisol wave the folded paper around.

"I hope not." He snatched it from her fingers. "There's blood on this."

His concerned eyes inspected her. "Are you all right? Are you hurt?"

"I'm fine."

"Marisol—"

"I'm fine, Luc."

"Then who's—Marisol, what did you do?"

"Never mind that." She must put an end to his questions and redirect his attention, for his sake as well as for hers. "Look on the inside."

Luc hesitated before opening it. Frowning, he turned the paper several times in his hands, trying to make sense of the writing.

"It's the rough coordinates and time for the interception of Windham's shipment of silver." She beamed, rather proud that she had deciphered the note. She had read and reread the message in her quarters under the dim flame of a single candle. Too much light coming from her room would have raised suspicion as they were barred from wasting the tallow unless needed. 'Twould do her no good to have been caught. So she'd memorized the words and blew out the candle before being discovered.

"How can you be sure?" Luc turned the page again.

"Really, Luc," she said. "You should learn to read."

She snatched the paper from his hands.

He clicked his tongue. "I know how to read."

"Something other than the names over the entrances to your favorite alehouses."

"Don't need to read. I just let Simone do the communicating for me," he said, patting the gleaming cutlass at his hip.

That was true enough. Luc exacted fatal precision with his sword. She had spent many hours watching him, learning from him, striving to be as good as he.

"All right, see here?" She pointed to the sole sentence. "*Gloria chante sept avec le lever du soleil des eaux nobles,*" she read. "Gloria sings seven with the sunrise of the noble waters. That is what it says." She looked up excitedly at Luc. "A ship called the *Gloria* will be coming from the east at high tide seven miles out." She could hardly contain her jubilation. "Windham has a ship named *Gloria.* Do you realize what this means?" Once she told Alain of the note, he would have to forgive her for disobeying his direct orders to not interfere.

"I know what you're thinking, Marisol, and it won't work." Luc shook his head. "He's not going to be pleased with you. He may even punish you."

Her smile faded. She knew what he would say next, dousing her mirth.

"You have no way of knowing if Monte is on that ship," he continued. "Alain is not willing to intercept a well-fortified ship to look for a ghost."

She puckered her mouth into a frown. Luc knew her well and he knew what motivated her. She had heard from a reliable source that her younger brother was seen in Santo Domingo and could be a sailor on one of Charles Windham's ships. Upon hearing the news, Marisol had decided she would find him at all costs.

"I miss Monte, too." Luc sighed. "But I've accepted him as dead. And you should do the same."

"His body was not found." Her voice caught in her retort. "He could still be out there."

"You and I both know Monte was an undisciplined bladder of air. Always impatient. Never following orders. I wish it weren't so. I really do."

He spoke true. Monte stubbornly believed he could outsmart anyone or anything. His arrogance got him into many brawls. Ask Monte and he would've said he never lost a fight, even when he was so battered, Luc had to carry him home. Aye, Monte was troublesome.

Luc put a comforting arm around her shoulders. *Here it comes. Here comes the same old drivel Luc spoon fed her when she insisted Monte was alive.*

"It was an accident, Marisol. It wasn't your fault that he didn't escape."

She refused to believe it. Monte was crafty enough to make it out alive. And if she ever stopped searching for him, her guilt would surely swallow her whole. It saddened her that Luc didn't believe in the possibility that Monte was alive. He was a great source of comfort to her, yet for some reason, he couldn't bring himself to support her quest to bring their missing brother home.

Well, if Luc wouldn't help she would continue her search alone. "I suppose you're right." She patted his hand that still lay on her shoulder. "Do you suppose Alain will still be interested in this letter?"

"Possibly." He paused. The shadows on his face only sharpened the tired lines around his eyes. "Do you want me to give it to him?"

She thought of Alain's punishments. As of late, she had been straining his patience beyond its tethered length. He wouldn't be lenient on her now, no matter her cozy position with him. What would he dole out to correct her bad behavior? It didn't matter. As part of his crew, she had to adhere to his orders. Her defiance really left him with no choice. She supposed she deserved whatever she would get. "No," she sighed. "I'll see to it myself."

Luc delivered a worried glance. She smirked, knowing she would likely talk her way out of trouble again if Alain found the note remarkable enough. He gave a low chuckle. He knew it, too. His laughter died as he returned his attention to the ship before them.

"What?" she asked. "Do you know this ship?"

"Aye," he answered. "The pirate ship, *Rissa.*"

Something in Luc's tone jogged her memory. It all came flooding back to her. She'd heard stories of the infallible ship and her conquests. Great battles she had won and immeasurable treasures she had garnered. It was believed among the tarry-breeks the sea over that the *Rissa* was cursed. For every voyage she embarked on, for every fortune she made, one on board must die. A trade for good fortune. Only those spawned from the devil could captain her.

"She's quiet tonight," Luc added.

Marisol hadn't noticed before. But he was right. There should be crewmen about. Even when the sailors caroused in port, some remained behind on duty to guard their ship and whatever she may carry in her hold. Marisol became more aware of the tenebrous brig and the ominous creaks of the quay around them. The darkened ship effused a foreboding sense. Bare masts like skeletal arms reached to the ebony sky. Ratlines resembled spider webs ready to snare a hapless soul who ventured too close. Somewhere in the shadows a door shut. They were being watched. Peripheral movement had her searching the vessel's bow.

"Why don't you go back to your cabin? You can give the letter to Alain later." Luc took a step back from the edge to the pier, pulling her along by her elbow. He must have felt the same baneful energy around them rolling in like poisonous sea mist from the ship. "Besides, you'll be safer there. I've got something important I must do. But if you want, later I can be with you when he returns."

"You know there is nothing you can do should he wish to punish me." While she appreciated his protective nature, she would not allow Luc to stand up to Alain for her. The act would be considered mutinous. She had no plans to be the cause of any more suffering to her brother. "I'll be fine. To prove it, I'll come directly to your quarters afterwards."

"Good." He nodded. "Later, then." He waved, casting one last glance to the *Rissa* as he turned toward the town.

She pretended to head for their ship for she knew Luc would look back. Let him think she followed his suggestion of returning to her quarters. She deliberately kept the letter within view a moment longer before returning it to her pocket. Then she, too, walked away from the docks and into the streets of Puerto Plata.

Alain had said they anchored here for the amber trade. Marisol wasn't so sure. He never revealed his true motives and they were most always selfish in nature. His rapacity played like a fine tuned instrument. If she struck the right chord, maybe she could pique his interest in the cargo the *Gloria* carried and convince him to chase her down. With the ship passing in the morning, she needed to get to him soon.

Crossing the square she spied Alain and two of his cohorts, Ben and Knuckles, duck under an open curtained doorway at the far end of the street. Another brothel. By now she should be used to his whoring. She blew out a disappointed sigh before she trotted after him. Marisol wished she could change him. God knew she'd tried.

She pushed through the red curtain. Several girls casually chatted with each other among the cushioned chairs and sofas in the room. An older woman wiping a glass clean behind the small bar looked up. Ben and Knuckles stood at the end of the counter. Three lusty molls negotiating socket money for their ribald services fingered the men's clothing, removing hats and running their hands through hair. The fellows couldn't have been happier with the attention.

Marisol caught sight of Alain in the back ascending the stairs to the bedrooms above. "Alain," she called.

"Marisol," he spat. "You'd better have a damn good reason for being here." He stood on the steps unabashed by the busty brunette beside him pawing her way over his body, tugging at him to follow her upstairs.

Maybe she should have listened to Luc and waited for Alain's return to the ship. Interrupting him now was a lousy idea. Leaving the ship against his orders and disturbing him in his leisure was bad enough. But once he found that she'd again left a little mess in her wake a few blocks over, the position of a silver shipment off the coast of Hispaniola would not be enough. She should have waited until after he had his pleasure. Then his mood would have been lighter.

"Out with it, woman." His growl filled the room like angry thunder. Alain's strumpet dropped her arms and frowned at Marisol for agitating him. Ben and Knuckles looked over. In fact, the entire brothel had come to attention.

Marisol bowed her head. "Pardon, Captain." When she looked up at him, she held her chin a bit higher. A gesture of courage she must always maintain, as she would not grovel to him. She doubted he took notice. "I have an urgent matter I would like to pass along to you. I can see you are busy—" she shifted her gaze to the woman, "—but it will only take a moment of your time, if you would allow it."

His stare bore into her. Oh great guns, was he displeased.

"Go on up, Zita," he said. "I'll join you in a moment." She squealed as he slapped her rear. "Be naked."

His heavy footfalls thudded upon each step. His knee-length coat buffeted around the arsenal she knew he concealed beneath it. He met Marisol at the bottom of the stairs. "This better be worth it." He led her to a quiet corner away from prying ears and sat down at a small tripod tea table. "Don't sit." He waved his ringed hand as she bent to take the seat next to him. He leaned back crossing his arms over his chest. "You have one minute. Go."

She tried not to let his gruffness upset her. Why did he have to act this way? She didn't need the constant reminder of his authority. "Very well," she bandied. "A shipment of silver is on a boat due to sail past on the morn seven miles out. It's the *Gloria,* a ship owned by Windham."

"Silver, you say?" Alain rubbed at the scruffy black beard growing in on his chin. "There's been talk Windham was moving riches. But it's been months." His scowling face darted up at her. His mouth twitched with admonition. "And how did you come by this information, *ma chérie*?" He stressed the endearment more than necessary.

She shrugged. "'Tis not important."

"I say it is."

An unexplainable apprehensiveness cautioned her from revealing the note. "I intercepted a message from a dying carrier."

Alain rolled his head back, stretching the tension she knew she caused to build in his neck. "So help me, Marisol, if I have to square away another one of your kettles of fish..." He let out a disgusted sigh. "How do you know there is silver on board?"

Anticipating his question, she withdrew two silver coins and laid them on the table. "I also managed to get these."

Lifting his eyes slowly from the coins to meet hers, he asked, "Is that all?"

"Aye," she lied. She would not break the stare. *Hold his stare.*

It took a great part of her will to stand very still, to not move as he took stock of her. Then a weak smile broke the stony facade of his countenance. "Well then." He slapped at his knees as he rose from the chair. "Your time is up." Swiping the coins, he put them in his coat pocket and pushed past her, heading for the stairs.

"What will you do?"

He did not break his stride nor turn around. "I shall sleep on it." His raucous laughter echoed throughout the room. "And when I'm done," he said as he climbed the flight of stairs to the dimly lit landing, "I will decide a fitting scourge for neglecting my orders." Halfway up to the landing he stopped. "Ben. Get yer hands off the jade's dugs and see Marisol back to the ship."

Ben scowled, but promised the woman he was fondling that he'd return for a bull's-eye's worth of tupping.

Alain moved from view on the landing. "Zita! On your knees, woman," he called. His door slammed shut.

So that's it, Marisol thought. Frustration warred with anger, swirling in her belly and tingling at her fingers. She had no idea if Alain would choose to hunt down the *Gloria.* No indication if the silver proved enticing to him. If he opted not to go after the *Gloria,* then what? She would have lost the opportunity to find Monte. Damn. She needed to captain her own ship. One day, she would break free from Alain. Slice through the ties that bound her. She wondered if she would ever have the courage to leave him.

And to think he relished the idea of making her stew over what punishment she would endure. Sometimes mulling over the atrocities Alain was capable of proved a worse sentence. Would he clamp the irons on and make her suffer the burning sun? Throw her in the brig without food and water for some untold time? Or worse, make her wash all the crew's nasty feet? Ugh, not again. Only once had the captain gone as far as having her flogged. To make the insult even worse, Alain had forced Luc to carry out her punishment.

"Please, Miss Marisol. Don' try an' rook me this time. Let's just go back ta the ship like Capt'n wants."

"Of course, Ben." Naturally, she had no intention of being escorted to the ship by him. She might as well earn her punishment. What was one more defiance?

The bordello suddenly burst to life. A group of young drunken seamen trooped in. Hollering and guffawing, they sank into the couches, ravishing the giddy girls. The woman behind the counter pulled out many glasses to fill with ale for the rowdy guests. Some were quickly led away up to the promises of desire in the rooms above. A tall man as drunk as a wheelbarrow grabbed Marisol, pulling her close. She pushed away from him, gagging on his breath stewed in booze as he tried to kiss her.

"'Ey, 'ands off, ya spoony bugger," Ben said.

"Who ya callin' spoony, nit."

"Nit? Ya lookin' to fight are ya?"

"Suppose I am."

"'Appy to oblige."

Ben struck the jack and the two locked into an ugly broil. Not to be outdone, Knuckles grabbed the nearest fellow and popped him in his nose. Those two were always looking to brawl. Why, they were as predictable as hungry dogs fighting over a meaty chop, sometimes just as dangerous. Marisol seized the opportunity and hurried out to the streets.

She took a deep breath of stagnant air and began to stroll back to the docks. With nothing left to do, she headed for the ship to wait for Alain's return. She would go to him then, prepared with an argument if he decided to forgo crossing the *Gloria.* Maybe she would embellish the ship's prize and dare him not to seek it.

She wished now she hadn't told Luc about the rumor of Monte sailing on a Windham ship. Without that knowledge, she might get Luc's backing to plunder the *Gloria.*

Luc. What business did he have this night? He wasn't with Alain and Alain never sent another in his stead where money or trade were involved. And if he was off sporting fun, such as night hunting or taunting the locals, he would offer to let her tag along. It struck her as odd.

She paused to peer in the glass window of an ivory tuner's shop and spotted a grand dagger with a bone handle. The fine detail of a sea dragon, the intricate pattern of vining knots and serpent scales, impressed her. She would like very much to have such a beautiful weapon. Leaning in, she stared more closely. The blade's clean razor edge gleamed and she wondered at its weight and how it would feel in her hands, how little resistance the flesh would lend upon penetration. Aye, a good dagger it would make.

A breeze swirled in, dusting up dead leaves and small clouds of sand. Marisol closed her eyes and straightened, facing the first welcoming cool reprieve to the humid night. The briny draft displaced the stale calm. But as soon as the wind swept over her face, it stopped. The air became thicker. She opened her eyes to a colossal black man looming before her.

"Uh." She huffed at his sudden appearance. She couldn't see his stare in the bleak light, couldn't gauge his intentions by them, but the smooth taut muscles in his arms bulging out of his sleeveless buckskin tunic cautioned that this man was an immediate threat. Instinctively, she moved back.

"Me capt'n says I need to fetch ya." His voice rumbled with a low strain, leaving her to question if the man had any occasion to talk.

"Your captain? And who might that be?" She feared she knew exactly who would want to see her.

"Capt'n Tyburn."

She winced at his name. Trouble brewed at the fringes of the moment. Under different circumstances, she would like very much to see the charmer again. And to have him touch her the way he had out in the street just a couple of hours ago, well, what sin wouldn't she commit for another such decadent sensation?

But leaving him as she had, making off with the shell cameo from his pocket, she should probably steer clear of the captain and his delicious body. No doubt he wasn't requesting her for a social call.

The pastel cameo bore the image of a mother and child under a leafless tree. Set upon a gray intaglio, the craftsmanship of the relief was amazing. Grape leaves and grapes twined through the mother's hair and she held her naked son close to her breast. Marisol reasoned the cameo to be a sentimental trinket and Tyburn would be none pleased with her for stealing it.

"Another time, perhaps," she said.

"I don' t'ink so." He placed a powerful grip to her upper arm. "What t'e Capt'n wants, t'e Capt'n gets."

"Hey, unhand me." Marisol struggled against his hold, punching him on his massive chest without effect whilst he pulled her along several feet. A cold wave of fear rose up inside her. So strong this man, that with a little more pressure he would snap her arm like a dry twig. Her knuckles burned from hitting her solid mark.

"You'd best stop fightin' me. Capt'n ordered me to get ya to him. Didn't say I had to keep ya in one piece."

She stopped, digging her heels into the ground, and looked up at him. His short tuft-like beard framed a taunting smile as he shrugged. Squelching the fear, she tackled her will. His sheer size had caused her momentary loss of control. He might be big, but big didn't mean smart. "All right," she said. "Take me to see your captain."

He did not loosen his grip to her arm as she had hoped. Wise he was for she would escape from the brute the first chance he gave her. But how smart could he be, after all? Any brainpower would have to be drained just to keep him standing upright. She was ready for the challenge. If only she could reach one of the three daggers she had hidden under her dress.

They made their way down the dirty street and cut across an alley. The man didn't bother sticking to the dark recesses away from the revealing street lanterns. He guided her along in lumbering strides aware no one would be foolish enough to confront him and his charge. She had to walk quickly lest he drag her. And if her feet failed her, she believed he *would* drag her, all the way to the tips of Tyburn's boots.

"Do you think you could slow down?" she asked.

"No."

"How about not holding my arm so tight?" A nasty bruise had begun to form where his sausage fingers dug into her.

"No." He kept his eyes forward.

Maybe if she kept talking, she could distract him enough to loosen his hold. Then she could get to a weapon.

"What do you suppose Captain Tyburn wants with me?"

"T'ain't me bidness."

"Where are you taking me?"

The beast gave no reply.

"Well, what's your name? What do they call you?" Silence. *Try again.*

"Not a man of many words, are you?" Nothing.

"Are you his slave?"

His short laugh ended in a sneer and a tighter grasp. "I belong to no one. Not even t'e devil has t'e courage." He laughed again, a booming boldness.

If Marisol could retrieve her dagger, she would merely anger him with a flesh wound. Nay, she would need to wait for when he let her arm go, reasoning she would be faster in a foot chase.

He led her down another narrow alley and knocked on the only door. She almost missed it in the blackness until it swung open to greet them. She couldn't go in. If she did cross the threshold, her chances of making a break drastically dropped. She had to think fast.

She looked to the gangly man holding the door open, ushering them in with his waving hand. His eyes darted to the obscurity behind them, restless in scanning the dark. As Marisol and the titan moved forward, the man stuck his head out to peer down the alley for anyone following them.

In one swift sweep, Marisol grabbed the doorman's gulley knife hanging from his belt. Thrusting up her elbow to connect with his jaw, she knocked him back with such force he slammed into the wall. She brought the blade down slicing at her captor's wrist. He howled and let her go, stumbling back with his hand raised before his face. Stunned, he howled again looking from the cut gushing blood back directly at her. Before he could react, she stabbed the knife into his thigh. Letting go of the handle, she spun around and ran back down the alley.

Challenge met. And she didn't even have to bloody her own knife. She smiled at her resourcefulness. Her heart raced with the excitement close calls always seemed to bring. That triumphant feeling of besting those who would see her ruin. What would that make? Her seventh? Eighth escape? And without Alain's help this time.

Glancing over her shoulder, she saw the large man yank the blade from his leg. His head shot up at her retreat, but he did not budge from the doorway. He wasn't following. Only his inflamed stare chased after her. She was almost out of the alley. Once she made the street, there would be no stopping her from getting away. Why wasn't he coming for her?

His words replayed in her mind. "What t'e Capt'n wants…"

She turned forward and slammed headlong into a hard wall. Falling on her arse, she cursed at the painful collision and looked up to see Captain Blade Tyburn scowling down at her.

"…t'e Capt'n gets."

CHAPTER 3

"Ah, Miss Castellan. Please don't tell me you mean to insult me by denying my company." Blade couldn't suppress the sharpness of his tone. He didn't want to. What he wanted was to shake her until his cameo fell free from wherever she kept it hidden. No one, *no one* touched his cameo. This wench would pay handsomely for stealing it. Oh yes, handsomely.

He ground his teeth as she skittered on her bottom away from him. "Didn't your mama teach you good manners?" He gave his head a disgusted shake. "It's condemnable not to give a man his respect."

The lass snorted at that, still putting distance between them. That is, until she backed into a pair of massive legs the size of tree trunks. Blade laughed to himself with the widening of her eyes. No chance for an escape now.

"Maybe someone needs to teach you manners right and proper." He smirked. Aye, he liked the sound of that. An image flashed into his mind of disciplining the naughty lass. But it faded just as quickly with the image of his precious cameo.

"For a man to get respect, he must first earn it," Marisol asserted.

Blade squatted before her, twisting his mouth into a contemptuous sneer. "Tell me, chit. Do you also think one must earn the right to keep her pretty little head?"

If the lass was scared of him, she hid it well. Instead, she stared boldly into his eyes. What was she thinking? If he didn't know better, he'd say she was assessing her situation. Calculating her next move.

"What? No opinion? Good, you are already learning your place. A quick study." He stood up. "Come. You must be eager to unburden yourself. Let Sam, here, show you the way."

Blade ignored the rough handling Sam displayed as he yanked Marisol to her feet and pulled her along. By the looks of the bloody wounds she inflicted upon him, the gargantuan buccaneer showed considerable restraint, if only because Blade expected it of him. As they passed through the doorway to the back room of a bakery, Lansky the baker stepped away, giving them a wide berth. The fellow rubbed at his chin, eyeing Marisol warily. A tendril of amusement twined around Blade's hostility. She must be crafty to evade two men at once. He would have really enjoyed witnessing her daring flight. Sam would have to tell him later how she did it.

Lansky closed and bolted the door shut behind them while Sam tugged the lass to stand in the middle of the room. They were in Lansky's kitchen. The brick oven behind them smoldered, the fire inside dying out from the day's last loaf of bread, and the space pressed in on him with heat. Flour covered every inch of the area. It shifted through the air with any movement someone made, settling on the table with the bowls, spoons and rolling pin, on the stools pushed to the side, and clinging to the walls in a dusty white layer.

Blade observed Marisol as she surveyed the room. No doubt, looking for a way out. Odd that she didn't show more fear. Odd that he found her confidence so alluring. Strong women had always held an attraction for him. Especially beautiful ones who didn't seem to know, or care, how much danger they faced. At what point did strength turn into rash stupidity? Being held against her will by three men who might have any number of horrific ideas in mind for her welfare should make her tremble in fright. But no, she didn't so much as bat an eyelash. Not even when he spoke.

"Allow me to get straight to the point." He paced directly in front of her. "You have something of mine. Something that you will return to me post-haste." He stopped and turned to face her with deliberate expectancy.

When Marisol made no move to oblige him, his patience palled.

"Where is my cameo?" He all but yelled at her, yet she didn't even accommodate him with a flinch. Palling, his patience, palling fast.

"I don't have it."

"Ah, so you admit to taking it." The wench didn't act as if he were demented, didn't question him about what he spoke of, and didn't inquire about *what* missing cameo. Aye, she knew exactly what he was after.

"If it means so much to you why do you keep it in your pocket where anyone with a deft hand could take it?" She dared him with such an answer. Her delicate face remained without expression despite her brazen tongue.

Fury invaded Blade's mind. Rarely did he lose control of his temper, even among his enemies. But now he felt a sense of hopelessness as the strange feeling heaved over his usually unyielding forbearance. "Most people are not so foolish."

"I prefer the term *enterprising*."

If Blade hadn't been trying so hard to keep from backhanding the woman, he would have laughed at her statement. It sounded remarkably familiar. Instead, he took a step back, an effort at restraint.

"I shall count to three, dear lady." He returned to pacing. "If by the time I make it to three and you have not produced my cameo, I shall search you for it myself."

"You may count as high as you like, but I do not have it." Marisol crossed her arms, like a child too big for her pantaloons.

Blade came forward, all too willing to search her. Whether to find his cameo or to rub his hands over her enticing curves, he couldn't be sure. But the lass dropped her arms and backed away.

"All right, all right." She held her hands up to shield herself from his approach. "I have it hidden in my boot."

Now they were getting somewhere. "Good," Blade said. She bent to reach into her shoe. "I'm glad you see that you have no other choice. Perhaps we can return to cordial—"

Marisol lunged from her crouch, wielding a small knife, coming close to stabbing him in his stomach. He hopped to the side and grabbed her wrist. The momentum of her rushing forward coupled with him forcibly wrenching her arm upward twisted her body into what had to be a painful contortion. She landed on her back onto the powdery floor, yelping as he still held her arm up. His boot to her shoulder kept her from squirming and hurting herself further.

That was the point of rash stupidity. Blade shouldn't have been surprised by her trickery. He had watched her carefully in the alehouse as she wormed her way around the aggressive sot. He knew then the lass could take care of herself. He had found it refreshing and attractive. However, he now retracted those earlier impressions and replaced them with one of annoyance. Blade recognized the fire in her eyes, seen on many faces of the brave before they met their fate by his hand. It burned with the light of intrepid spirit. Blade considered the felled warrior's demise as honorable. Any life he had taken that fought with courage was a life well deserved. Anything less seemed such a waste.

Maybe he shouldn't be hasty about her will to survive. "I wish you hadn't done that." He brought her to stand again and plucked the knife from her. Sam and Lansky stood by with their drawn pistols. Blade tossed the knife to Sam, who tucked it under his waistband.

"I do, too," Marisol replied. "I should've waited for a better chance."

This time Blade chuckled, shaking his head at her brass. "You give me no choice but to go ahead with searching you. Do take into account you will be shot should you try another half-witted attempt to flee."

"Understood." She dismissed the gravity of her predicament with her nonchalant demeanor.

"Fair warning, lass, my search will be thorough." He smiled, adding, "And you may very well enjoy it." But not as much as he.

She stiffened under his touch as he placed both hands on her hips and rubbed upward along her close-fitting bodice to under her arms. She sucked in her breath when he slid his thumbs along the underside of her breasts, cupping them. Their shape was perfect, filling his hands nicely. The seams of his trousers strained under her subtle response. How many times had a woman held her breath while he caressed her in such a manner? The simple action had never gone unnoticed. He thrived on every movement, every minute reception, every sigh and every quiver a woman gave him under his touch.

"I once knew of a lady who hid a valuable medallion between her breasts." He drew his eyes up to meet her stare. They flickered, but not with fear. Nay, there was something else lying in those eyes, something less lucid. "I can't risk not being sure." Satisfied she hid nothing there, he lingered before he continued on lower. Her bodice concealed nothing, nothing but naked flesh underneath.

Damn, he needed to stop thinking of her that way. He reminded himself that she stole his cameo. Focusing on that should keep him from wanting to throw her on the table and roll around kneading some dough of their own.

He patted down her skirt. Feeling something round, he smiled at Marisol, confident of his find. He reached in her pocket and pulled out a folded paper and a silver piece. Holding up the coin, a heartbeat passed. This wasn't his cameo.

"What the hell is this?" he asked. Where the hell was his cameo? Panic surged, crashing through him with the thought of never holding his cameo again, of never rubbing his fingers over the raised relief or the smooth shell underside. Without his cameo, without its unrelenting, unforgiving memories, he would go mad.

A hatred for the woman standing before him snagged him like rusted trolling hooks. He clenched the coin tight and shook his fist at her, startled by his building ire. He had never had such a feeling over a woman. No, he adored women. Women of all kinds, all shapes and sizes. He loved their smiles, their smells, their dispositions, no matter what their faults and shortcomings might be. In everything about a woman he could find a bit of paradise.

But this one, well, he found himself wanting to strangle her, to take her cherished life from her as she took his cherished cameo from him. Oh yes, and she had made it easy. Especially since she seemed unconcerned with his being in high dudgeon. Rather, she showed more interest in the letter he held.

The letter. No, it couldn't be. He opened his palm to the coin and watched as Marisol tore her gaze away from the letter to the silver piece. Realization sank in. This vixen was responsible for the trouble back at the tavern. "Well," he said. "It seems you are quite the pickpocket." Opening the letter, he scanned the coded sentence quickly, pocketing the coin.

"I believe the letter was intended for you," Marisol stated. "By the queer way it was to be handed off to you, I've got to question if you are not some sort of charlatan yourself, sir."

Blade ignored her remark and refolded the paper. Someone else knew of the hefty silver shipment and they sent this trollop to ferret out information. Blade's commission just got more interesting, and more dangerous. Maybe this voyage wouldn't be as dreary as he first thought. But who would send a mere lass to do something so foolish and deadly as to cross him? "Who sent you?"

"No one sent me." Her answer was tinged with gallantry and he thought of the dead messenger.

"Who else knows of this?" He flashed the letter before putting it in his coat pocket.

"No one."

"You lie." He leaned his back against the table flush with the wall. "It will be in your best interest, Marisol, if you would be forthcoming."

"Or what, Captain Tyburn?" She fixed one hand to her hip. "Will you torture me until I talk? Are you that kind of man? Cruel and sadistic?"

For finding out who sent her, no. But for his cameo... "Perhaps." He repeated his question. "Who else knows of the silver shipment?"

She leaned forward, stressing her words. "No one."

She would've been convincing if not for the way she looked away and raised her arm up as if reaching for her ear.

Breaking glass shattered from the front of the bakery, startling them all. Blade grabbed Marisol's arm and drew her with him to see what caused the loud crash. Better he keep her close than to have her use the diversion and take flight. They entered the small front room and stopped short, Sam and Lansky bumping into them from behind. Men were racing along outside on the sidewalk brandishing blazing torches and hurtling bricks. A large torch flew through the jagged window igniting the lacy curtains and erupting into hungry flames as it landed in the middle of the floor.

"Ack! My bakery!" Lansky grabbed a huge flour sack from the counter. He slung flour out of the open bag, sifting all of them heavily in the white powder. Thick puffs of the flour made it difficult to see and Lansky twirled around trying to get his bearings. His frantic movements caused more flour to fling out of the sack blanketing everyone and everything within its radius. Desperately waving their arms for clean air, the group wheezed and coughed. Blade sneezed on the fine meal clogged in his nose. Inhaling, he gagged at the grainy taste coating his mouth. With the dust stinging his eyes, he could barely make out Lansky's silhouette holding the half-full bag.

"No." Blade hollered at Lansky, but he was too late. Lansky tossed the flour over the fire. The flames flattened then exploded, raging into bright life, reaching for the ceiling as it spread across the room, swallowing everything in its path.

"Shit." The heat seared at Blade's exposed skin and his eyes burned. "Get out! Everyone, get out!" He still had Marisol by the arm, pushing her toward Sam as they retreated. "Lanksy! Come on! You can't save it!"

Lansky grabbed a pitcher filled with water and sloshed it onto the flames. He jumped at the liquid crackling and popping, and then the water disappeared as if the fire drank it away.

"Lansky!"

The baker turned and followed Blade on his heels, out the back and into the alley.

The foursome stopped at the street, dust clouds settling around them as they coughed.

"That was close." Blade smacked at the bland paste in his mouth. "Any longer in there, and we would've been baked into crispy meat pies."

He patted at his clothing in a futile attempt to remove the layers of fine grain. As he waved away another wafting drift, he heard giggling. Marisol covered her lips with both hands, making a miserable attempt to conceal her laugh.

Her giggles aggravated him. Given that they barely escaped with their lives, she should be quaking in her boots, not tittering like a schoolgirl. Blade glanced back to the open door. Smoke rolled upward then caught on a breeze. Eluding another brush with death 'twas nothing to him, but to the lass...he should watch for signs of hysterics. Maybe she'd already cracked.

"What?"

Without removing her hands, she said, "I was just thinking you look as if you fell into a vat of King Louis's makeup."

Lansky began to chuckle, as well.

Blade looked at them. They were as white as bleached sails. Flour clung to their clothing, matted to their skin and dusted their hair. What a sight. He reached for a sprinkled strand of Marisol's wayward hair. Smudges of white smirched across her high cheeks from where she rubbed at her watery eyes. Her smiling lips were rosy from licking them wet and clean. "And you could pass for a tasty tart." He couldn't resist the tease. She looked good enough to eat when she laughed.

"But I assure you, I'm sour on the inside." She winked.

"You couldn't be any worse than Lansky," Blade replied. "He looks like a battered chicken leg."

"Aye, and a skinny one at that," the baker retorted, making Marisol burst into more laughter. Blade couldn't help but join in.

Turning to Sam, their laughter died. His stern, annoyed countenance bore no indication that he shared in their humor. The white powder starkly contrasted with his dark skin. The wrinkles around his eyes and mouth grossly outlined his features. The flour stuck in the dark hairs of his beard served to bring to mind terrible table manners and accentuated his deepening frown.

"You got a little something right there." Blade pointed to Sam's chin.

"Humph."

Blade clapped him on his back and Sam broke his caked mask, smiling and joining in the mirth. Fine mists of flour billowed all around them.

A quick shift in Marisol's movement during the distraction alerted Blade to her attempt to flee. He snatched a broom leaning nearby on the wall, smashed it across his knee breaking it in two, and threw it at her feet. Her legs tangled upon the dowel causing her to crash to the ground in a most ungainly fashion. Skin and skirts lay exposed. Glory be! If she wasn't tantalizing off her feet.

"A courageous effort, chit." He didn't hide his amusement as he pulled her up, even as she glared at him.

A bloodcurdling scream pealed from down the street. A bullet ricocheted off the wall behind them. Blade threw up a protective arm and pushed Marisol back into the shadows. Chaos rampaged, pouring from doorways and darkened crevices. Running, screaming villagers barreled toward them, and clashing armed men made their way out into the open. Fires flared, destroying buildings and plunderers carted off armloads of goods and valuables.

"A raid." Marisol voiced the obvious on a breath of excitement.

"Aye," Blade replied. "Carrion."

Her brow knitted. "Huh?"

A crackling pop diverted her attention. But not before Blade caught the expression of perplexity skip across her face.

Flames burned from the roof of the bakery beside them, licking down the walls and closing in on the alley in which they stood.

"I'm sorry about your place, Lansky." He placed a hand on his friend's shoulder. Lansky stared at his burning livelihood, his eyes heavy with grief. "Don't worry, mate. I'll see to it that the bakery will be rebuilt. On my honor."

And he would. Having any dealings with the ship would likely result in a date with the executioner. Blade and the *Rissa* crew made sure those who precariously allied themselves with their ship reaped protection and a tidy compensation. It was an unspoken gift in exchange for whatever services her captain and crew might require from loyal friends. For Lansky, it would mean keeping him from homelessness and starvation.

Lansky turned sharply to him, smiling, shaking his hand. "Oh, thank you, sir. Thank you."

Blade nodded. "Go see Kate down at The Harpy Wineskin. Tell her I sent you."

"Yes, sir." Lansky bowed, not letting go of Blade's hand. "Yes, sir."

"We'd best be on our way, then." Blade looked toward the docks and the concentration of billowing smoke smothering the night sky. "Before one of us takes a wayward bullet." He pulled on Marisol's wrist.

"I'll take my chances," she contended.

"Aye, you will. With me. Come."

She pulled back, releasing herself from his grip. "No."

This woman made no bones about testing his temperament. She must have coughed up her scruples from the caustic mixture of smoke and flour if she thought he would allow her to merely leave. "You have stolen not one, but several items that belong to me. You wounded one of my men. And…" He stepped in close to her, close enough that her breath fell on his face. "You tried to kill me. I don't believe you are in a position to argue."

"Maim you."

"What?"

The tips of her lips curved up into an impish grin. "I tried to maim you."

What a devil of a woman. Cloaked in beauty, she was wicked. Wicked and deceptive and, oh so close to finding herself naked beneath him. He groaned inwardly. He wanted her, despite the urge to strangle her. And that peeved him.

"If I wanted to kill you, I would have aimed higher."

Blade smiled at that. "Not likely, love." He grabbed her again by her wrist and her other arm. "Whatever it is that you've gotten yourself into has ensured that you belong to me."

She struggled against his hold. A new fire raged. It fumed in her eyes, her expression. "I belong to no one." She swung her free fist but their closeness kept her from hitting anywhere but his shoulder.

"Aye, keep fighting me, chit." His skin prickled with both anger and arousal. "Make it easy for me." He enjoyed the control over her, enjoyed letting the ire course through him. "You gave up your freedom the moment you chose to steal from me." He enjoyed feeling her strength slacken upon his words. Never had he let iniquity obscure his mind. He was a better man than that. Yet he was beginning to see how weaker, evil men could lose their temper, their morality on a witch of a woman like Marisol.

He laughed. "Aye, your freedom is mine."

She stopped squirming. Her jaw set rigid and her expression turned cross. "Never."

Wooden crossbeams moaned and cracked as fire ate away at the bakery roof. It collapsed a moment later. The heat from the flames grew in its intensity and Blade knew the four of them would have to vacate the relative safety of the alley.

He drew his pistol. "Let's go."

Marisol gave him no resistance and he pulled her along, hurrying to his ship. His crew would be waiting for his return, ready to move out of the bay, and armed for anyone anxious enough to lose their life trying to board her unwelcomed.

In and out of side streets and alleys, they hurried. The closer they came to the docks, the more the melee thickened. Thieves ransacked homes and businesses, laying waste to everything in their paths, taking anything they desired or could turn a coin on. He held Marisol tightly by his side, pulling her through the clumps of men fighting in the streets, drawing fists and drawing blood. Women dashed in directions of safety, fleeing from the horrors of rape and death, cradling their children and meager possessions to their breasts. Shouts and screams carried over the crackling, hissing sounds of burning wooden buildings, dying in the bright orange glow.

Blade had to extinguish the urge to join in the affray. 'Twas hard to turn his back on a chance for a good fight. But he had other dogs to whip. Although he now had the information to continue his mission, he still was without his cameo. He figured he would be long tired of whipping before that wench stopped toying with him and returned it. Enough. When he got her back to his ship, he would spare no time stripping her for it. No more distractions. He would get his cameo back.

They crossed the square, Blade heading them to the long street leading to the quay. The raid was at its densest here.

This had to be Carrion's doing, no doubt. But why would he choose Puerto Plata for a raid? This port served little more than to replenish ship provisions and perhaps dally in amber trade. Carrion wouldn't be interested in amber—there was simply not enough profit. Something didn't make sense. It didn't feel right.

He cursed to himself. Searching for Marisol instead of meeting with Carrion like he had intended had cost him time. If not for her… He ground his teeth.

He stopped them at the other end of the square and clapped Lansky's shoulder. "Good luck to you, my friend."

Lansky nodded and hurried away into the night toward The Harpy Wineskin on the other side of the bay, a flour cloud swirling behind him. If he made it, Kate would take care of him.

Beside them, glass burst and a chair crashed through a nearby mercantile storefront window. They needed to keep moving. Blade pulled at Marisol to follow, but she stood steadfast, staring at the broken window. He pulled again and she refused to move. She kept staring at the window, beyond the window. Her eyes seemed sad, and the look of pain unexpectedly moved him like a glancing blow.

A tall, young man stepped over the broken pane, his boot crunching on tiny shards of thin glass. He clutched a sack full of stolen goods in his hand. Curly brown hair just covered his eyes as they met Marisol's in stunned silence. He took a crushing step forward onto the glass-littered sidewalk.

"No," Marisol mouthed.

That was all Blade needed. He tugged her along as she continued to look over her shoulder at the man beginning to follow.

CHAPTER 4

Blade shoved Marisol's arm to Sam. "Take her on board," he ordered. He only just caught the look of trepidation flitter in Sam's ever-deepening frown. He swung around with his pistol raised to meet the man following them.

"I think it unwise to come any farther," he warned.

The young looter stopped dead in his path. His brow knitted in anguish when he spoke. "But...but that's my sister."

"Well, well." Blade snorted. "It seems thievery is a family affair."

"You have my sister." He dropped his sack, reaching for his rapier.

"Do you wish to engage me, son?" Blade glared at him. The man's fingers twitched over the sword's handle as much as the indecision flickered in his eyes. He must be handy with the weapon to think he could incapacitate Blade while staring down the barrel of his gun. Either that, or he was extremely stupid.

He watched Blade's trigger finger for a moment then met his stare. "What do you want with Marisol?" he asked.

The way the young man pronounced her name caused a lurch within Blade's chest. He said it with such love and it sounded so musical. Ugh. He hated having a conscience. Made it hard to be ruthless. More so since it involved a woman. He was not used to acting fierce with the fairer sex. Unless, of course, it involved a bit of play acting between the sheets.

Blasted wench.

He shook his head. "You can have her back as soon as she returns what she took from me," he replied.

The man sighed heavily and looked away. "On your word, Captain Tyburn?"

Blade tilted his head at the man's recognition of him.

"Aye. I know you. Any sailor worth his salt knows of the legendary Captain Blade Tyburn and the brigantine *Rissa.* And I know I cannot fight you for my sister and win. Not this time."

Not so stupid after all. Blade especially liked the way the young cunning shaver subtly predicted a future confrontation with him. Strong will and courage, another family trait. "On my word, son."

"When?"

Blade shrugged. "'Tis up to her how soon I will release her." He lowered his pistol. "The sooner, the better," he said as he turned and walked away.

* * *

Marisol watched from the deck of Tyburn's ship as Luc grabbed his loot and ran off into the midst of the pandemonium. So, this was why Luc wanted her in her cabin. For her safety. Bah. Rioting—his important business. Damn it. Oh, she hoped Alain wouldn't find out. He would not tolerate it. Her brother would be lucky to survive their captain's wrath for violating his command. She lowered her head with a weighty realization.

"What ye got there, Sam?"

She turned to the sound of the gruff voice behind her, but nobody was there. Crewmen milled about the ship deck, checking lines and climbing up the masts to the crosstrees, preparing to sail.

"Capt'n ain't got time for a lass t'night."

Marisol lowered her gaze to a stocky stump of a man. He wore his gray beard decorated with tiny red bows that framed a viciously foul scowl. His trousers were bright green and his red beaded vest reminded her of the crowded streets of India. She found the man a ridiculous parody of a play actor in women's fashion on the losing side of a drunken bet. She stifled a grin.

Beady eyes upon his weathered face scanned her suspiciously. “And he don’t tend to want ’em on board, no how.”

“Followin’ me orders, Henri.” Sam shadowed the little man. They were like a mountain and a molehill.

“Criminy, tar. What the bloody hell happened to ya?” Henri’s missing teeth notched his nasty grin. “Ya git the color scared outta ya?”

“Careful, squatty. Ye may find yerself scrapin’ t’e bottom of me shoe.”

“Whaddya call me?” Henri came forward, his chest puffed outward.

Sam stared directly down at Henri. “Squatty.”

Marisol took a step back. She didn’t think there would be much of a fight between a giant and a tiny troll, but she didn’t want to find out firsthand by standing too close.

“Name callin’, eh?” She didn’t think it possible for Henri’s jowls to frown any lower. “That makes me mad.” He wagged his finger. “Why, I oughta ration ya rum.”

“No, sir. M’ apologies, to ya, Henri.” One corner of Sam’s mouth curled up as if he enjoyed the scold.

Henri reached up and patted Sam on his forearm. “Let that be a lesson to ya, mate.”

What just happened? Where was the fighting? They just insulted each other. If that happened on her ship, there would be an obnoxious scuffle to break up and Luc would have to carry on with lashings. But these two men acted as if they were...*friends.* How very strange.

“Miss Castellan.” Captain Tyburn called out to her.

He took the gangway in long hurried strides. As he approached, she noticed the determination etched across his austere face. His bearing, his movements, they were powerful and fluid, but precise. He carried the posture of a man who commanded the world around him. Confident, fearless. And most maddening—arrogant. It was no wonder she felt the pull of his allure.

Accustomed to men snarling at her, Marisol expected his disappointment when she did not shrink under his harsh tone. But none came.

"This is your last chance. Hand over the cameo and you will be free to go."

She was in no hurry to leave his brig. She knew well enough he would not steer his ship out of port solely because of some riot. He'd set his course straight for the *Gloria* and her shipment of silver. Exactly where Marisol wanted to go. If Alain didn't see fit to load himself down with the riches, she'd use the roguish Tyburn's beloved bauble as bait and let him take her to the vessel. He would lead her to her brother. She just knew Monte would be among the *Gloria*'s crew. She felt it in her gut.

As it were, she would trade her freedom for the boat passage. Once reunited with Monte, she simply would stay with him. Tyburn couldn't keep her.

"Then I am your captive, Captain Tyburn, as I shall not hand over your cameo." She had to buy herself enough time to make him keep her on his ship. She must delay him from getting his embossed stone and ridding himself of her. "I cannot."

"What have you done with it?" His snarl bit with venom.

"Do you fear that I profited from it already? Aye, it is a pretty piece. The detail on the shell is remarkable. A fine price it would bring." The workings of his jaw reined in her taunt. She didn't want to push him to the point where he tossed her into the bay. But she did like to make him uneasy. Empowering, it was, to have a man squirm. "Not to worry, sir. I still claim it."

"Then hand it over." Each articulated word marked his growing impatience.

"What? Here? Come now, Captain. I thought you a gentleman. You know from your initial hunt I don't have easy access to it. I require privacy."

The captain's frown disappeared and consideration lifted his eyebrows. "Privacy," he repeated. She could swear she caught the glimmer of a grin as his eyes raked over her.

She wondered if she led him to think about his exploration. And what inquisitive hands he had. He'd come close to rendering her as helpless as a virginal bride on her wedding night under his unabashed heated touch. His strong hands rubbing her body, cupping her breasts, had sent blazing chills from her fingertips to her toes. She thought a rousing game of hide-and-seek with the captain would be more fun than she could handle.

"Very well." A cruel, rascally smile curled with those words. "If it is privacy you require then it is privacy you shall have. So much so that I'm afraid you will miss the *Egeria*'s departure. You are now in custody of the *Rissa.*"

She was not pleased with the manner in which he phrased her temporary circumstance. Just what did he have planned for her? Nonetheless, she *had* manipulated her way on his ship and it *was* to be temporary. Tyburn would have to shackle her in the pit of his ship to prevent her from leaving, and even then she was clever enough to escape.

"Willie!" he barked. Tyburn walked to stand in the middle of the ship, waiting for a sea dog, not much older than the captain himself, to descend the ladder from the deck above.

Marisol recognized the man who came forward. Not that she knew him at all—she didn't. But she saw him as a man born of the sea. A man seasoned to a life on the back of the vast ocean. Someone who probably would die by it, too. Cropped brown hair topped his square face, making his crooked nose and long chin the focus of his tough visage.

"Miss Castellan has graciously taken the place of our missing messenger," Tyburn said. "We need to shove off immediately."

Willie glanced at her. The helmsman's unpleasant scrutiny made him appear hardened, but his small eyes belied a softer side of him, sympathy perhaps.

"Aye, Capt'n." Willie wheeled around and made his way back to the quarterdeck shouting orders. "Fetch up your hook! Man all canvas! We set sail!"

The weak breeze drifted the *Rissa* away from the quay. Marisol stood at the rail to watch the docks slip by. Pockets of yellow balefires lit up the night, casting the flickering light upon plumes of blackened smoke.

Alain marched down the pier. A pang of regret cramped within her chest. Even from the distance she could make out Alain's anger in the workings of his posture. There would be hell to pay when she got back. She turned away, not wanting to change her mind and spare herself his fury later. Besides, the damage had been done.

Captain Tyburn joined her at the edge. "A friend of yours, I presume?" He jutted his chin toward the man she had given her back to.

"No." The truth would only complicate her plans further.

"Uh-huh. No need for concern, then."

"Concern?"

Tyburn stopped a passing sailor to give more orders and then strode away.

What does he mean?

Shouting and the popping of gunfire spun her back around. She gripped the railing as she helplessly watched Spanish soldiers storm in to corner Alain and Luc, who'd just joined him, on the pier. Alain walked in an eerie calm toward the firing line, squeezing off shots from the pistols he held in each hand. Whilst Luc charged forward at the line with his sword drawn, a boat docked alongside the landing blocked her view of the combat. Desperate to see what was going on, she stood on her tiptoes then ran down the rail to catch a glimpse of the fight, with no luck.

What was going on? Where were Ben and Knuckles and the rest of Alain's men? Surely Alain and Luc would overcome the soldiers. They'd make it out. They always did.

Still, she watched until the wharf was too far to make any distinction. She could no longer smell the putrid fishy scent mixed with the heavy odor of burnt timber. A hefty dose of guilt replaced her regret. Aye, hell to pay, indeed.

"Set an easterly heading, Willie." Tyburn's command traveled to her ears, recapturing her attention. "We should meet our mark by sunrise."

"East?" Marisol made her way to the middle of the ship where the captain stood shouting his directions. East? If he sailed east, the *Gloria* might already be past a point of intersection. He was sending them in the wrong direction.

"You should take a westerly course," she said as she reached him.

"Oh?" His eyebrows lifted with an incredulous look. He rested his arm on the hilt of his sword at his hip. "By what reason?"

"The letter said seven miles out from the east."

"For a lass who pretends to know nothing, you sure have an opinion."

"You didn't ask me if I knew what the letter said. You only asked me who sent me for it." She gave him a dismissive look of her own. "If you go east, you'll miss her. For a captain of the fabled *Rissa,* you surprise me by your lack of knowledge in this matter."

He must have been using a heroic effort to control himself. She sensed it in his wrathful smirk.

"And if I listened to the twaddle of a meddling woman, then I don't deserve to captain a jolly boat." He leaned forward, as if to impart a prized secret. "The code meant for *me* sends me east to the noble waters. Tell me, chit, do you know of the noble waters?"

That part of the code she could not make sense of, she had to admit. "Well, no." She crossed her arms.

"Of course not." He straightened. "The noble waters refers to the Mona Passage, the treacherous waters which lie between Hispaniola and Puerto Rico. So you see, Miss Castellan, if we go west as you suggest, we might as well be skipjack fishing. You will be merely wasting my time. We go east."

Was that her pride she heard deflating? A nod seemed the only response she could muster.

"Henri." Tyburn waved over the small sailor. "Take Miss Castellan to the guest quarters. She needs her *privacy.*"

"Uh." Henri groaned. "Not again." He exaggerated his apparent dislike of the order with an eye roll.

"See to it that she makes herself presentable to me before I come to her cabin." He scanned her dusty clothing and with his heated expression she swore he could see right through her dress. "You *will* make yourself presentable to me."

"Perhaps you should do the same for me." Though, she imagined, if the circumstances were different, she wouldn't even mind if he were covered in fish scales.

"Perhaps I shall." He circled around her. "But not because I find it necessary." He leaned over her shoulder to let the last of his words drip into her ear. "Nor would you, I think." His breath sent shivers of desire to her most coveted sweet spots. *Think smelly crusty fish scales.*

"Half an hour." He dismissed them both and walked away.

Marisol followed Henri below deck, listening to him grumble

the entire way. He favored one leg as he hobbled along and she wondered what hazard had befallen him to result in his limp. He couldn't be much help as a pirate with such impairment.

"You're kind of old to be a cabin boy," she said.

"Cabin boy?" He jerked around. "Watch your tongue, lass. I'm not above cutting it out."

"Hmm. I think you'd have a hard time catching me." She smiled.

"Aye. But I can poison ya."

Oh. She didn't like the sound of that.

"That's right, dearie. I'm this ship's cook and I can whip up a nasty blight." He turned to unlock a door. "Cabin boy. Humph."

She stepped into the small room and her jaw dropped. The cabin was an indulgence of beautiful blue fabrics and textures. Silken pillows and spread covered the plush bed flanked by a small writing desk and chair. An ornate chest of drawers marked the opposite wall next to another door. Painted blue flowers and sweeping vines adorned both pieces of furniture in astounding craftsmanship.

"I'll git you clean water to wash with," Henri said. "Clothes are in the dresser."

She hardly heard him as she stood in awe of the lovely room. Not what she would expect on a vessel full of hardened seamen. She kneeled to the floor and let her hands caress the smooth bedspread before laying her cheek down on the cool satin.

Closing her eyes, she relished the softness. Alain would never allow such frivolities on his ship. Nay. The luxuries of money were best spent in port. His crew threw their earnings at whores and bad liquor. As for her, she had her share of boozing. But her weakness came in the form of finely crafted knives.

Someday, when she captained her own ship, she vowed to furnish her quarters with sumptuous style, such as in this room, in her favorite color. Blood-red.

After Henri brought her the water, she cleaned up and changed into a tunic and pair of trousers she found in one of the drawers. She had just finished combing out her hair with a silver brush she found in the dresser, when there came a quick rap on her door.

* * *

Blade smiled as he put his hand to the doorknob. He had a special fondness for this room. The blue hues and silky sheets were perfect for a seductive night with a lucky lady. He reserved bringing women on board for the few he coveted the most. And never did he allow them in his own quarters, in his own bed. As much as he loved his bonny girls, there must not be any confusion in their relationship with him. No woman could claim to be anything more than his lover for the night. Each time he crossed the threshold to his blue paradise was like stepping into a lover's arms.

But there was no lover waiting for him on the other side. Not this time. His smile faded.

Blade pushed his way inside. "Games are over, Miss Castellan," he said.

Something in his chest hitched at the sight of Marisol stroking a brush through her shiny black hair. She stood and crossed to the dresser. He could see how well the trousers fit, how nicely they molded to her firm backside. Her tight-laced tunic did nothing to hide well-rounded bosoms, tucked in under her corset, that jiggled with each of her movements. He would have to concentrate, really concentrate on the task at hand. Not on what fantasies he would like to carry out on her.

"Games." She turned around, her back against the chest of drawers. "Right."

"My cameo, Marisol." He didn't have a good feeling about this. She avoided eye contact with him, glancing to the floor, then to the door.

"You see." She paused, looking to the floor again before settling on him. "I don't have it."

"What?" The bile of anger curdled in his gut. "You said you had it on you."

"No. I said I still claim it. I never said I carried it with me."

"Where is it then?"

"In my cabin."

"Your...cabin." Scorn tinged his words as if he could taste the bile in his mouth.

"Aye, uh, on the *Egeria*." She reached up to tug on her ear.

He came forward, crowding her in. “You lie.”

“No.” She leaned back placing her hand on the dresser, trying for a comfortable distance. “I speak the truth. ’Tis in my cabin.”

“Darling, I know you are not sailing with the *Egeria.*” Some things were not worth his patience. “What are you hiding?”

“All right. Fine.” She straightened, trading her space for boldness. “I lied. I deliberately misled you so you would take me along when you seized the *Gloria.*”

Interesting. “Why?”

“I believe my missing brother to be onboard. I’m desperate to find him.” She grabbed his arm. “Please, Captain Tyburn. Take me to my brother.”

“Why in the name of Davy Jones would I do that? You’ve robbed me of my personals and of my time. And you’ve not spoken a truthful word.” His ire grew into a churning angry sea. “You’re lying to me even now.”

“No.” Her eyes widened as she wildly searched his face. “Please, you must take me to him. I know he is on the *Gloria.* I’m not lying.”

“I say you are. I met your dear brother on the docks. Taking care of business. You remember. You lied to me then, too.”

“I suppose I did.” She leaned wearily back against the dresser. “Luc *is* my brother, my older brother. But I’m looking for Monte.”

Suspicion rang in his ears. “This is a trick. You’re only interested in the cargo.”

“I swear to you. I only want to find Monte. Please, Tyburn. I’m not used to begging.”

Blade found it difficult to have any sympathy for the lass. With the idea that she played him for a fool, no amount of pleading would sway him to help her.

He shook his head. “And so you hide my cameo to ensure I help you.”

“I saw an opportunity and I took it. How could I know that you have some perverse obsession with women’s jewelry?”

He slammed both hands down on the dresser, pinning her between them. “My cameo has value only to me. Do you understand? Value that you could never comprehend.” He ground out his declaration between clenched teeth.

She flinched at his actions but she did not recoil from him. Instead, her eyes traveled down to his mouth. The blistering smolder within them fueled his temper and sent a jolt of heat to his groin. "You will give it to me." He spoke slowly, wanting the form of his words on his lips to sear into her gaze. "You will."

"Take me to the *Gloria* and you will have it." Her mouth hardly moved with her reply.

He laughed in spite of her, a welcome distraction to what he reckoned could be had—or could be taken. "Bargaining with me, are you, chit? No. We turn this boat around and return to Puerto Plata. You board whatever vessel it is that you sail on, with me and a few of my most persuasive men as your personal escorts. You give me back my cameo and I spare your life."

"But, the *Gloria*. You'll miss her."

Curious that she would be more concerned about that ship than the threat he just made on her life. There had to be more to it than what she was telling him. Never mind. Her plans had failed.

"We are less than an hour from shore." He pushed away from her, moving to the door. "It will be but a minor setback to return. Besides, I see no reason to dock. We'll simply ferry to the wharf." The farther away they sailed, the smaller his chances were for getting back the one thing that embodied his world. That special piece of ornamental shell that reminded him of the man he was cursed to be.

Windham's merchant would wait.

"Yet precious time will be lost." She beseeched after him as he moved away. "I can promise you the cameo is safe. Don't let the *Gloria* slip away, Tyburn."

He didn't fear losing the *Gloria*. She was under the protective escort of Captain Drake and his brigantine, the *Widow Maker*. Charles Windham made sure to hire the most cunning and feared of sea wolves available to protect his treasure; Captains Quint, Drake and Tyburn. They were to keep the *Gloria* safe from other predators, such as turncoats of the brotherhood like Carrion, and get the vessel in her berth by the end of the month. Windham staked that with the three pirates working together, no one captain would betray the others and make off with the treasure. As an added incentive, once the cargo reached Windham's greedy hands, he would reveal the locations of some corrupt landowners ripe for lucrative plundering.

As long as the wealthy man was willing to pay handsomely for the protection, the three of them wouldn't let the profitable opportunity fall to someone else. It was something of a precarious pact made amongst devils. Stripping Windham of his silver would be simple. Any one of them could do it. But a pirate worth his merit wouldn't give in to the temptation of treasure whilst a bigger prize could be had.

Captain Quint had led the vessel from Havana to the tip of Cuba where Drake took over. Drake was to accompany the boat until the *Rissa* could escort the *Gloria* and her valuable cargo the rest of the way around Hispaniola through the dangerous Mona Passage, waters which few could maneuver through better than Blade, to Santo Domingo and Windham. To help keep it a clandestine mission, each captain sent a messenger ahead detailing a point of contact. Delays were inevitable. Drake would wait until Blade made the rendezvous.

"You mustn't risk losing her." She was as stubborn as he. But he was the captain and his decision was final.

"Don't underestimate me and my ship," he said.

She came forward, following him to the door. "Will you take me then? I mean once I return your cameo to you? Will you take me to the *Gloria?*"

Blade faltered for a moment staring down in her creamy brown eyes haunted by mania. How could he deny her this one simple wish? He'd be taking the *Gloria* anyway. How much trouble could this lovely woman be? This shifty, thieving, infuriating woman.

The onslaught of a headache gripped him, a vise squeezing his temples. Maybe if he quit grinding his teeth, the pressure would lessen. Somehow, he didn't think that would relieve the ache. Lightening his load was a different story.

"Deception among men is to be expected." He stepped across the threshold. "However, it is very unsavory when a woman spouts lies." He pulled the door behind him, adding, "I won't help you," just before the latch clicked.

CHAPTER 5

"I mean no disrespect, Capt'n. But it will be daybreak in a few hours."

Willie's statement cut into Blade's quiet contemplation. He understood what Willie had been trying to say minutes ago, and why he had asked to speak to Blade in private upon being ordered to turn the *Rissa* back. Willie objected to the decision. Even in the dark, Blade knew his quartermaster frowned at him. As he probably should. Blade let the matter of his cameo get the better of him.

He leaned on the railing with crossed arms. His gaze dropped to the prow slicing through the water below. Black ridges with fleeting white crests rolled then disappeared into the dark. The ship creaked as she stretched forward into the salty night. If he returned to Puerto Plata now, he would indeed lose precious time. Sailing along the Mona Passage was tricky with its twisting tidal currents. He'd need as many days as he could afford to make it through safely.

As for his cameo, he suspected it lay with other ill-gotten trinkets someplace Marisol regarded safe enough. A thief wouldn't be irresponsible with her booty, and she didn't act as if she'd be careless. He had to trust that it was in this cabin of hers and that she could get it back to him. The Spanish soldiers of Puerto Plata wouldn't release any ships from port for several days following the raid. The likelihood that his cameo would be there by the time he returned from his encounter with the *Gloria* was high. Still, it sickened him to be at the mercy of her word. Mercy was his to deal out, not the other way around.

He resented being caught between Marisol's treachery and his commission. Bitterness soured in him like rancid meat roasting in the muggy hold.

"Willie, we've sailed together for many years, eh?" Blade turned to look at him, seeing little more than his silhouette. Willie faced him, holding on to a line of the rigging.

"Aye."

"Do you doubt my leadership?" His question was blunt. He wasn't angry with Willie's resistance to his orders nor did he fish for selfish validation. Nay. There were few who could captain a ship as well as he. Yet Willie would speak not as his first mate, but as his friend.

"No, sir." Willie shook his head. "But I wonder if the woman has muddied up your objective."

Blade nodded. He hated it, but Willie was right. And he supposed he knew what he was to do all along. He pushed off the rail. "My objective remains the same. Continue the course."

He took the companion ladder leading below to his cabin. Maybe some sleep would clear his mind. He plopped down onto his bed without removing his boots. Tucking an arm under his head, he closed his eyes. This night had certainly been exciting. Laughable how the clumsy feet of a dancing lass could muck up everything. She spun around in his mind to some distant music he could not recall. He summoned up the feel of her slender body, her firm breasts, when she'd crashed into him after tripping, and smiled. An unorthodox way of meeting a bonny girl. Who knew her cunning matched her beauty?

Where had she come from? Whom did she work for? He had a nagging feeling he didn't want to know. What he wouldn't mind knowing was how good her lips would taste. Or how she would look naked beneath him.

Damn it! He didn't want to think of her in that way.

She couldn't be trusted.

Ah. But when there's nothing between you but naked flesh, there is nothing to steal.

He smiled at the thought.

* * *

The thin morning fog hung low over the water, hugging the sea in the last minutes before the early rays of the sun absorbed the briny mists. Marisol paused at the top of the ladder of the quarterdeck to take a deep breath of the fresh new day. The clean air filled her with a renewed joy of finding Monte. Today would be the day.

"Stop dallyin', girlie." Henri's tone barbed with impatience. "Come along. Capt'n is waitin'."

She let him lead her along the deck, though she didn't need the little man's guidance.

Tyburn stood with his back to them, next to the wheel like a hardy beacon. His shirt strained against the defined muscles across the expanse of his shoulders as he scanned the horizon with his spyglass. The sharp lines of the sword that hung from his hip rivaled those lines that rounded in the seat of his pants. She bit her lower lip.

Henri grunted. "Ahem."

She tore her eyes away from the captain's arse. Henri shook his head as she mouthed the word *What?* at him.

"The lass, Capt'n." He hobbled away and continued to shake his head.

"A fair morning to you, Miss Castellan," Tyburn said. Still searching the sea, he didn't wait for her reply. "After leaving your chambers last night, I took stock of the situation. The winds have favored us and I decided to make good use of the generosity. We should be upon the *Gloria* soon."

So much for the humiliating show she'd put on. Obviously begging had not worked. She had known better. Begging had never swayed Alain, either. She needed to do something to preserve her dignity. Perhaps she should start by helping him survey the sea properly.

"Shouldn't you be looking beyond the bow with your bring-em-near instead of behind us?" By the way he brought down the telescope to stare at her, questioning his tactics was not the way to redeem herself.

"That's why I have a man on the fighting top." The breeze distracted her from his sharp tone as it rustled his sandy hair against his whiskered cheeks.

"Then someone is following us? Is that it?" She sidled up next to him to get a better view of the ocean spanning in their wake. The haze had all but disappeared from the farthest reaches of the open water. Nothing there, nothing but the masculine presence beside her that sucked up all available good sense. His musky smell wafting on the wind sent awakening signals to all her womanly parts that would betray her rationality. How nice it would be to see him smile again. Even if not at her.

"Aye. A light was spotted on the break and stayed with us for some time." He slid the telescope short. "It disappeared about an hour ago."

"Undoubtedly falling back out of view before the sun gave them away."

His eyes tightened with suspicion. "A probable stratagem."

"Be at ease, Tyburn. I told you I'm not working with anyone to steal that silver cargo. I'm only interested in her crew."

"You'll excuse me for taking your words with a shaker of salt."

"I suppose I deserve that." She knew she did. Tyburn had every reason to call her a liar. She hadn't exactly been forthcoming with him. Though he would claim she deliberately deceived him, she preferred to term her behavior as bending the truth. She only did what she felt was her right in her means to an end. Besides, her falsities were far less harmful than those with no moral boundaries.

She might live amongst the belly of scurvy men, but the inherent good her mother had fought so hard to teach her children had taken root within Marisol, just as the stubborn impetus of will lent from her father had seeded deeply. All too often, her paternal traits were stronger than those of her mother's and she hated that people got hurt. But once she got an idea stuck in her mind, nothing would stop her from seeing it through. Whatever it took to get what she wanted.

"Let me explain how this is going to measure." He shoved his scope into his pocket and faced her. "Once we make the *Gloria,* you will stay here on my ship until she is secure. Then you will be allowed to board with me as an escort. You find your brother and return to the *Rissa.* You will not be permitted to stay on the *Gloria.* If your brother is a free man, he may join you. If, however, he is under contract with Windham's captain, there is nothing I can, or will, do. He will stay on his ship. But, again, you will not."

"But, Captain Tyburn, you know he will be under contract. A sailor not signed on to a ship's crew would be either a prisoner or a fugitive. You're being unreasonable."

He tilted his head. "Am I?"

"Yes. I've waited a long time to be reunited with Monte. It's beastly to let me see him just to separate us again." She wanted so much to embrace Monte, to tell him she was sorry for not saving him. She needed time with him. For Tyburn to dangle a reunion in front of her then rip it away before the warmth of a cheerful hug faded was cruel.

"You seem to forget, lass. I am in no way obliged to reunite you with your brother. I find it a kindness to have permitted you to board the ship in the first place. You can do all that mawkish reunion rubbish when we get to port."

She stiffened her spine at his rude tongue.

"After, of course, you return my cameo," he added.

What was it about this cameo of Tyburn's? Why was he so determined to get it back? Beautiful the shell was, but a treasure worth risking a fortune over it was not. It had certainly been a good bargaining tool. She shouldn't forget it had been her decision to stay on his ship.

"All right. I'll play by your rules, Captain." That was, until she could make rules of her own.

He gave her a nod but his drawn brow negated that she had him convinced.

Still no smile. She wished he would, even for a moment. He had such an attractive mug when he grinned. She longed to see those dimples of his.

"Why did you kill him?"

Stunned by the turn in the conversation, she frowned. "What?"

"Why did you kill him?" Leaning his hip against the rail, he crossed his arms, obviously expecting her answer.

She stammered, unable to speak the words that were not there.

"My messenger. You killed my messenger. Why?"

"I..."

"And don't lie to me, Marisol."

Trepidation flushed over her. She felt like a rodent caught by a stalking cat—trapped and about to be devoured.

She sighed and looked to the brightening sky. Pity about the poor fool. Talking about the man humanized him, something she struggled not to do. If only the light of the new day could bleach away her crime.

"I overheard him on the pier talking to a fish just arriving," she said. "I happened upon them quite by accident." *While sneaking away from Alain's ship looking for an evening of excitement.* She had found excitement, all right.

"From what vessel?"

"The *Sugar Lady,* I believe."

Tyburn scratched his chin. He looked straight at her, but for a moment, seemed to not see her at all.

"I heard them speak something about Windham's ship," she continued, hoping to regain his attention. "If the rumors I'd been hearing were true, I knew this time I might find Monte. There was an exchange but I couldn't see what it was. So, I followed him from the docks into the alley. I was simply going to pick his pocket but the idiot pulled his pistol. We scuffled and, well..." Would it be too much to ask to let the matter drop? She offered a sheepish smile.

"I'm to believe you were defending yourself?"

Nuh-uh. No letting the matter drop. "Believe what you like, Captain. He pointed that pistol at me claiming he'd see the devil before he'd let some woman foil his mission." Men, humph. Always failing to appreciate a woman's ambition. "I merely helped him see his proclamation through."

"You raise another question." He lifted his brow in mild curiosity. "Where is it you lay your head at night? Where do you call home?"

He was crafty. Her answer would tell him much about her. If she told him the truth, that is. She would reveal nothing that could get her further into trouble. "I come from Île-á-Vache.

Cow Island."

"Nice try. But I was referring to the ship your cabin is in. Forgive me for saying as much, but you are no windswept flower plucked from the grassy dunes of paradise." His stare grazing over her was no less sharp than a scythe cutting down a ripened harvest. "You're more like a scavenging gull circling a fishing vessel waiting to snatch a prize while no one is looking."

A fair assessment. She'd been called worse. "I told you, Cow Island. My mother was born in Spain to a mercantile family. During Queen Anne's War, she fell in love with a French seaman. Against her family's wishes, she married him. Together they absconded to Cow Island where she raised three children and he took to sailing on merchants. She has a cottage near the wharf. There she plies her trade as an apothecary, selling healing herbs."

For a moment, Marisol could smell the spicy twigs laced with leaves and flowers her mother hung in the windows to dry. Warmth spread throughout her as she thought of her mother, of sitting at the table watching her prepare the small pots of remedies. Marisol missed her, missed the way she hummed while she worked, missed the love and understanding only a mother could give.

But not Cow Island. She did not miss that wretched spit of land.

"That is where I call home," she said.

"You live by the sea, that much is clear."

"I have occasion to sail at times."

"Ah, yes. Especially after pillaging unsuspecting victims, beguiling them with your beauty."

"Victim? I wasn't aware you consider yourself a victim."

"Hardly, that. I would never allow as such. But that is why you are here, is it not?"

"I detect bitterness."

"Ho, ho." His fleeting chuckle gave way to what she'd been waiting for.

Delighted, she smiled as those dimples made an appearance. Her knees weakened with his trifling grin. She knew why he reserved his good nature in her presence. There would be no mistaking his intentions and what he expected from her. This had all been unpleasant business to him. She felt saddened by the thought, saddened that he didn't smile at her more.

"I harbor much more than bitterness, sweet lady." He closed the gap between them. "Would you care to find out just what I harbor? Or where?"

His crude remark did not appall her like she imagined he intended. Living among a ship full of scum counting down the days until they would make the next port so that they could prig a cheap blouse, she had heard it all.

"I'm uninterested in the docking habits of a draughty dinghy."

His deep laugh lengthened the cut of his dimples. "'Tis a shame, I'd say. Wherever I drop anchor, my man-o'-war is usually well received in berth."

Ah. Now she remembered where she'd heard of him. The girls in Port Royal. They had treated her with tales of raunchy affairs about the man standing before her. Captain Blade Tyburn, the libertine, known to seduce women all over the Caribbean and the far reaches of the Atlantic with his charm. 'Twas said that fathers locked up their daughters or sent them to the country at first mention of him sailing in nearby waters and that women of all statuses swooned at the sound of his name.

Well, she could certainly see why. No doubt he was a dashing rogue spreading devilish fantasies meant to make the heart flutter with unbound desires. But she had no use for being another conquest. She had grown tired of being insignificant, of being little more than a strategic ornament. A swift rendezvous would serve to fortify his debauchery while lessening her own feelings of importance. Unless *she* seduced *him*. As tempting as that seemed, she had a more pressing objective.

Besides, Alain would flay them both alive should she indulge in such a dalliance. Especially after that incident with Bobby Bones in Tortuga, God rest his soul. What was good for her captain was a far cry from what he permitted from her.

But Alain wasn't here, was he?

"I don't doubt your influence over the childishly lovesick lasses pining for a tryst with a legendary lover blowing in from the high seas. Aside from your mildly pleasing features, I see no other reason to entertain the idea of testing your mariner skills."

"Skills beyond your imagination, to be sure." He reached out to brush the loose strands of her hair behind her ear. The backs of his fingers trailed down her neck to her collarbone, scraping immense rifts in her composure. "No worries, though. I've no intention of entertaining a troublesome showpiece with a wily tongue such as the likes of you."

"Bastard."

"Guttersnipe."

Ooh. Her bosom to her ears prickled in heated anger.

"Ship ho! Portside!"

Marisol looked up to the sailor. He pointed north off the masthead.

Tyburn had already made his way across the deck and Willie had joined him. "What does she hail?" Willie asked. "Is she our quarry?"

Tyburn adjusted his scope. "I can't tell. She flies no flag."

Marisol leaned over the rail, straining to see the ship in the distance. The faintest of haze lingered, clinging to the only solid object on the surface of the sea. It was as though the vessel strove to disappear. An eerie feeling crawled across her skin.

"Take us to her," Tyburn said to his first mate.

"Aye, aye." Willie strode to the midship and hollered up to the helmsman on the quarterdeck. "Two points forward off the larboard beam, lad!"

The *Rissa* cut through the waves as she turned on her larboard. Marisol held on to a ratline with the sudden shift of the ship. The rise and fall over the swells sent shallow gusts of wind across her face, blasting a feel of urgency in her chest with each dip of the bow.

That could be the *Gloria* out there. Monte could be on that ship. Oh, to see him again. The ache in her heart dwindled with the swell of anticipation.

"Do you mind, Captain?" She wanted to take a look for herself at the target.

The corner of his lips twitched with unmistakable enjoyment and he placed the scope in her outstretched hand. "By all means, dear lady. Take a look."

She sighted the ship in the scope. In the rounded distortion, the image in the center cleared. It was difficult to keep it in sight with the swaying *Rissa.* But even with the unsteady movement, she could tell something was not right. Her intuition triggered a chilling warning signal.

"Something is wrong." She passed the telescope back to Tyburn.

He peered through it for a moment. His facial features hardened into stony severity. He paused to take in the currents of the ocean then focused again on the nearing vessel.

"What is it?" she asked.

"Tell me what you see," he said.

She took back the scope and scanned the ship again. Her heartbeat picked up in pace as she realized what she saw. Or, rather, what she didn't see. "Nothing. I see nothing."

"Exactly."

No one on deck milling about, no crew manning the sails, no one at the wheel. She swept the boat from bow to stern but saw no signs of life.

"It may be a trick." He spared her another cynical glance. "They could be trying to give us a false sense of safety."

"Another pirate ship?"

"Hiding below deck ready to attack is a reasonable tactic among buccaneers. But brethren don't usually attack brethren." He pushed off the railing. "Or do they, Miss Castellan?"

A captain who takes nothing for granted, including a woman. He must think her a pirate. A pitiful excuse for a pirate, too. She didn't know if she should be insulted or laugh.

He called to the crew. "To arms," he commanded.

A seaman brought up a crate from below and dropped it in the middle of the deck. He cast off the lid and handed rifles to the eager tars.

"Man the guns, men." Tyburn directed the gunners. "Be ready for an attack."

As they neared the other ship's starboard, Willie shouted, "She's the *Gloria,* Capt'n. Right and true, she is."

Tyburn called up to the lookout. "Any sign of the *Widow Maker?*"

"Nay, Capt'n!"

"Bring her alongside, Willie," Tyburn said. "Let's see what this is about."

Willie called the orders to the helmsman.

Marisol's grip on the rope line tightened as they sailed closer. Still, the ominous deck on the ship cloaked in thin mist remained empty. It drifted aimlessly as it rolled along the tidal flow. Sagging ropes drooped from spars. Slackened sails flapped without any acceptance of wind. The rustle of the canvas and the bumping of an overturned barrel sounded like a spectral warning to stay away. Marisol shuddered as an uncanny sense of dread seeped into her every pore.

She stepped closer to the captain.

"Watch it, lassie," Henri snapped. "Damn near broke me toes with yer big foot."

"Pardon, Henri. I didn't see you there."

"Humph." He grumped before stretching his neck up like an old turtle to peer over the side.

"Ship ahoy!" Tyburn called out.

No answer came.

"Willie, give the command. We're to board."

With one hand on his hip and the other leaning on the rail, Tyburn reminded Marisol of Alain. Relaxed by his outward appearance but poised for deadly action.

Willie hollered out the order and grappling hooks flung across the span, drawing the ships together.

The men poised around the cannons and readied their weapons. Every passing moment came wrapped in a cocoon of tension. Marisol wanted to take a gulley knife, cut open the constricting wall of disquiet and step through. She felt she would seize up from the strain. And she didn't dare break the silence with a twittering faint. She'd die from embarrassment.

And still nothing disturbed the empty boat.

"Capt'n, look." Henri pointed to the sky. Seagulls flew in, a half dozen or so, circling the two ships in an aerial frenzy.

Marisol froze. This was bad.

"Blimey." Henri reached inside his vest and pulled out a flask. "Those be the souls of dead tars, they be." He pulled a hearty swig from the flask, wiping the dribble with the back of his sleeve across the red bows in his beard and smacking his lips.

"Stow your gab, you old superstitious fool." Tyburn shook his head.

The birds glided through the rigging and around the masts then came together.

"Look." She gently shook Henri's shoulder. "Look what they are doing."

His eyes grew wide. Mumbling curses, he put his flask back to his mouth, emptying it.

"The gulls," she continued. "They're separating. Two sets of three. Do you know what that means?"

Henri nodded so that she thought his little head would pop off. She would rather be witness to that than the omen the gulls had brought.

"Death will be soon coming."

"Quiet, woman." Tyburn whirled to face her, snarling at her through clenched teeth. "I'll not have you scaring the crew with lamp swinging tales."

"But, Tyburn."

"Capt'n."

"Enough!" He slammed his palm down on the rail. "You two dupes want to trade ridiculous superstitions, then go below."

A large gull lit on the *Gloria*'s railing across from Tyburn. Its white head tilted to one side as the black abyss in its eyes studied the captain. He stared hard back at the bird.

Marisol wondered who would look away first. She'd put her money on the bird, doubting Tyburn would be outflanked by a flying rat.

She and Henri together took a step away from the captain in shared superstition. The gull squawked so loud, they both jumped.

Clutching at his chest, Henri did some squawking of his own. "Bloody bird. Nearly made me heart give out. If it weren't bad luck, I'd shoot the bastard."

"I'd give you the bullet," she added.

Henri smiled at her but the kind gesture melted away while the silence surrounding the ships stretched on. The *Gloria*'s decks remained still. If something didn't happen soon, Marisol was sure to chew off her bottom lip.

The gull squawked again. Taking flight, it buzzed Tyburn's head before joining the other birds withdrawing to the distant sky.

"Ye be a marked man, Capt'n," Henri said. "A marked man."

CHAPTER 6

Blade's footfalls reverberated on the wooden planks of the *Gloria.* The cavernous thuds announced his arrival, but it was the silence that prickled his keen defenses. He trailed his gaze along the vessel's barren structure. The solicitude burrowed deeper into his bones. Drake would not desert such a profitable commission. Something had happened. But what?

He motioned for several men to fan out, to skulk and search for anyone on board.

They found no one.

"Where do you suppose they've all gone?" Marisol asked.

Her voice hummed barely above a whisper, and for him that was too loud.

"I gave you no permission to leave the *Rissa.*" He had wished not to keep an eye on the troublesome woman. Not right at the moment, anyway.

"Didn't you?" Marisol scanned the ship before settling her brown eyes on him. "Well I'm here now. You really must make yourself more clear."

If he had been any clearer, she would see through him like a pane of glass.

"And stop staring at me so."

That strange, ugly feeling for her began to ferment in his gut once more. He swallowed his peevishness before it could boil over. A woman had never angered him before. Never in such a manner as she. He'd played the fool a time or two. Always by way of romance. But never had a woman caused him to lose control. He would not let her push him toward that path. He feared he would not be able to return.

"Keep yourself in check, chit. I'm not above shackling you up for your careless sauce."

Her impassive shrug left Blade to wonder if she hadn't suffered such a fate before. Had her flippant tongue been the cause? Or perhaps it had been her larcenous tendencies. Either way, he wouldn't blame the man holding the keys.

"Capt'n." A crewman poked his head out the main hatch. "You'd better come take a look at this."

Blade followed the man below deck. Marisol stayed close behind. The sea dog swung open the door to the master cabin but stepped aside, shaking his head and refusing to go back into the room. As he passed through the threshold, Blade noted the man's complexion drained of color. What had gotten into him?

At first glance, the room appeared unassuming. A table had been laid for a meal. But a closer inspection rendered the unassuming cabin into a sinister scene. Forks speared with half-eaten fish lay askew on plates. A knife sat on top of a cheese wheel ready to cut the rations. Dying bands of smoke from a fat cigar butt curled up from a metal dish at the end of the table. The salted meat mixed with the tobacco left the stagnant air smelling fusty.

"They were in the middle of eating their morning meal." Marisol looked at the contents of a full tankard.

"No." He moved around the table "See this trail of ash?" Picking up the butt, he rolled it between his fingers. "This cigar was lit hours ago." Something was amiss, to be sure. He snuffed the cigar out in the dish.

"What could have happened?" She picked up the knife, eyeing the blade as she turned it in the light.

"I don't have an answer." Her sedate inspection of the burnished tool intrigued him. How soon before she tried to steal it?

"There is no evidence of a battle," he continued. "No sign of unfortunate weather or a sudden outbreak of disease. They all seemed to…" he hesitated, not wanting to say the obvious, "…have vanished." Even as the words fell from his mouth, her eyes darted up and rounded the size of pieces of eight.

"Do you suppose the ship is cursed?"

"Nay. I don't believe in such things."

"A ghost ship. We're standing on a ghost ship."

She spoke more to herself than to him as she peered into the corners of the cabin shrouded in shadows. Her anxiety grew palpable and Blade knew by the stiff way she stood that she held her breath. Had he not felt a dire need to understand the situation, he would have found her laughable.

"No—"

"Now *we're* cursed." Her voice raised up a notch, drowning him out from speaking further. "We've come on board and now we're cursed, too."

"Oh fire and death—"

Willie burst through the door. "It's gone!"

Marisol swung around and flung the knife at the helmsman.

"Bloody hell!" Willie yelped. With the knife embedded in the frame just inches from his head, his eyes widened as he realized how close her mark was.

Blade suppressed a smile. Marisol had a growing list of surprises. He should've guessed her to be handy with sharp cutlery. Best not to encourage the lass or her skills further.

"Apologies, sir." She strode to the threshold. "You gave me a fright." She grabbed the knife handle and yanked it out of the door casing.

Willie's mouth gaped. He struggled to reply but his jaw could only tremble in disbelief.

Blade saved him the trouble of accepting her apology. "What's gone, Willie?"

"Uh." He dragged his eyes away from her upon answering. "The silver, Capt'n. It's not in the cargo hold. It ain't nowhere on board."

Tyburn snorted out an obscenity and shook his head. "Are you certain?"

"Aye. No silver, Capt'n. From stem to stern, we checked."

Blade swore again, sending Marisol a heated glare.

"What? You don't think I have anything to do with the

missing silver, do you?"

"Things do seem to disappear when you are around." He crossed his arms over his chest. "How do you explain that?"

Her back straightened into that defensive posture he was beginning to come to know well. "I told you. This ship is cursed." She pointed a slender finger at him. "*You* are cursed."

"Now *that* I know to be true. I am cursed." His tone sounded more detractive than he intended.

In a few strides he stood in front of her, staring down upon her. He rushed not as he studied the soft lines of her lovely face, lingering perhaps too long on her lips. Her cheeks rose with the corners of her smile. He would only have to bend slightly to seize those inviting lips with his. Perhaps someday. But not today. "Aye. Cursed," he said again. "Bloody cursed with you."

Her smile gone, he pushed past her out the door. "Topside, Willie." He shoved his quartermaster forward. "I need to address the crew."

As they reached the hatch, he turned to face Marisol who was just a step behind. "I'll be taking that." He grabbed her by her waistband.

"Hey."

Her objection mattered little to him and he removed the knife she had tried to hide under her tunic.

"I can't risk you *maiming* any of my men." He held up the knife eye-level before slipping it under his sash. "I'll just put it here for safe keeping." He patted the handle against his hip.

"That's anyplace but safe." She gave him a coy downward tilt of her chin.

Though he didn't want to, he couldn't help the twist of his wicked grin. *Perhaps someday.*

Outside, the sun now shone vivid. A moment passed before Blade's vision adjusted to the light. Already warm this early in the morning, the heat promised a sweltering day ahead. Hot days on the sea were as expected as a pirate's death. Yet, this day, the air seemed, well, drier. He sensed a change blowing in the wind. By the fidgeting of his crew, they sensed it, too.

"Capt'n on deck," Willie hollered at the seamen.

Blade climbed the ladder to the quarterdeck and looked down at his gathering crew and over to his remaining men on the

Rissa.

"No doubt by now you are aware of this ship's missing crew and cargo." His voice carried loud over both ships. "This is a mere impediment to our task. We will find who is responsible. And they will pay dearly. We sail back to Puerto Plata post haste. Are you fellas up for a hunt?"

Their cheers were hearty. He nodded, satisfied with their enthusiasm.

"We will bring the *Gloria* in as well," he added, "and drop her anchor outside of the bay. We don't want any unnecessary attention bringing her in without her crew."

The zest died in an instant. The men hung their heads, muttering and avoiding eye contact with him.

"What has gotten into you men?" He knew the answer and it sickened him.

"Capt'n." Willie spoke up. "No one wants to work this ship. They believe she's cursed."

A frown tugged on his mouth as he scanned the crew.

"Lily-livered is not a pirate's mettle. When did my men turn craven?"

"Pardon me sayin' so, Capt'n, but you hafta admit there is somethin' unnatural here."

"Nay. Stint this foolery. There is not." He shot Marisol a stern dare to say otherwise. "The men are to draw straws," he announced. "Those who oppose their duty will take a turn with the gunner's daughter. On with it. I want to be under sail right away."

The men scattered back across to the *Rissa* to draw their lot. Willie met with Blade when he came down the ladder.

"You don't believe in this rubbish, do you, Willie?"

"Nah. I was just speakin' on behalf of the men is all." Willie took out his little sack of tobacco. "Some tend to let their heads get jumbled. Probably should add more water and less rum to their grog."

"Try that with Henri's ration and he'll hang you from the yardarm." Blade shared a chuckle with his first mate at the thought of the cranky little man without his normal strength of tot.

"Whaddya think happened?" Willie stuck a pinch of the

tobacco into his cheek.

"My guess is someone boarded this ship under the cover of darkness, taking the crew by surprise. They must've been loaded up along with the cargo. We're going back to Puerto Plata to talk with our stalwart landlubber friends, see what news there is—if anyone has produced silver coins or a fresh batch of slaves for auction."

Willie nodded as he chewed on his wad.

"I'll captain the *Gloria,*" Blade continued. "You, of course will be in charge of the *Rissa.* Have Sam join the others who find themselves unlucky enough to pull the short straws. When we get to port, we won't dock but take the longboats in."

He had been aware that Marisol had eased herself closer to eavesdrop the entire length of their conversation. Though she was still a good distance away, he knew she'd heard every word. Blade finally turned to acknowledge her.

She joined them at the jerk of his head. "Shall I draw a straw, too?"

"'Twould be foolish of me to allow you the odds of escaping my hospitality, don't you agree?"

"I should think it foolish keeping me at hand."

"True." Her smile bewitched him, but her efforts were lost on him. "The alternative is to throw you overboard."

"Ah, then I most certainly would be your curse, for I'd haunt you from my watery grave until the end of your days."

Blade internally shuddered. What in the blazes would that be like? In the short time he'd known her, Marisol already had made his life hell. He would think to seek a quick death should her wraith plague him. The sooner they got back to Puerto Plata, the better.

"Stay out of the way, Miss Castellan, and we can unburden ourselves of such terrible doom." He turned his back to her and saw Willie onto his ship.

* * *

Marisol straddled the cat head at the bow of the *Gloria,* letting her feet dangle just above the secured anchor. She had been ordered to stay within sight and forbidden to wander below deck. The crew kept an eye lifted on her to make sure she behaved. A grin slipped at the thought that she kept them on their toes.

Stray strands of her hair blew across her face and she tucked them behind her ears. Breathing deep, she closed her eyes. She found this spot peaceful. An occasional spray of water from the main stem slicing through the sea below splattered cool upon her exposed ankles. She felt so alive.

She imagined herself as if she were the ship. Her wooden hull skimmed over the glassy ocean, her sails full and stretched wide from the good wind. The warm sun soaked into her smooth planks, invigorating her as its rays pointed the way to far off mysteries waiting for her to unlock.

Marisol wouldn't need a captain. She could see her own way. But if one should ever be required, she would think of no one better to unfurl her sails than Captain Blade Tyburn.

A devil, he was. And a devil to be had. His crass affronts rivaled with his lust-filled eyes, even when she angered him.

Dare she admit that she was smitten by him? Everything about him struck her as foreign. My, but it wasn't simply his handsome features or the sinful tight curves and planes of his body. There, too, was his whip and pickle banter. A pleasure she verily enjoyed, no matter the sting.

So unlike Alain.

Tyburn's command over his men was stern but not menacing. Despite his threat to lash anyone who flouted his orders, she believed his men were loyal enough to follow him into Satan's fiery mouth of hell. Not because of the pirate code, but because they genuinely respected him. She'd seen it in their actions, heard it when they spoke. Not once had she heard a crewman complain about his leader. It was odd to see so many in good spirits and without squabbles. These men trusted their captain even as they feared the damned ship they sailed.

She admitted she had been spooked, too. 'Twas not a good omen, happening upon a ghost vessel. And the seagulls. Every sailorman, young rooster and old pigtail alike, knew that seagulls flying in groups of three were a warning of death soon to come. She could not believe the pattern of the birds as a coincidence. Although, Tyburn gave a credible explanation about the disappearances of both the cargo and crew, she wouldn't feel relieved until they made port. She planned to stick close to him when they reached the island. She had to find out what happened to the *Gloria*'s hands. She had to find out about Monte.

Was he on board? Was he safe? Was he even alive? The questions burned in her gut like last night's dinner. The ship couldn't arrive fast enough if Neptune, himself, picked her up and set her dockside. What desperation her need to find her brother had become.

He must know she did not give up on him. Never had she given up on him.

A commotion drew her attention to the deck. Several men were hollering, pointing up into the rigging. She focused high up the main mast. A topman hung precariously upside down from the edge of the yardarm, his ankle wrapped tightly by the halyard cord and he flailed his arms wildly. Men on the arm shuffled out to reach him. Below, several men climbed the ratlines to help. One lost his balance. Marisol flinched as he tumbled, causing another shipmate to fall with him into the water below.

"Man overboard! Man overboard!"

Bedlam broke free as the men rushed about and down the length of the ship. Feverish irrationality spread like a wildfire and they seemed momentarily disoriented. She heard Tyburn's mastery, his steady voice shouting commands, pointing at various tars, delegating his men and regaining control.

Crewmen threw down a rope into the water, then another. One of the thrashing men grabbed a hold and it pulled him through the water with the ship's momentum. The other unfortunate lad missed the lifelines. Tyburn ordered more ropes to be thrown.

Everything happened so fast. The man suspended above twisted in a panic, trying to grasp for anything within reach. Two men sat on the arm, both clutching the breeches of their mate.

Frightened by the scene unfolding before her, she brought up her legs and crouched on the cat head. She needed to get midship. She had to help. Those men were in danger and she had to do something.

Standing up, her right foot slipped off the beam and she toppled forward. She flung out her arms and slammed into the side of the ship. The air burst from her lungs. She couldn't breathe as she struggled to hang on, clutching the edge of the rail. Her chin smashed into her wrists, but she had to keep her head up. If she slipped lower she'd have no strength to pull herself back up. Falling in front of the vessel, it would plow her over and she would be lost.

She pawed with her feet for the hull, scraping it with the tips of her shoes. She grunted from the effort of lifting her upper body. It was all she could do to bring herself up an inch or two. Strength gave way, dissipating with her lack of leverage. Landing the ball of her foot to the hull, she took a moment to still, to reclaim her calm.

She planted the other foot. *Another sorry plight I've gotten myself into.* Her toes dug into her shoes as she slid a foot slowly up the bow, then slid up the other. *I won't scream. I'll get myself out of this one, I will.*

She would get back on that ship, willing herself to push her body up. Shifting her foot another notch higher, the *Gloria* dipped on a swell. She lost her footing and slipped once more. She bit her tongue when her chin smacked down upon her wrists. Searing pain and the metallic taste of blood filled her mouth. She let go.

Something caught her arm. Her weight yanked at her shoulder from which a new pain radiated. She flung her head back to see what had snagged her. Torrid green eyes stared down at her.

"Give me your other hand."

Relief whooshed through her chest and Marisol took Blade's outstretched hand. He lifted her easily enough to her feet on the bow and, taking her elbow, led her down to the forecastle. She chose a weathered barrel to sit upon, shaking out her arms that burned from the exertion of hanging on for dear life. Midship, the crewmen had pulled the second man from the sea and the topman had safely climbed down from the rigging. 'Twas a lucky thing not losing a man to the sea.

"Thank you." Hugging herself, she kneaded her fatigued muscles and tried to catch her ragged breath. "Almost made good on that curse I promised you."

Tyburn rubbed at the back of his neck, apparently not amused by her feeble attempt to detach from what could've been a dreadful ending to her grossly misunderstood life.

"Must I always keep an eye on you?" Frustration was etched in the lines of his frown.

"Am I so unpleasing to look at that it causes you pain?"

"On the contrary." His countenance softened. "Your beauty exceeds that of the most gracious of all God's golden sunsets."

An odd sensation fluttered in her stomach as if a mass of butterflies burst free from a flowering bush. Heat steamed her cheeks. She opened her mouth to say something, a retort perhaps, but the words escaped her. No one had ever said such glorious words about her. Whatever could she say?

"Beauty such as yours must be heeded most carefully, for it makes a man blind and inadvisable. 'Tis not a position I care to revisit."

She knew his meaning. Another woman might take it as a slur. But he meant no disrespect. In fact, Marisol found it flattering. It was her craft to distract with her well-honed feminine wiles. Moreover, she prided herself in her ability to take from others what she needed using her assets, and with none the wiser.

Accepting his remark along with his smile as praise, she would not forget he had his own acute craft. Left in the path of his craving stare, geysers of heat seethed at all points womanly.

"Then I shall be wary of the watch from a man whose reputation is morally unrestrained, lest I fall victim to his depraved behavior."

"You'd be wise." Darkness passed over his stare like a cloud blocking out the sun's bright beams.

Sounds from excitable shipmates clamoring over the near disastrous events pulled Marisol back to the *Gloria.* She hadn't realized the world had fallen away, as though it were her and Blade alone drifting on the vast sparkling ocean. He, too, seemed to refocus on the action around them.

The rescued men recalled the accidents. They spoke in hurried cadences of invisible hands pushing them, of the breath of death blowing them off the ropes, and heads bobbed with similar stories.

Beside her, Tyburn shook his head.

"I'm not clumsy, you know." She added more to the overture of the crew. "This ship has a shroud of affliction upon it."

"I will hear no more talk of this blight," he told her.

Tyburn jumped up onto the starboard rail. "Lend me your ears, lads." He hung from one line as he spoke. "You've been yammering like cowards. This mayhem is not some unseen evil. Letting old sea tales and unfounded beliefs soften your brains. Bah. 'Tis your own fault, these burdens. Toss them out with the bilge water. Any more clack about ghost ships and, mark me, next port you'll be finding your feet dry. There'll be no sailing under me. Am I clear?"

Marisol watched the taut workings of his face as he emanated his anger and frustration toward his crew.

"There is no evil on board other than the evil spawned by our name and cultured in our hearts. Rightfully so, I'd say." He drew his cutlass and brandished it skyward. "Let us sail with unyielding confidence. We are the terror of all the Caribbean!"

The men harrumphed and roared, rallying their collective deviant cheers loud enough to send ripples of fear across the ocean surface. Tyburn impressed her by how he relieved the crew's skittish minds in so few words.

He hopped off the rail and returned to her side. "I won't tailor my expectations," he said. "I require the same from you as I do my men."

A simple order, she wouldn't challenge him. Not if she intended to use him to find her brother. "Very well, Tyburn. No more talk of curses."

"Good." He returned his sword to the green sash wrapped around his waist. His large fingers tied the corded string holding the cutlass in place with dexterous ease. She wondered if he was as deft in all things he handled.

Too easily he distracted her with the most minute action. And she still wished to see him smile. *Focus. You've no place for silly stargazing.*

"Might I ask what you will do once we drop anchor?"

"About you?" He looked up. "Well, yes."

"Only circumstance has changed, not the goal." He propped up a foot to the rim of a cask on which she sat and leaned his arm on his knee. "At least not mine. You will still return to me my cameo." His casual tone grated against her already sensitive nerves.

"And what if I cannot?" What if Alain sailed without her?

"You will give back what has been stolen from me one way or another." He bent close, stressing his answer as a threat she should take seriously. "You can count on that, love."

"What about Monte?"

"Your brother is no concern of mine." He stood, ready to move on. "Should I learn the fate of the *Gloria*'s crew before you have been released from my custody, then I will pass along the information. Otherwise, you are on your own."

"Just as before," she mumbled.

He studied her for a long moment, nodded once and turned to leave.

Delicately she touched her tongue with the tip of her finger and felt the gash that had swollen there. The initial pain had given way to a dull pulsating ache.

"And stay off the bow," he called over his shoulder. "I may not be there to save you next time."

She sighed. She could add Captain Tyburn to her other ailments. He was definitely a pain in her arse.

CHAPTER 7

Twilight painted the sky in deep shades of blue, ushering in the long creeping shadows. Silence suffocated the incoming night except for Sam turning the oars of the swaying rowboat that carried Marisol and Blade to shore. The water lapped gently at the sides as they crept closer to the docks and the town beyond, which huddled in the glowing orange embers and rising thin trails of gray smoke. Wet ash besieged Marisol's nose once they reached the pier.

She had not before returned to a victimized port after an assault. Never mind the detail that she'd never been allowed to take part in the thrill of plundering. Alain would order her to stay behind on the ship. And he trusted she would not listen, as he should. He'd always assign a guard to keep her locked in her cabin. Poor saps bartered with their earnings to avoid the unlucky job.

But Luc, her loving Luc, always made sure to bring her a special gift with each pillage. He never let an occasion pass without reinforcing their father's decision to keep her out of harm's way and from the action. Madness, danger, terror. No place for his little sister. Besides, he would add, she was certain to get herself into trouble. He sounded a lot like Alain.

She grabbed Blade's extended hand and allowed him to pull her up onto the wooden pier. Waiting for Sam to secure the longboat's rope, she took sight of the quay. They were at the far end, a distance from the main dock. Only one ship remained tethered and it wasn't Alain's. Neither were the two anchored in the bay.

The subdued activity at the center of the docks sent shivers down her spine. There was something wrong, very wrong.

Her intuition drew her in and she walked toward the small crowd gathered there. A makeshift gallows cross stood amid the onlookers. She swiped at the cold sweat beading upon her forehead.

Spanish soldiers posted at attention around the perimeter of the gibbet. She quickened her pace. Five lifeless bodies dangled from the wooden crossbeam, wilted and flaccid. Someone called out her name.

Dead men on display, a warning. A warning to all looting pirates.

No.

She broke into a run, racing down the remainder of the dock, pushing her way through the dreary crowd. Glimpses of dark heads hung at crooked angles that would not afford her a clear look. Brown curls. One definitely had brown curls. The panic blasted through her veins and she frantically shoved her way past somber spectators, bursting through to the front. A hand grabbed her arm, halting her from rushing headlong into a soldier.

"No!"

Her panic exploded into a detachment of horror hovering all around her like a leaden shade, as her worst fear became realized. Luc swung slowly around, the full of his body facing her, arms and legs bound. Cuts and blood covered his distorted face, frozen in a slacken frown.

"Luc." His name hitched in her throat.

Voices sounded muffled in her ears. She tried to breathe but a painful lump lodged itself in her chest. She sank to her knees as the spinning world pulled her down into a hollow of nothing. No feeling. No life. No meaning. The blanket of hurt smothered her and swirling black spots blinded her vision. She gasped for air but there wasn't enough to fill her shrinking lungs.

An arm wrapped around her, helping her to stay upright.

Wailing, someone was wailing, a mournful and desperate cry.

The sound peeled away her soul. Only till she choked for more of the soiled air did she realize it was her own godforsaken cries she heard.

My Luc. Why? Oh God, why? Luc.

She willed herself to see him. The injustice of it. Luc, her beloved Luc, hung without the dignity he deserved. Anger shattered through her and she scrambled to her feet.

"Get him down!" Tears stung her eyes as she screamed at the soldiers. "Get him down, now!" In a blur of speed, she shoved her way past the soldiers, snatching out one of their swords with both hands in the process. Taking the steps by two up the gallows, she swung the sword high to slice through the rope stretched tight over Luc's head. His heavy body crumpled to the ground.

She spun around. The crowd erupted in protest, pulsing forward against the soldiers, calling for a traitor's head. Her head. Two soldiers aimed their muskets at her and demanded she lay down the sword. Like hell. She tightened her grip on the hilt.

"Put down the sword, Marisol."

Tyburn stood right beside her. She hadn't realized he'd been there at all. She met his eyes, tender in their sadness. He gently placed a hand over hers and lowered the angle of her sword.

"But they killed Luc," she cried.

"And they will kill you if you don't put down the sword." His words rustled her reason, stirring what little sanity she had left.

The unruly crowd raved on, the soldiers appearing more anxious with each passing second. Luc lay crooked in the dirt below.

"There's nothing you can do for him now." His voice, it sounded so…affected.

She let him remove the sword from her grip. He kept his gaze locked firmly on her even when he tossed the weapon to the feet of the soldiers. Hot tears flowed freely down her cheeks as he pulled her close to his chest, wrapping his arms around her. She hugged him tight, desperate for control.

Luc is dead. Luc is dead. Dead. Dead. Dead. Panting again, everything around her began to spin.

"Come." He stroked her hair as he pulled back. "It's not safe for you here."

He took her hand and led her down the steps to where Sam stood, parting the crowd with his menacing size and scowling frown. She had no clue how she made it to the end of the docks, back to where the longboat waited. Maybe she floated along the wharf. Certainly her numb legs didn't carry her there.

Tyburn made a gesture to Sam, who nodded in turn and gave them distance. He guided her to a batch of wooden crates stacked up on the platform. The damp stench of musty fishing nets grew strong, disturbing the air when he tossed them off the crates. Tiny fish scales glimmered in the pale light of a nearby dock lantern. He swiped them off the box and she sat. Her legs gave out, no longer willing to support her. Tyburn sat with her, quietly, his arm around her. She nestled her head on his shoulder and cried.

She cried for Luc, cried for her mother, cried for herself. Never again would Luc tease her, fight with her, instruct her, hug her. What was there left but memories? And it was too soon for them. Her soul chafed raw and bled.

The warmth from Tyburn rubbing her arm spread, thawing the chill that frosted her heart as he let her cry. He had no idea the comfort he brought. Or how thankful she was to him that he said nothing in her grief. There was nothing he could say. Words were veiled attempts to be sympathetic and he couldn't possibly know how she felt. His silence, his thumb caressing comforting circles on the hand he held, was exactly what she needed.

When she had no more tears to spill, the sea breeze cooled and dried her wet face. He kissed the top of her head. The simple act bestowed upon her brought a solace unlike any she had ever received. She couldn't explain it. It felt wholly different than anything her brothers or even Alain had given her when she needed strength.

"Thank you," she said to him.

He brushed aside the damp hair stuck to her cheek. "For what?"

She pulled back slightly to look him in the eye. "For not abandoning me." He had to know she meant it.

His benevolent smile weakened any resolve she had left. Her world had been shattered. Broken pieces lay all around her. She could never put those pieces back together as they were before.

Her life would never be the same. And at that very moment, it didn't matter. All she wanted, all she needed was *Blade.*

So close, his mouth. She leaned into him. Parting his lips, he let her waver. Her desire grew too strong. She kissed him. His lips felt soft and wonderful. Marisol suddenly felt as if she'd been starved. She needed more. She needed to be sated. Pressing harder into him, he took control, voraciously feeding her. Grabbing the back of her head, he became wild, pushing his tongue through, probing her mouth. Her mind spun with the dizzying effect of his responsive passion. She opened for him, lapping up every heated morsel, taking all he had to give. She sighed as he broke from their kiss.

He wanted more, she read it in the way his lips twitched with arousal, felt it in the way his fingers threading through her hair tightened. But he let out a frustrated breath and relaxed his hold.

"I'm sorry, Marisol. I shouldn't have taken advantage of you like that."

"I'm not." She still hungered. Yet, when he pulled her into a hug, she knew he would take, or give, no more.

Just as well. Her bare soul needed time to heal. A wanton pirate with his own charted course would only lead to more misery.

"Your ship is not here, is it, Marisol? And don't lie. Those anchored aren't passenger vessels."

She wondered what he would do with her once she gave him the answer. His tenderness would surely disintegrate into anger. It would be what she expected.

* * *

Blade leaned his shoulder against the rough brick wall in the shadows across the street from the Harpy Wineskin drinking house. This corner of Puerto Plata went largely unscathed by last night's riot, as here flourished the port's belly of scourge. No valuables or treasures could be pinched here. The best rum and carnal women were the preferred riches, just as they were in the rotten abscesses of every town. Those who wished to destroy were more likely to spare favored drowning pools.

He watched two men exit the tavern, but he did not move. Not yet.

He hated to leave Marisol the way he did. She suffered in her pain. He wanted nothing more than to ease her sorrow, to kiss her tears away. Suffering was his to bear. He'd grown tough as old leather hide from its constant battering. God willing, he would take all her agony and accept it as his own if it were to give her happiness and peace. He could have sat with her in his arms all night. And when she kissed him, a fire ignited within him. He didn't understand it. It burned too hot. He'd had to force himself to stop. She was broken, laid bare, and yet he felt her tangible heat. So close to the point of no return, he wanted to take her right there on the docks. She was damn near irresistible. He'd had to leave her with Sam and Henri, to clear his head.

What better way to cool off than to solve the challenge of the missing silver.

Three men came around the corner, pirates from a familiar crew. Blade pushed off the wall and crossed the street as they entered The Harpy Wineskin. Not surprisingly, the place reeked of sweat and ale, sousing him with thoughts of very fine times. A harpsichord twanged out an upbeat ditty for the dancing girls up on the small dais in one corner of the room. Men closest to the stage offered the pretty lasses flipping their dresses and kicking up their heels encouragement by tossing ill-gotten coins to them. The gals snatched them up as they hit the stage.

Blade found it easy to locate the man he sought. A wide berth had been given to the table at which he sat with his cronies near the rear of the tavern, his back to the wall. Crocodiles lying in wait for any hapless soul to wander too close. Amused with the perceived danger, Blade crossed the room.

"Captain Tyburn." A voice as sweet as nectar called to him.

"Kate. My darling, Kate." Blade smiled at the petite brunette who sashayed up to him and gave his arse a playful squeeze. Her ginger-colored dress fit snug along all the luscious curves he so fondly remembered, mapping out every soft detail.

"Tell me, my valiant prince, that you've come to my alehouse for a bit of personal pleasure. It's been far too long since we last parted." She ran her fingers along his biceps, a caress he had missed.

"That it has." Kate was a jewel in the Spanish Main, a real

vision of beauty with an unbridled skill to match. Never had Blade been more gratified by a woman than with her. But tonight, Kate's beacon of light did not gleam so brightly. "Regrettable it is, but my visit is purely business."

"'Tis a shame." Her wayward hand boldly continued downward to the front of his breeches, stirring a titillating arousal, then slowly up again to rest upon his abdomen. "I've missed your company."

"I must admit escaping with thoughts of you during my long travels. Your image has often brought me a welcomed relief." Her hearty laugh eased the trouble from his mind and he, for a moment with her touch, slipped from the turmoil which surged through his life since a certain fluttering dove fell headlong on top of him.

Marisol. His senses returned with the force of a breaking tidal wave. He shifted his weight away, away from Kate's distractive contact.

"What is the word on yesterday's raid?" He had to get back to the matters at issue. "Who was behind it?"

"Ah, yes," she chimed. "Some say it was Carrion's men. But Carrion denies any involvement."

"Aye, so he does." Blade began to believe this was bigger than Carrion. No one would risk losing their life over any small gains in Puerto Plata. Something else lay in the muck.

"I trust you took care of my man Lansky?"

"Aye. He's been set up with your provisions." She shook her head. "The world is full of corrupt men. Even the pious are tainted. But you, you are a good and decent man."

"A lie."

Kate rested her hand on his chest. "You have a heart of gold, Blade."

She couldn't be farther from the truth. His heart beat cold and black. A cameo proved it so. He wondered now if he would ever hold it again. Hold the one thing that kept him from ever forgetting the past. From forgetting what he had become.

He removed her hand and brought it to his lips, planting a kiss. "Thank you for your help, dear lady. You will be compensated for your secrecy." A guarantee that he would be able to depend on her. Now and in the future. Free-handed wealth was a persuasive tool. No one was immune from its glittering allure.

"I'd rather you come to my bed."

"Consider that a debt I will be happy to pay during another visit, with added interest." He bowed. "Until then, darling."

He left her standing there with a smile of unchaste anticipation. Though he meant every word, he had a queer feeling that he would never lie with Kate again. The reason clipped at the recesses of his mind but disappeared as he reached the table in the back of the room.

"Captain Thayer Drake." Blade addressed the man who wore his tricorn hat low on his brow, hiding his eyes. Blade didn't need to see his expression. The menacing malignity hung heavy in the air surrounding him. His men at the table repositioned themselves in their chairs so they might draw their weapons more easily. Blade sized up the four of them with a sweeping challenge. Should they draw, he would take out the man to the left of Drake. He wagered by his relaxed posture, leaning back into his chair, that this man was the faster, more deadly of Drake's pestilent companions. The others he could take down in turn. Should he need to, of course. But Drake was not a foolish man.

"I've been expecting you." He did not look up from his tankard.

"I imagine you would be. Now that our profit has gone missing."

Drake's men rose quickly, knocking back chairs and readying to arm. Drake put up a hand to stay them. "Leave us," he commanded. "You too, Valeryn." His mate gave Blade a piercing eye. He rose to join the others, grunting out his disapproval.

As the men left, Drake pushed out a chair with his foot. "A joy to see you again, my friend."

Blade took the proffered seat. "And you, as well. 'Tis been some time since we last crossed wakes. Speak to me your tidings."

"Better than our brethren with the hemp fittings."

"Aye. A damned disgrace, it is."

"What happened out there?"

Drake thumbed his hat up on his forehead. Dark circles hung low under his red-rimmed eyes. He looked tired, mad and mean. And he was drunk.

"We were befooled under the cover of darkness. Following at two leagues by the foretop lantern. On middle watch, the light disappeared. Once we spotted it again, it wasn't until morning we realized we'd been following the wrong vessel. A merchantman called the *Sugar Lady.*"

Blade bristled at the name. The *Sugar Lady* again. Warning bells clanged in his ears. He would need to find out where the vessel had headed.

"We turned back but couldn't locate the *Gloria.* Thought it best to come to Puerto Plata and give you my account. Lest you think I went rogue." He chuckled, amused by his own irony. "Well, any more than I already am."

Blade related to Drake. Accursed men, they were. An incongruity among pirates. "I've landed the *Gloria.* She had neither crew nor cargo. I'm looking to get some answers."

"I can help you there." Drake pulled a swallow from his ale. "We plucked us a few barnacles out of the water. Said they were part of the *Gloria*'s crew."

A serving wench stopped at their table. She smiled shyly at Blade. He took a tankard from her tray and winked at her. She giggled and she rushed to another blushing maid waiting by the bar.

"What did the lads say happened?" He returned Drake's attention from the wench's backside to their conversation.

"Wouldn't say. Only that they were spared." Drake focused back on Blade. "Clammed up tight. Two of 'em anyway. The third crowing princock wouldn't mind his tongue, practically begged for a beating with his back talk."

"So they were boarded." Just as Blade suspected.

"Aye."

They were spared. That doesn't make sense.

"There was no sign of a struggle. It would've taken time to unload that silver. Why not take the vessel? Why would three seamen be cast out only to leave an entire ship drifting?"

"Something smells foul," Drake agreed.

Blade thought on this, taking a deep quaff of his ale. Its

warmth and bitter taste slid down his throat. He welcomed the heavy-bodied brew, heartily finishing it off. Yet with the way his night had been shaping up, he'd rather enjoy a strong whiskey to dull the edges.

"Carrion is in these waters." He motioned to the serving wench to bring a fresh tankard.

If black had been a light, it shone bright across Drake's face at the mention of the erratic pirate. And with reason. Carrion was known by all who sailed the Caribbean as a murderous scab. The man set about to surpass the legacy of Blackbeard. In Blade's opinion, the pirate had a long voyage ahead.

"Ah. I'd like to pipeclay that bastard. He needs to be put in his place," Drake said. "Do you suspect he's behind this?"

"When has Carrion not been suspect? He's ignored the pirate code countless times. We only put up with him for when we need his guns."

"To hell with him and his guns," spat Drake. "I've managed fine without him and I don't have a need for a rotten traitor."

"Up for a cast about, then?"

"Always, mate. No one makes a mockery of me."

"The man foolish enough to cross the brethren will pray for the devil to take him. He will show more mercy." Blade clanked his tankard in a toast with Drake then swallowed his ale. "How about those men you picked up? What did you do with them?"

"Saved them for you, my friend. Truth is, I'd have been inclined to feed 'em to the sharks had I not thought you'd want to take a crack at them."

Drake tipped his head to a point beyond Blade's shoulder. Blade turned in his seat to peer at a table across the room. Three men huddled around their ale while two others sat at guard. The seamen kept their downcast eyes on Drake. With a quick wave of his hand, the men rose to the command. The guards unnecessarily prodded and shoved them forward until they stood before their table.

"Don't be so rude, gentlemen," Drake said. "Introduce yourselves to Captain Tyburn."

Blade looked to each man in turn. They were a pitiful parcel of lackeys, unkempt and wild-eyed. He wondered if these lads had seen more than a month's time at sea.

One of Drake's men popped a fellow upside his head. "Well, go on. Tell the captain yer name."

"Rip McLaughlin." The man nodded his head in greeting as he rubbed at the spot where he'd been smacked.

"William Bell." The next man spoke without hesitation. "Pleased to make your acquaintance, sir."

The last man stared hard at Blade, unmoving. Contempt roiled in the depths of his dark eyes. Intimidation hardly ever worked on Blade but the man seemed determined to do just that, capping it off with a disgusted frown.

This man must have been the one with the loose flapper. Seemed he had nothing to say now.

Blade recognized the type. A man with something to prove. Usually this kind of fellow was too arrogant and thick-skulled to know his proper place among the hierarchy of men. A fatal mistake for most. Would this dog know enough to keep his life?

Now was as good a time as any to find out. "Remove your hat, lad," Blade said, "and address me."

Making no move to comply, the miscreant continued to stare at Blade.

His crew on the *Rissa* was a loyal bunch of tars. Rarely had anyone flouted him or his command. So unused to disrespect, Blade narrowed his eyes on his offender while anger dissolved his usual good nature.

He rose slowly from his chair and crossed to stand an arm's length from the bloody fool. "I said, remove your hat, boy."

Still, the man remained motionless.

Blade drew a pistol from his brace and aimed it within an inch of the man's mouth. "Let's try this again." He pulled back the hammer. "Remove your hat and address me."

To anyone watching, it would seem the fool would take the bullet before speaking. In fact, the tavern had grown quiet as if the whole building held its breath, waiting for the explosive pop of Blade's gun.

But Blade picked up on the young man's fear. It glinted quickly through his black pupils, before being chased away by indecision, but it had surely been there. The fellow reached up to swipe his hat off his head.

"Good man." He lowered his gun. "Now, your name."

"Monte. Montenegro Castellan."

The lad might as well have kicked Blade in the stomach. He'd have been less surprised by the impact. The rules of this game had just changed.

CHAPTER 8

"He's outta his bloody mind if he thinks I'll pay that price for a barrel of pork."

Henri and Marisol walked outside the chandler's storefront and down to the corner of the street. The lantern hanging from the post cast an illuminating pool around them. Marisol had listened to the cook haggle with the shopkeeper to the point of name-calling. Yet, Henri did not threaten him with what he could *take.* Pirates have a way with convincing people to be generous through fierce intimidation. With all the tales of the feared *Rissa,* one would think a member of her crew would ravage and pilfer whatever they wanted from whomever. Instead, Henri sputtered obscenities and hobbled away.

"You'd think they used up all the bloody pigs puttin' out fires." He scratched at his wiry beard, his bows tightly knotted for the occasion to come ashore. "Why, I oughta..." Letting out a resigned sigh, he huffed over his shoulder. "Rook."

Marisol produced a ripe mango from her woolen pants pocket. He eyed the fruit, then her. His scrubby brows hung like drooping eaves over his wary scrutiny. "Where'd ya get that?"

She shrugged. "I hate crooked merchants." She handed him the mango. "Especially ones who cheat hardworking folks out of their money."

A smile slowly broke through his bearded chin. "Aye. None

other are as hardworkin' as we."

Shopping with Henri for provisions had been a welcome distraction. Blade hadn't left her to stew in her grief. She needed to be with someone, not be alone by herself to brood into a woebegone waste. He understood that when he sent her to the crotchety little man. Something else to appreciate about the pirate captain.

But just to ensure she didn't run off, he had Sam remain close by. She glanced over at the looming pirate at the edge of the ring of light. Positioning himself to take up as much space as any one man possibly could, he stood hulking with his massive tree logs crossed. Amazing those arms could even make ends meet over the expanse of his chest.

"Doesn't he ever talk?"

"Sam's a man of sparin' words," replied Henri. What he lacked in speech he made up for in brawn.

Did Blade believe her to be dangerous enough to require his bulk to keep in line? The crazy thought gave her a momentary lapse of relief.

Yet even poking through foodstuffs with a coifed troll couldn't stop the sands of despair from sifting through her. Nothing had seemed real. She felt empty. A shell. Without Monte and now Luc, she was nothing more than a shell.

The life of a pirate was short indeed. Luc and Monte had accepted that inevitable fact when they joined Alain. She had too, not wanting to be left behind like her mother. Dried herbs were fine but she didn't belong onshore. She didn't want to waste her life planted on soil. She traded it for the rocking swells of the sea.

It had been a dirty trick, one he never fully appreciated, but she trapped Alain into taking her along onboard with her brothers. For one voyage, a short one. Not a man of sympathy, she convinced him she would have no meaningful livelihood at home pruning and drying plants. What adventures could she possibly have without her brothers? The excess rum which she made sure filled his bottomless cup had helped. He had been so drunk they were well under sail before he realized he'd been duped.

Two years later, she still sailed with him. She'd proven her worth, shared in the profits and seen many perish. Death had been indiscriminate and came often. But never so close to her own kindred.

Empty. She didn't even remember taking the fruit. Under normal circumstances, that feat would send a bolt of giddy excitement bucking through her. Not this time. Her brother was gone. She was angry. And there was no one to blame.

She retrieved another mango from its hiding place and then bent to draw out a small knife from under her pants leg.

"Criminy." Henri gestured to the weapon she used to slice the mango's orange-yellow skin. "Tyburn know about that?"

"What? This?" She cut the mango into square chunks. "Does he need to?"

"He'll take it from ya."

"I'll just get another." She popped a piece into her mouth. The juice tasted thick on her tongue.

"I reckon ya will."

She held up a chunk as an offer to Sam, still brooding nearby. His grunt shook the boulder that sat on top of his neck, no.

"What's the matter? Don't you like fruit?"

He grunted again.

"He prefers raw, steamin' flesh," Henri said.

"That so? I'd say he likes something sweeter." Taking the final mango from her pocket, she tossed it to Sam. He snatched it from the air and crossed his arms again, giving her a subtle nod. She nodded back, the gratitude duly noted.

A rowdy bunch of men rounded a corner across the way from the three of them. Scruff of collar, singing terribly and waving around brown bottles of liquor, they shoved and stumbled along the sidewalk toward their small group. As they neared, one caught sight of Marisol. He held out an arm to stop his comrades.

"My, oh my," the man said. "Isn't she a pearl of a girl, lads? An hour with her and I be a broke bastard."

"Ha, poor lass would be powerfully disappointed. She'd be cheated after three minutes," one fellow quipped.

"Lucky she'd be is more like it," another said.

The men laughed and jostled about. Their good humor fell flat with Marisol. She had no use for their boorish fun and knew well enough how the encounter with them would end.

The drunk fool came forward and made a mocking bow before her. Sour booze permeated the air as he pulled himself upright, swaying from the quick movement. "How about it, sweetling? Want to find out how long we go for a few coins?"

"What you seek would cost you far more than what you carry to compensate for—" her eyes dropped to his crotch, "—what you so obviously lack."

The liquor hadn't flooded his mind enough to miss her meaning. "Mercy me, a smartin' hussy."

Beside her, Henri bristled. His little body seemed to grow as if every hair and whisker on his body stood on end, puffing out like a threatened alley cat. "You fellas need to move on," he warned.

"Isn't that something? The dwarf here is telling us to shove off. Whatcha goin' to do? Punch me in the kneecap?" Their laughter filled the night.

"He ain't no dwarf." Sam's statement rumbled quick and deep. He took a step farther into the light. His dark skin soaked up the lamplight, making their corner appear darker.

The laughter died. Seriousness replaced the jest and the drunks came to attention.

"Go on," Henri said. "Git."

"No," the sot said. "Not without the woman." He pulled out a pistol and pointed it at Marisol.

Good god. Not again. Bloody men. Bastards think because they have an extra appendage a woman must submit to their demands. Was waving a gun at her supposed to scare her and keep Sam at bay? She glanced at the behemoth. His arms remained fixed, relaxed across his chest. A wee smile flitted at the tips of his mouth when he returned the quick look. Poor Sam. He'd already found out firsthand how ill-natured she could be when bullied.

"Come." The man snatched at her wrist, causing her to drop her mango. It plopped to the ground, splattering juice and releasing a delicious fragrance.

"Me and the boys here are gonna show you a good time."

"You should let me go," she snarled.

"Nothin' doin'."

"Let go, you lobcock!"

Marisol yanked back her wrist, forcing him forward. He stepped on the fruit and slipped into her. Sam took a step forward. Henri poised with daggers drawn against the other troublemakers. Lacking any restraint or hesitation, she stabbed him with her small knife into the arm holding her. He yelped and bumbled backward. Everything happened so fast, Marisol had no time to react to the man's next move.

He leveled his gun at her. "Bitch!"

A shot pierced the night and the gun flew out of the brute's hand. It clattered to the cobblestones and slid from reach. "Son of a…"

"My next mark will be your head." Blade stepped from the shadows, a puff of smoke still visible from the pistol's discharge.

Whew. Another close one.

A group of men stood at Blade's back shrouded by the darkness. The faceless pack poised deadly in their silence. "You men best move on before my benevolence runs aground."

Stanching the blood flow from his fingers with his other hand, the napper studied Blade hard. No contest could be had. They were outnumbered.

"Let's be on our way, then, lads." He frowned at Marisol. "We'll find us another poppet to play with, eh?"

He took a bottle from one of his friends and the gang disappeared down the street.

Blade strode over. His powerful pace had her wanting to shrink like a swooning genteel lass. He commanded the world around him to bow as if no man could conquer him. The elements were his to rule. And with those haunting eyes staring through her, she would be his loyal subject. Blast! Where had that come from?

"You, dear lady, attract all sorts of trouble. How you have managed this long without a guardian, I'm certain I could not fathom."

"Did you not bear witness to his stab wound?" He hadn't been contemptible, yet she would not admit to him how right he was with his remark. She wiped her knife on her hip and bent down to put it away under her pants leg.

"Aye. A favorable event to have him fall on you."

"The happenstance means little as long as the end result

keeps me alive." She smiled at him as she stood, conceding to the obvious. "Thank you, Blade. I dare not think of what would have happened had you not come."

"Saving you has become something of a habit. Twice in one day." He pursed his lips into a smirk.

"I suppose now I'm beholden to you." She winked and his smile spread.

"I believe you are right, in more ways than one."

What did he mean by that, more ways than one?

"Henri." Blade turned to the little man. "I've made arrangements to have poultry brought to the *Rissa.* Cook us up a feast. We're having guests dine with us tonight."

"Guests, Capt'n? Are we celebratin' somethin'?"

"Nay. But a man's gluttonous stomach full to bursting is the best way to start a hunting party."

Her heart picked up speed. "You found out what happened to the *Gloria?*" Did he know what happened to the cargo and crew? More importantly, did he know what happened to Monte? Was he alive?

"Not entirely. But we will be chasing down a couple of suspected targets."

"A couple, Capt'n?" Sam moved to stand with them, now soaking in the growing anticipation.

"Captain Drake and the *Widow Maker* will be joining us." He motioned to the shadows concealing the group of men. A tall man came forward. A white feather plume bounced on the hat covering the flips and waves of unruly dark hair as he neared. His long coat flapped open with his confident gait, revealing his brace of deadly weapons strapped to his proud chest.

"Milady." He inclined his head to her. She nodded back and he stepped aside.

"Drake will follow one lead and we shall follow another. I am certain one of these vessels will have the silver and the answers we seek."

"But what of the *Gloria?*" Marisol chomped at the bit for whatever it was that Blade knew. "You said 'not entirely.' What *do* you know? You must have found something."

Blade took her by the shoulders. "You're right. I do have something else I have found." He let her go and motioned again to the group in the shadows.

The rest of the figures pushed away from the darkness and came into view. There were eight of them but she locked on only one. Could it be? A painful lump lodged in the back of her throat. Tears, which she thought she had no more of, sprang from the corners of her eyes. She couldn't breathe. But this time, these reactions were not because of sadness. These were born of joy.

Monte. Her little brother Monte. He lived. He lived and walked toward her. She broke into a run.

"Monte!"

His broad smile warmed her as he raced to meet her. They embraced, hugging tight. She did not want to let him go. Ever. "Monte. Thank God. You're alive. I've missed you so. Oh, Monte, you're alive."

"Sister. Of course, I'm alive." He pulled back to look at her, his loving gaze accentuated with the crow's feet of his eyes. He had aged. His youthful countenance had been replaced with harsh lines. "I've missed you, too." He kissed her cheek.

She had so many questions for him. "What happened at Matanzas? Were you injured? How did you escape? I tried to get Alain to go back. Are you a member of the *Gloria*'s crew?"

"Whoa, Marisol. Slow down. None of that is important right now."

He was right, of course. She let her excitement carry her away. This was a matter to be discussed among themselves, not openly in front of strangers. Each of them watched their reunion. She didn't care. She'd been searching for Monte for months. Every port, every passage, she culled for any information about her brother. The tip that he sailed for Windham had paid off. The messenger, taking Blade's cameo, the ghost ship blunder, it had all been worth it. *My God.*

The elation overflowing in her heart made it so. She should feel repentant for those ill fortunes. She didn't. Not anymore. Here they stood, together again. She had the urge to sing. If only she could carry a tune.

"I can't believe I've finally found you. I never gave up hope. I told Luc. I told him you were still out there."

It hit her again. The deep dread of losing Luc. How unfair that life had wreaked such havoc upon her. Losing one brother and regaining the other. Why couldn't they both be there, with her, like old times? She would have to tell Monte about his big brother.

"Monte." She looked to the ground before summoning up enough courage to give him the news. "Luc is dead. He was hanged for last night's raid here in Puerto Plata."

Monte pulled her back into their embrace. "I know, Marisol. I witnessed it."

She jerked back, shocked at what he'd said. "And you didn't save him?"

"There wasn't anything I could do."

Something she couldn't explain, a darkness perhaps, drew down his demeanor and his stance. She hadn't noticed before, but he seemed rigid.

Wasn't there anything? If she had been there she would have fought tooth and nail to free Luc, even if she had to pay for it with her life.

"Come," Blade said.

She was glad for the interruption. She couldn't trust herself for what she might have said next.

"Let us return to my ship for supper. There we will eat, drink and talk of tomorrow."

Tomorrow. For far too long, tomorrow held little promise. Although tomorrow would be a fine new day, Marisol was not ready for tonight to end.

* * *

Marisol sat at the captain's table with the men as they discussed the plans for their hunt the next morning. Five of them gathered there, Captain Drake and his first mate, a brawny beast he called Valeryn, Blade, Willie and herself.

Blade thought it best she dine with his company, not as his guest, but to ensure she remained on board the *Rissa.* She had what she wanted. But she still had an obligation to return Blade's cameo, and until she did, she remained under his custody.

Empty plates sat before them, nary a crumb left, and fresh tankards of ale had been poured. The smell of meat lingered in the air from their earlier feast of boiled chicken, potatoes and bread. The meal tasted hearty and satisfying, settling deep within her and making her fight a drowsy tug. When was the last time she felt full enough to want to curl up for a nap? She should consider stealing Henri away. He was a master cook fit for the kings.

Monte had not been allowed to dine with her in the captain's quarters. However, she had a nice long stroll with him on deck before the meal. They reminisced about fairer times—as children gathering shells and crabs along the beach, their mother's baked tarts, of adventures sailing with Alain. They talked of Luc and his mastery at swordsmanship. It must've been difficult for Monte to talk of their brother. He spoke little more of him, dodging any other subject about Luc, most notably, Luc's death. That had been fine with her. Her grief had been reeled in. She controlled it now. But if Monte wavered and gave way to the hurt, she probably would, too.

Perhaps he wanted to spare her from his terrible ordeal, and time and again, he avoided retelling what had happened to him at Matanzas. She hadn't an inkling of how he escaped the Spanish soldiers in the raid gone horribly wrong. Never mind. They were together once more. That was all that mattered.

Marisol looked about the cabin as she drank her ale. It was only a bit like what she expected from a pirate captain's quarters. Functional but without the spoils of victories displayed throughout. Bookshelves secured books, maps and nautical instruments. Various painted lockers were pushed into available nooks, a small gilded mirror nailed to a post hung over a barrel and a peculiar painting of a naked woman embellished a wall. The most impressive piece in the room was the intricately hewn black desk. With a golden candelabrum casting a flickering glow on the matching set of scales and inkwell, the desk made a grand statement. Black hemp drapes were drawn, most likely hiding the bed Blade slept in. What wonders lay beyond those curtains? She would like to find out.

Licking her lips at the thought of the captain tangled up in the blankets of his bed, she set the tankard down. He sat across the table from her and she caught him staring on several occasions. Not that she minded. She'd sent him a coy smile, or two, herself. This night, he had given her more than anyone before him. He gave her comfort, friendship and a spicy kiss to top it off. She had done well in getting him to help find Monte, even if it was accidental.

Now she and Monte could return to Alain. Wouldn't he be surprised? He'd be so thrilled with her and her relentless will, bringing Monte back. Especially with losing Luc and other crewmen to the gallows. She would be back in his good favor.

Yes, she owed much to Captain Tyburn.

"We'll send the *Gloria* back to Santo Domingo." Blade's rich voice lured her away from her thoughts. "The three ships will sail together until we reach the Mona Passage."

"Are you sure the *Sugar Lady* headed east?" Captain Drake relaxed in his chair, absently tapping the rim of his cup.

"Aye. A seaman on board pawning off pouches of tobacco mentioned to Willie, here, their next port of call to be San Juan."

"Smugglers?"

"Perhaps." Blade propped his leg up onto the table. "She'll be going against the easterly trade winds and will have to tack across the passage. My waters." He chuckled. "The *Sugar Lady* will be easy prey."

"So you are wagering this mystery ship is making a quarry of the *Sugar Lady.*" Drake nodded his head slowly and smiled. "I like this. Hunting the hunter. Jolly good fun, my friend."

"A glorious thing, to be a sea devil." The room bellowed in laughter and the men raised their tankards high.

After they settled down, Blade continued. "Mr. Castellan can pilot the *Gloria* back to Windham."

Monte? Why him? She just got him back.

"He can give Windham his account of what happened."

"But Blade—"

"Not now, Marisol." He set his cup down and leveled his stare at her. "We've already discussed this."

"You can't—"

"Enough."

"What about—"

"You may excuse yourself from the table."

She clamped her mouth shut. She'd learned long ago arguing with a bullheaded captain would do nothing more than blow hot air. Never argue in the company of men, either. A man doesn't appreciate a woman criticizing him in front of his mates. Blade's mates waited with stringent expressions, fully expecting she follow his orders.

She brooded. "Very well, Captain."

"Willie, see Miss Castellan out," Blade said. "Assign a man to her cabin."

With his cameo gone, she was to fawn under his command. It would be a whimsy notion to think he would let her go with her brother. Obviously talking to him about it now was out of the question. No, she would need to take a different direction if she were to stay with Monte.

"Very well, sir." She pushed off the arms of her chair, rising tall. "Gentlemen." She inclined her head to the men and left.

* * *

Blade added a final detail to his log and replaced the white quill in the inkwell. Leaning back in his chair, he clasped his hands behind his head. Another long day. Exhaustion threatened to seep into his soul. But sleep remained a stranger. He hadn't had a true night's rest since, ah, well, it didn't matter. A few winks would be enough. It always had been.

Thoughts of Marisol wandered forward, sending missing silver and ghost ships evaporating to the back of his mind. The bonny lass sure had a go of it that day. He admired her for all that strength she shouldered. He had a special affinity for strong women. Especially those with overmodest smiles and eyes that batted at him during supper. Remaining focused on the business at hand had been a real challenge. He kept finding himself wanting to kiss her lips again. At least now, he could let her be the fetching obsession in his brief dreams.

He rose from his desk and stripped his tunic from his body. A muffled knock tapped at his cabin door. Who would disturb him at this hour?

"Enter."

When she stepped through the threshold, he silently cursed. Having Marisol in his dreams would be a pleasure. But having her come to his quarters to argue about her brother...well, that didn't sit well with him at all. Couldn't she wait until the morning to fence him? He would have a harsh word for the fellow guarding her quarters. If she hadn't incapacitated him permanently.

"Sorry to disturb you, Captain."

"As am I." He shook his head, instantly feeling bad about his curt tone. "My apologies, Marisol." He moved around the desk and motioned for her to close the door. "What can I do for you?"

"I am looking for relief," she said.

"Oh?" This could get interesting.

"I understand if you feel I am stepping over any boundaries but my curiosity is eating me alive."

Curiosity? I've a bit of my own. "Go on."

"Your cameo. Its value undoubtedly pales to what meaning it holds for you. Please. Tell me what secrets it keeps. Tell me why you would torture me for it."

She had come to him to inquire about his cameo? "Torture? Dear lady, I believe you've toppled too much drink tonight. I've shown you leniency. Besides, I reserve my torment for when it behooves me most."

"Please, Blade." She closed the distance between them. "I must understand why I'm being kept from my brother. I'll be happy to return the damned thing to you, if you'll just tell me why it is so important."

"Why should I relieve your misery while I remain in mine?"

She sank down into a chair, dropping her hands into her lap. "You're right. It's just...I've just lost one brother." She sniffled back her surfacing tears. "Getting Monte back, well, it would help if I knew the reason for giving him up so soon."

Ah, that fleeting relief of peace. He knew well the euphoric end of suffering and how quickly the false sense of freedom could be replaced with something beyond horrendous. He knew suffering. More than she could ever know. Her blind madness on the gallows with Luc's body was only the tip of what torment could be, but time would numb her loss. Blade was not about causing her more pain. He needed her to understand that his motives ran deep and that their arrangement was merely provisional, not like the lifetime of suffering he endured. He'd never have peace. But she would. Soon enough, she would.

He took a knee before her. "I was just a boy when I was taken from my home and sold off as a sailor to a savage master of a merchantman." She raised her eyes to him, dams ready to burst. Oh how he hated to see a woman cry. He didn't want to tell her about the cameo. It wouldn't put her at ease. But then, he hadn't been at ease since she stole it from him.

"He had many boys, all of us slaves. We worked long hours in the scorching sun, during dangerous squalls, among vile conditions. Disease ran rampant, as did abuse. We had to be tough. We had to learn quickly. If we didn't, we died. Young boys were easy and cheap to come by."

Sadness furrowed her brow. Her earlier claim of occasionally sailing had been falsified by the bow of her head. Aye, she knew of these hazards he spoke of. But he doubted it was firsthand.

"You speak of torture. You know nothing of torture." He no longer saw Marisol, no longer sat with her. His mind whirled back to a dark place. The dank cell in the belly of that hellhole.

"He starved us. Deprived us of food, water, dignity. I had angered the master. I don't recall what I had done. Only that he beat me and chained me in the bilge."

The smell of human filth assaulted him as if he were still shackled to the rotten hull. He heard that familiar drip, that slow steady leak that had kept time with the unraveling of his sanity.

"Another boy was there," he continued. "Starved just as I." Few words had been spoken between them. It had been forbidden. "We grew feral in our hunger.

"The master." His cruel face flashed before him and he growled. "He thought to play with his lackey toys. He unshackled us, brought us on deck for entertainment. *His* entertainment. He held up a small loaf of bread. It had smelled so good. I had never wanted something more in my entire life than that one piece of bread."

He swallowed the saliva that pooled in his mouth. "We were to fight. Fight until we could fight no more. If we refused, we would both be tossed to the sea. The reward, the loaf of bread. Someone pushed him at me and I attacked. We fought, clawed, bit."

Cheering among the older men filled his ears. A glimpse of the master's vicious guffawing forever seared into his mind.

"I managed to land him on his back. I sat on his chest and

pummeled his face. Over and over I hit him."

Blood ran from the boy's nose, his mouth. Red all over Blade's knuckles, splattered across his shirt.

"He stopped blocking me, stopped moving. I had killed him."

No more cheers. The only sound had been his own heavy breathing. The master tossed the bread to him. He snatched up the loaf and devoured it, weevils and all. "Well done," his master had laughed. "You've become a man, today." 'Twas then Blade had understood what he had done. Aye, from that day forward, his lot had been cast to a life of hell.

"The cameo had fallen out of the boy's pocket. No one had seen it. But I had. I kept it. As a reminder of the beast I had become. To honor the boy's life I'd taken. To never forget my deserved perdition."

Marisol slid to kneel before him. Her beauty returned him to his cabin. He hadn't realized he had sunk back on his knees to the floor. She placed her small hand to his cheek.

"I'm so sorry, Blade." Tears flowed freely down her soft face. "I never should have taken it. I promise I will get your cameo back. I promise."

CHAPTER 9

Never had Marisol been sorry for stealing. The thought of an object meaning more to someone than for its coin value failed to ever cross her mind. Yet, Blade's cameo pulled tight on the fiber of his soul. She might as well have stabbed him in the back in his sleep. How could she? Her own permanence crumbled under the weight of her shame. A simple flick of her hand and she had put his world in an upheaval. It was a wonder he'd shown her any kindness at all. Her heart ached to ease his pain.

His face warmed on her palm as he closed his eyes and leaned into it. He reached up to take her hand and placed a gentle kiss on the inside. Cupping her face with his other hand, he wiped at the tears streaming down her own cheek with the pad of his thumb. The intimate touch sent shivers down her spine.

"I shouldn't have told you about the cameo." He shook his head with his whispers.

"No. I needed to hear it. I've been selfish. I know that now." She offered him a smile. He needn't worry about her. She would be all right. "I did a terrible injustice to you. I will make things right."

His green eyes captured her, held her fast. "Yes, you will." Desire swirled in their emerald crystalline depths. Time seemed suspended. She couldn't break free from their magical binds. When his gaze traveled down to her mouth, their pull loosened and she felt as if she'd lost something. Just as before, when she wished he would smile upon her with those sinful dimples, she longed for him to look at her again with that needful want.

Blade leaned in. His hand remained on her cheek and he still watched her mouth. His earthy scent filled her head. A heady aroma she inhaled deep. She lifted her face to him and met his lips. Tender at first. But then something she couldn't identify flushed through her with such force it took her by surprise. Consumed with desire, she crushed into him as he grabbed her close.

Their kiss turned wild, rough. His tongue slashed through her mouth and she responded in urgent kind. She pulled herself into his lap and rubbed her hands against the bare flesh of his back, grabbing for him, pressing him even closer.

He shoved a hand into her hair and yanked her head back to expose her neck. His kisses burned along the sensitive column of her skin. She drew a ragged breath. And then another. The stubble encasing each kiss shot thousands of tiny arrows of arousal to every part of her body. She roared alive.

Moving up to her ear, he ran his tongue along the ridges. His hot breath tickled and she swore she would shatter from the excitable prickle spreading down below. "Oh dear God." Her voice sounded distant, raspy. He delved his tongue in and then nipped her earlobe. She nearly unraveled.

A whimper escaped when he pulled away. He studied her. She hoped he could read her mind. Unabashed as her dirty thoughts were, she refrained from begging him to take her. At least not out loud. *Oh please, Blade. Do what you will, but please have me.*

Peeling her from his lap, he stood. From her vantage, he towered over her. The dim light danced across the taut planes of his bare chest, parting in a ripple of magnificent muscle. Broad shoulders rounded into sinewy arms extended, to help her to her feet.

He cupped the back of her head and found his way to her neck again. Growling, his breath moistened the base of her throat in the recess above her collarbone. "Strip for me." His words rumbled through her as the thunder would roll through swollen rain clouds. "Strip for me now."

Music to her ears. “As you wish, Captain.” She could not deny him anything while he branded her with those searing full lips.

He stepped away and leaned against his fancy desk; to watch, to wait. A glow from the flames of the candlestick on the writing table permeated the shadows around him. An aura encircling a bronzed god. His golden hair swept across his shoulders and feathered along his face almost concealing his lust-laden gaze. He dipped his head for her to begin.

Crouching down, she retrieved the small hidden knife from under her pant leg. She held it up to show him she removed the threat then tossed it aside. Blade’s eyebrows shot up as she pulled out the second knife from her other leg. Handsome, he was, in his mild surprise. She suppressed a giggle when she stood to remove her last knife from under her waistband. Blade, however, appeared less amused.

He tilted his head, questioning her over more concealed weapons. She shook her head. No, she had no others.

Sliding out of her shoes, her feet touched the smooth, cool planks. She pulled the drawstring to her trousers and shimmied, letting them fall into a puddle at her feet. Blade’s gaze fastened on her bare legs. The shirt fabric brushed against her thighs, a stark reminder that she wore nothing underneath. Could he tell? He’d find out soon enough.

A twitch played at his mouth. He inclined his head for her to continue. Watching him observe her through a thick fog of desire endowed her with the courage to disrobe fully for him.

She crossed her arms and took the hem of her tunic up and over her head. Thick waves of hair fell soft, cascading down her back and coming to a rest on the rounded curve of her breasts. Was it the sudden rush of cool air or Blade running his tongue across his bottom lip that made her skin pucker into gooseflesh? Fingering the laces of her corset, she took care to be slow in slackening then removing the unyielding clothing.

Standing in all her glory for him, she might have felt intimidated, powerless. Instead, his seductive study of her body, his eyes raking ever so slowly over her breasts and dipping down to her juncture, empowered her. She straightened her back, just to give him a little more chest to look at.

Blade came forward. The desire that stiffened in the air became more solid. He brushed aside a tussock of hair covering one breast. Her nipple hardened in response to the strands whisking across its peak. He reached out, his hand spread wide over her breast.

Fingers twitched as his hand hovered, ready to take hold. Her breath caught when he grasped her and she leaned into him, pushing forward against his hand. The pressure was painfully sweet with each careful squeeze.

He took her mouth again. She urged and cajoled, taking in little pants each time their lips parted. He moved down to take her breast into his mouth, suckling her. The sensation raced down to her buzzing core. His hand slid down her back to her buttock. With fingers callused and domineering, he caressed the crease above her thigh as he cupped her. She uttered a sweeping sigh, arching farther into him.

The rough strain in his trousers grated against the naked flesh of her belly. The texture heightened her awareness that he remained clothed. That would not do.

She planted her palms on his chest and pushed him back. He groused his displeasure from being refused. A wanton smile she could hardly contain slipped across her mouth. "Your turn," she said on a breathy moan. "Now you must strip for me."

Chuckling low, he pursed his mouth, contemplating her proposal. "No."

"No?" *He has brought me all this way to deny me?* She must have pouted for he chuckled again.

"That's right. No." A most larkish grin snuck in the impressions of his dimples. "I want *you* to undress me."

Heat flushed throughout her, stoking the flames of raging need out of control. What a wicked demand. One she would relish.

She placed her hand on his firm stomach, slowly dragging her fingertips down, following the dark flaxen trail of hair disappearing below his waistband. Breathing quickened as she loosened the tie of his breeches. Was it his breath or hers? She couldn't be sure. His skin felt smooth as she slipped her hands to the narrow of his hips. Tucking her thumbs over the fabric, she rubbed her open palms down his powerful legs, pulling his trousers down with them. He hissed as he sprang free and she continued her descent until the breeches loosened from the breadth of his thighs, falling the rest of the way to the floor. Much farther down and she would be eye-level with his stretching member. She stared at it for one moment. Saint's blood, he was magnificent. Thrusting high and proud, she craved to touch him but dared not. Wielding a sword as aggressively large as he was bound to be dangerous.

Rising, she arched in close to his body, lightly brushing her nipples along his hardened chest. She reached his lips and planted a languid kiss to his open mouth.

Blade moaned. "A lusty one, aren't you?"

"I prefer hot-blooded." She could kiss him like that until morning. Quite possibly even longer.

"Let's see how hot-blooded you are."

In fluid motion, he moved to the curtain screening his sleeping quarter and yanked the heavy drape back. She hardly noticed his bed lacking the plush pillows and soft coverings such as in her own cabin. No, the window his bed jutted against ensnared her. It must be beautiful to lie there at night with the sea below as a mattress and the stars shining their endless sparkling lights as the blanket.

He turned to her and, quite sudden, she knew she was prey. Scooping her up, he tossed her to the bed. She rose to her elbows and almost protested to being thrown around like a child's rag doll. Almost. Perched with his knee on the edge of the mattress, his primal gaze boring into her, she burned for him. She burned hot for the feel of his rough hands handling her. She wanted to relinquish her control to him, for him.

He crawled across her, wedging himself between her legs, pinning her beneath him. His weight settled upon her, comfortable and moist, and he ravished her body with enchanting kisses. Made barbaric by his torturous lips, she caressed his back, his arms, his shoulders, and any exposed part of him she could reach in a frantic need to touch him, to mold to him.

Nipping, mauling her breasts, the pain he inflicted sent ruptures of liquid heat pooling between her thighs. Her whimpers rose with each sharp pinch of his fingers and teeth.

One punishing hand rummaged down her side, pausing long enough to squeeze her hip and then moved to her hammering center. He stroked her there. His fingers were brutal, raking up and drawing down across her soft sheath. Her body responded uproariously as she lifted herself to take in more. *Please, more.*

Lower he took his kisses, down, down, to her throbbing mound. *Mother of Heaven.* His tongue flicked and swirled within her pulsating folds. Never had she felt such delirium. Her head spun in dizzying circles and her rhythmic breathing gave way to uneven gasping. He drove her mad.

"Blade..."

A swell of sensation whirled with the friction of his relentless tongue. Building, churning, she grabbed a fistful of his hair. What sweet death he brought her. She seized, squeezing her thighs, lifting her buttocks from the bed to clutch into his mouth, the crest of throes spilling over in wave after wave of spasms. She rose into a void of sheer pleasure only to sink helpless into his sheets.

"Mmm." Blade slipped his way up her body. "Delicious."

His lips tasted warm and smelled musky as she rewarded him with a kiss, deep and appreciative.

She wanted to take him to the same wondrous place he had taken her. A precious gift she intended to share. Slipping her hand to reach for him pressed solid against her belly, he grabbed her wrist.

"No." Something mischievous clouded his countenance.

He sat up and reached for the candelabra sitting on his desk. Plucking out a candlestick, he returned to straddle her. His corded legs tucked next to her hips and his rigid length remained at full attention. But the flickering flame of the candle held her mesmerized. And as she looked past the yellow flare to his bold grin, she squirmed in uncertainty.

"Have I brought you pleasure?"

She nodded. More than any man before him.

"Will you trust me?"

Glancing at the candle, she had no idea what she should trust him to do. What could he mean to do with the little fire stick? His smirk dared her with a reply. She doubted her actual answer mattered. She nodded again.

He grabbed her head, lifted her up to smother her with a torrid kiss. Letting her back down to his pillow, he cupped her face and rubbed his splayed hand down her throat and the middle of her chest to rest below the rise of her breasts.

"It will burn, but only for a moment."

Burn? What did he mean?

Blade tilted the candle to let droplets of melted wax slide down the side of the stick and drip into the valley of her chest. She yelped as the heat seared her skin. The burn, it felt…remarkable. A devilish pleasure broiled deep within her core and she shivered with the hot chills of the initial singe blending with the seething heat of his palm caressing, groping at her flesh. Dear Lord. How could something so painful bring such intense enjoyment?

"Aye," he said. "You like that, don't you?"

She succumbed to his rich voice, writhing under him. "More."

His throaty laugh accompanied another dose of wax. She cried out as it ran down her side before cooling. Gripping at his knee with one hand, she pulled at her hair with the other. Mad. She would go mad. His free hand continued to knead her body. Still, he poured more wax on her, bringing her to begging. He sprinkled it closer to her nipple. She yipped with the sting on her tender skin. She had known no pleasure such as what he doled. She fought back tears of dire abandonment.

"You've had enough, dove."

Snuffing the candle flame with his fingers, he tossed the spent stick to his desk.

"Please, Blade. Haven't you tortured me enough? Won't you have me?"

She shrank into the bed from his grin. He descended upon her, raining her with more lascivious kisses.

"I've wanted you from the moment you fell on me." He ran his hand down her thigh and nudged her to open for him.

She did as he bade, no longer wanting to play with his fire. She inhaled him, breathing in as much of him as she could take. He smelled of brimstone. And why wouldn't he, the devil.

He growled in her neck as he eased himself into her. She tensed but as she stretched for him and fastened down around him, she felt full. He edged out then pushed back in and she lifted her hips to meet him. He picked up his rhythm. Wanting more, needing more, she rocked up burying him as deep as she could make him go. She dug her fingers into the curvature of his back, taking in all of him.

His panting in her ear, landing warm and wet on her neck, unleashed a wanton flurry. "More." She sobbed on the intolerable ecstasy of his possessive thrusts.

He plunged into her harder, faster, sending her closer and closer to the edge. Her body petrified and he gave her a final lance. She screamed and shattered into hundreds of tiny pieces, showering her soul in bursting hot cinders. And with one last thrust, Blade pierced her into two, groaning on his own climax, quivering on each tiered release.

Weakened, she relaxed, languid with contentment. He gathered her into his arm while bending the other under his head. She nuzzled into him, wrapped up in his cocoon of sticky warmth and sweat and planted a kiss on the salt-tinged skin of his neck. His exotic spice lingered on her lips. Sampling more, she suckled a band along his neck, savoring the tasty tang. He pulled her closer, petting her.

An unfamiliar feeling crept up on her. Peace. Comfort. Very much like what he had given her earlier in the evening on the wharf. It scared the hell out of her. Had she given up so much of herself? She'd relinquished her self-control. And not to just any man. But to a dangerous man who could see her ruined over her thievery should she fail to return his cameo.

She'd come to his chambers to persuade him to send her with Monte. Distract him with bawdy talk and empty promises over the return of his cameo. That was the plan. Her plan failed. Somehow she strayed. She hadn't expected Blade's cameo bound him to a hellish nightmare. Nor did she expect his story to affect her so. She lost her way in his suggestive jousting. Wicked. He was simply wicked. And she was more of a woman because of him.

Damned if he hadn't stirred up a long dead emotion.

Compassion.

Bah! Compassion was for the weak.

However, she couldn't overlook the fact Blade showed

considerable compassion. He was far from weak. On the contrary, he appeared to be more powerful than any other man she had ever been acquainted with, including Alain.

Alain. Oh God. He mustn't know about Blade. Alain would kill him. Quite possibly, kill them both. What had she done?

"I should go."

"Aye." Blade let his hand drop away.

He would let her go so easily? After what they shared, after what he did with her, *to her?* A painful knot constricted in her chest.

He rolled out of bed and slipped back into his breeches.

No. No feeling of remorse. She wouldn't allow it.

And absolutely *no* shame.

Gliding off the mattress, she gathered her clothes and redressed. He poured himself a tankard of ale from the table and watched her over the rim of the cup while she slipped on her shoes. He did nothing as she picked up her knives, shrugging when she replaced them in their proper hiding places. Infuriating! She wanted to scream at him for his flippancy. How dare he no longer see her as a threat. *Ooh!*

Her heart sank once she reached his door. He had said nothing to her. The cool metal of the doorknob diverged from the humid cabin around her. The smell of copulation and spent candle stained the air, a hint of their unity minutes earlier. She didn't want to leave without him saying something, anything. She looked over her shoulder at him. If she hadn't known better she would have sworn she saw sadness in his eyes. Was that because of what they had done? Or was he thinking of his lost cameo? Either way, she was to blame.

"Well, good night, then." What else could she say?

"Good night, dove."

* * *

The door closed with a soft click. Blade let out an audible sigh in his cup and swallowed the rest of his drink. What in the name of all that was holy had gotten into him? Why had he let that happen? Bedding the woman. Here, in his cabin. He turned to the tousled bed. The only place he kept for himself, his safe haven.

A place where he dreamed, suffered alone.

He sank down in his chair and picked up the candle off the desk. The yellowed tallow had congealed its waxy drippings. A cavity along the burnt wick testified that much of the stick had been used up. Marisol's yelps and moans as he trickled the wax onto her creamy skin still reverberated in his ears.

Sins of flesh. The more iniquitous, the sweeter the deed and it always had been worth it. It would someday be the death of him. He enjoyed women more than he should, and too often, too easily. But enjoy them he did. Admittedly, his appetite for a woman's body teetered on greedy and insatiable.

Yet with Marisol, that delectable creature, the desire had been furious. So strong, their passion. He wanted to hurt her with his lovemaking, be rough with her. Enact a gratifying punishment for her intolerable wrongdoing. She had enjoyed it as much as he. The bonny lass was a rare and delightful surprise.

He stiffened as he remembered the feel of her supple skin, the sounds of her uneven breathing, and the taste of her drenched core. She was something he had never imagined. He couldn't put it to words, but she stirred something within him.

Damn it! He slammed his fist down on the arm of his chair, clamping tight to the candle. She collapsed the crusty stronghold of his number one rule. *Never in his bed.*

Oh, she had tried to lead him away from his refuge, rattle him from his sanctuary, and lay claim to him in the bed he shared with no one. She tried with those carnal eyes and provocative smile. She tried when she reached between their naked bodies to take him in her hand. It had been laborious to stop her. No doubt she would have brought him to his knees.

He snorted. As if he would relinquish his control to her. No. He deprived her of that victory. His bedchamber, his terms.

Damn her!

* * *

"Does he let you wander alone around his ship at night?"

Marisol looked up from the black water below. Monte leaned next to her on the railing, bringing her back from distant thoughts. She had spent the better part of the half hour oscillating between dreamy fantasies of Blade and bloody humiliation-fueled anger.

"Does it matter if he didn't?"

Monte smiled. "No. I suppose not. You aren't one for doing as you're told. You continually kept Luc and I busy covering your hide."

"At least I staved off boredom." They shared a quiet laugh, but it ended all too soon.

"Why didn't you send word?" She tilted her head to see his face better. The *Rissa*'s lanterns had been extinguished for the night and she couldn't see her brother clearly in the dark. "Why didn't you let us know you were alive?"

"Nothing would have changed. Alain had made a decision." He had snarled out Alain's name. "You know he never changes his mind. He took his ship and left Matanzas and he didn't look back."

"He thought you were dead," she said. She understood Monte feeling abandoned but something more malicious lay in his harsh tone. "If you would have sent word, I'm certain he—"

"Don't bother, Marisol. We both know Alain cut his losses." He spat to the planks. "To hell with Alain."

Blame him for his resentment, she could not. She had her own to keep in check. Like it or not, Alain was her master. He'd given her access to the sea. For that, she would continue to serve him. At least until the day she procured her own ship and crew.

Monte stared out across the bay at the anchored *Gloria.* The mood had made a notable shift. One she could not entirely miss. One that made her feel…uncomfortable.

"He means to send you with the *Gloria,*" she said.

He nodded. So Blade had already spoken to Monte of their plans. She shouldn't be surprised.

"You'll be her captain."

He nodded again. In the dark, she couldn't gauge him. But she knew him well enough.

"If you vanish with her, how will I find you?"

He turned to face her. Even without the benefit of light, Marisol saw the flash of his spiteful smile. Aye, he was a Castellan man through and through. A conniving pirate with unscrupulous designs. He might even make a father proud.

"Don't you fear, dear sister. I will find you."

CHAPTER 10

Damn if it wasn't hot. Blade took his green kerchief and wiped at the sweat stinging his eyes, then tied it tightly around his forehead to protect against the harsh midday sun. The brittle wind left his skin tight and parched. Grueling heat scorched so that even the wooden rails of his ship burned to the touch. He shielded his eyes to view the bright sea, taking note of the two distant vessels in his wake.

The three ships had set sail early in the morn, before the break of dawn, leaving Puerto Plata for what Blade hoped would be the last time. Once they reached the Mona Passage, he and Drake would head for Puerto Rico and the wayward *Sugar Lady*. Monte would take the *Gloria* down along the coast of Hispaniola to avoid the deadly currents and return to Santo Domingo.

Although he told Monte he would recommend him as a captain to Windham upon returning, his gut told him the boy likely had other plans. Blade was no fool. The arrogant dolt knew more than he was telling. Monte refused to give any information about what happened on the *Gloria,* claiming he saw nothing. He and his cohorts had been blindfolded and set adrift. A lie. To what purpose would someone kill off or suppress prisoners only to let three go? And leaving a ship behind? No purpose Blade could imagine. Unless, of course, they both were meant to be found. But why? These questions bounced around in his head.

He couldn't be bothered with the minor details of a scheming dog. His mission was the silver, which he would find. Let the little arse cross him. He expected it.

Blade hadn't become a successful pirate by being naïve. Rules to live by: Never be unarmed. Never give a man your back. Anticipate your foe's next move. And know when to show no mercy. Monte was unimportant. But his sister? Perhaps Blade should apply these same rules to her.

His thoughts meandered to their tryst the night before instead of centering on what lay ahead. Blissful memories ousted the edgy thrill of sniffing out prey. That annoyed the hell out of him. In part because of the space Marisol invaded. But truly, nothing should get in the way of a good ole dirty pursuit. Oh, but those beautiful eyes, fine pair of breasts, supple hips…

"Capt'n? Did you hear me?"

"Hmm? Um, no. What is it, Willie?"

"Smoke. Gunfire. Someone's having a party without us."

Blade heard it, the next blast. He'd been so distracted with ruttish reflections, he hadn't noticed the low rumble of round shot blasted from shipboard guns. On the near horizon, two ships engaged in a sea battle.

"One of ours?" he asked.

"I reckon that depends." Willie passed a spyglass to Blade's waiting hand.

Blast after blast sparked the gun smoke that hung between the two ships. He scanned the masts of the ships for their colors.

"Of course. *Sablewing.* Carrion's brigantine." He groaned. What was the renegade up to now? "Who the hell is the other ship?" he muttered. "A red flag. Do you recognize the ensign?"

"Nay, Capt'n. I thought you might."

Blade had not seen the skeletal hand and sword flag before amongst the brotherhood. A buccaneer invading these waters was either a newcomer or immeasurably stupid.

"Looks as if Carrion is getting a right good flog." Carrion's ship had taken several direct hits. Shattered rails and a damaged mizzenmast had the vessel faltering to hold her own.

Blade spun around and looked past the stern on the larboard quarter. Drake sailed at some distance behind with Monte and the *Gloria* off to the right. The *Rissa* would be upon the ongoing battle long before Drake.

"We'll be on them handsomely, sir. Are we to intervene?"

"Clear for quarters and look for my signal. There may be no need to engage. If we get close enough and the fighting doesn't end, we'll send a warning shot to Carrion's offender." He scratched his chin and chuckled. "With any luck, we'll accidentally hit the *Sablewing.*"

"'Twould be a shame." Willie laughed as he left to give the orders.

After another look through the lens, Blade followed Willie down to the ship's waist. Excitement vaulted through him. Leaning over the rail, they had sailed close enough to see clearly the silhouettes of the battling ships. He almost prayed for a stray shot to splinter the *Rissa* just so he could join in the affray. Aw, hell. Why wait? It'd been a while since the lads had seen any real action.

He called out to Willie. "Make ready. No mercy given to either ship."

Willie smiled and nodded. "Make ready," he yelled to the men, repeating the orders.

"Wait!" Marisol grabbed Blade by the arm, turning him to face her. He frowned at her sudden appearance. Wild trepidation skipped across her eyes. "You can't."

"And why not?"

She pointed to the *Sablewing.* "Because if you destroy that ship, you lose your cameo."

Did he hear her right? Blood rushed to his head with a flash of pulsing anger. Grabbing her arms, he jerked her close. "What did you say?"

"That is the ship I sail with." Her chin lifted a fraction with her words. "Your cameo is on the *Sablewing.*"

A shell ripped across the *Rissa*'s deck narrowly missing the mast and sploshing into the waters on the other side of the ship.

"Capt'n!"

Blade heard Willie's call. He waited, standing with the gunners, for the orders to be given as they drew nearer to the fierce battle. Blade ignored his first mate. "Carrion is your captain? Why didn't you tell me this before?"

"You didn't ask."

He clenched his fingers, cutting deep into her arms. If he hurt her, she gave no sign of it. She only returned his glare. It all came clear. When he spirited her to his ship that night on the docks, she had lied when he asked her if she knew Carrion. He dismissed it. And her brother, Luc, stood beside him. Idiot!

He shoved her away, not trusting himself to withhold the pain he wanted to inflict upon her.

Another volley blasted, falling shy of the hull.

"Capt'n!" Willie shouted over his shoulder, his face gathered in a critical furrow filled with censure.

Blade bared his teeth in rage. They were under fire. And now it became apparent he would have to try to deflect the rounds shot at Carrion. "Spare *Sablewing,*" he ordered.

Willie motioned to a master gunner. "Stay guns two and five."

"Fire as you bear!"

"Fire!"

The ship rocked with the succession of gun carriages jumping back whilst firing deadly missiles. Pungent, spent gunpowder flushed the air as smoke billowed forth. Gunners and the firing crews called out their positions over the deafening booms of gunfire—firing, swabbing the bores, ramming shot and firing again.

Blade prickled with a tempest of agitation and thrill. Battle was strategic sport, one he usually enjoyed. Having to save Carrion, however, stuck in his craw. The battle would have to end before Drake caught up. Drake would certainly take the opportunity to destroy Carrion just as Blade wanted to do. And there would be nothing he could do to stop him. Damn it!

"You." He pointed at Marisol. "Stay down."

He grabbed a musket from the open gun chest in the middle of the deck. The *Rissa* was coming up the aft of the desperado ship's stern.

"Broadside!" he hollered.

They slid alongside the ship on the outside of the ensuing fight. Bracing himself against the rail, he prepared to shoot. Blade aimed for any man barking orders. Any man who might claim a leadership role.

A burly fellow racing along the rail, brandishing a barker, caught his attention. Not a captain, but most likely second-in-command. A good start. Blade aimed. A shot rang out, popping in his ear. The first mate buckled with the slug and fell to his knees. But Blade hadn't pulled the trigger. From the corner of his eye, a musket lowered. Beside him, Marisol removed the ramrod to reload the gun she held propped with her knees.

"What the devil?"

A salvo of bullets bombarded past, sending them ducking below the railing.

"You've got a lot of explaining to do," he shouted.

"Can we talk about this later?" Huddled against the side, she shoved a ball down the musket bore.

He leaped up and fired his long-arm musket.

Crouched again, he said, "No."

She swung up, pulled off a shot and dropped back down.

"What were you doing with Carrion?"

"Not now."

"Does Carrion know about the silver?"

The ease and speed with which she primed her weapon meant she had been in battle before and likely more than once. Blade grunted then darted up to send off another shot.

Damn Carrion. How long had he had a woman on board? With his flagrant penchant for trouble, how could he be so irresponsible? He could get her killed. "Answer me!"

"Later."

"Now!"

A bullet nicked the rail above them. In an instant, she returned fire. Settling with her back against the sidewall, she glared at him. "All right. Yes, he knows. I told him about the silver."

Fury clouded his vision. It wasn't that Carrion knew of the treasure. That, Blade had already decided. But this one woman and her criminal ways had muddied up his waters into sludge. This had been her fault.

She must have seen his ire. In truth it would have been hard to miss. His hand hovered between them with his fingers bent as if he warred with himself to not strangle her neck.

She looked up from his trembling hand of death. "I thought

he would take us to the *Gloria.* I did it because of Monte."

"You play pirate games, puppeting men for your own gain?" And to think she manipulated him like a bloody marionette.

The blast from a ship's gun drowned out her answer. *No* formed on her lips, but the fierce explosions of gunfire fueled his fury. He tossed his long-arm aside and bolted upward. She wanted to fight? Let her. Pulling his two blunderbusses from his leather brace strapped across his chest, he stormed the length of the ship, firing his weapons.

Rissa and *Sablewing* hemmed in the trespassing intruder. The battle lasted a few minutes more before the outnumbered desperado ship steered away rather than risking defeat. The winds lifted the gray smoke in wispy vapors taking with it the acrid smell of burnt gunpowder. Blade marched the decks, surveying what little superficial damage they had incurred. Fortune smiled upon the *Rissa* and her crew. There were no injuries to tend and the men were free to make necessary repairs and clean the guns.

But not until after he made sure Carrion posed no threat. With Drake sailing up along the other side of the *Sablewing,* he doubted the swivel-tongued captain would dare.

"Ahoy there, Carrion," he called. The proud man stepped forward flanked by scowling seamen covered in blackened smudges from the fight. "What's your trouble?"

"Bastards attacked without cause." The mystery ship had tested him, and it showed. After he plopped his feathered tricorn hat onto his head, loose scraggly hair protruded from their binds behind his neck. Dried blood and sweat clustered around the small cuts across his hardened face. "We came upon her as a merchant. Didn't know she was disguised until she opened her gun ports on us."

Undoubtedly Carrion planned to take an easy quarry not suspecting he could be on the losing end of a clash. "How do I know you weren't the one attacking?"

"Come now, Tyburn. You don't think I would confront a vessel if I couldn't beat all hollow and sail away fat and happy, do you?"

No, he didn't. The men on that ship had been well trained in the verse of battle.

Blade smiled. "No need to thank me." He motioned to several of his men and pointed to the *Sablewing*. "We'll be coming aboard now."

Grappling hooks from both his and Drake's ships flew through the air, landing with a thud on the planks and snagging deep into the wood. The men pulled the vessels together, three ships joined as one on the rolling sea.

"I give you no permission." Carrion reached for his cutlass but as men from both the *Rissa* and the *Black Widow* poured over onto his ship, his hand went no farther than grasping the hilt.

"My apologies, Carrion." Blade hopped onto the *Sablewing* and strode over to the pirate captain. "It is quite unacceptable to disrespect a brother's ship. However, Captain Drake and I have reason to believe you are after something which we have vowed to protect. With the recent goings-on, I'm afraid we must search your vessel."

He nodded to Drake, who sent armed men swarming about, keeping the *Sablewing* crew at bay and ducking below deck to check the cabins and holds.

Carrion upturned his lip and blatant hatred abraded his scarred visage. His men all around itched to pounce on their surly captain's orders to fight. With odds against him, the scug could do nothing about Blade and Drake scouring his ship. "I know nothing," he spat.

"Don't insult me, Carrion." Although he wanted to throttle Marisol for her recklessness, Blade wouldn't implicate her for their actions. It would only bring her harm. If he knew Carrion, which he did, the captain would spare no rod on the likes of her. "I don't believe it has been by chance that you and your cronies just happened to be where the trouble is."

"If you search my ship, that must mean you've lost the silver." Carrion laughed, nodding and coaxing on his guffawing men. "Bungler is a new title for ya, Tyburn."

Blade grinned again. "I said nothing about silver."

"You didn't have to." The renegade's gaze landed beyond Blade. He knew even before he heard the subtle footfalls that Marisol had boarded the ship.

Carrion opened his arms wide. "My pet." The endearment

made Blade's skin crawl.

She stepped into his embrace and kissed his filthy cheek. Blade forced himself to remain rooted to the spot. She belonged to Carrion, not him. He didn't want the fighting wildcat anyway.

"I hope she hasn't caused you too much misfortune, has she, Tyburn?"

"Plenty." She descended on him like a plague. In spite of that, he wanted to cut off the arm Carrion draped around her. The idea bewildered him.

"I should apologize on behalf of Marisol," Carrion said, "but then, better you be afflicted by her calamities than I."

Marisol rolled her eyes and sloughed away from him, disappearing to the interior cabins through the forecastle hatch Drake's mate, Valeryn, held open. Blade wanted to go after her. He imagined her settling herself in Carrion's quarters, Carrion's bed, to wait for her master. Marisol's naked flesh against Carrion's putrid body, the image summoned a rabid reaction. His fingers cramped from crushing the smooth handle of his flintlock.

He checked himself, keeping in mind that he had taken control of the *Sablewing. Clear your mind, man. She's retrieving your cameo.* If she didn't uphold her end of the bargain and return his cameo, he could tear the ship apart looking for it.

"You waste my time." Carrion blew out a frustrated breath. "Your men will find nothing. Perhaps you should give chase to that mangy tyke getting away."

"Should I?" The answer came as an impassive shrug.

Valeryn bent to Drake and whispered in his ear. He nodded. "He's clear. No silver," Drake said.

"As I have said, Tyburn. You waste time."

"Aye, and yours will be up soon if you do not heed my warning. You would do well to not interfere in my business." An empty warning. Carrion would do as he pleased regardless of the brotherhood. One day, he must be dealt with.

Drake moved to stand beside Blade, his back to Carrion. Lowering his voice, he spoke. "Our mystery ship is the same vessel that overtook the *Gloria.*"

Blade looked over to his friend. "How do you know?"

"I recognize it. The morning before the *Gloria* disappeared, I saw a vessel on the horizon traveling west. It looked like any other merchantman. But I remember a red flag. When I tried to focus on it, the flag was gone. Thought maybe I made a mistake. Now I'm sure. It's one in the same."

"Damn." If he had known, well, he wouldn't be standing around trading pleasantries like spars with Carrion.

At once, the hatch door crashed open and a man skittered backward to the deck. Marisol stepped through the threshold after him. "Lay a hand on me again and it'll be your head I put my foot through."

Carrion's laughter resonated around the crowded deck. "That's my lass."

Blade had to agree and containing his smile was near impossible. Marisol smirked at him. She was a spitfire, all right.

He leaned over to Drake. "I suppose our quasi captain sheered off with the *Gloria,* as well."

"Headed northeast."

Just as expected. Monte took to the open seas.

"Should we put a bounty on him?" Drake asked.

"Let him go. There'll be time for that. He may yet surprise me." Blade redirected his attention to the impatient captain who had returned to glowering and stood with his arms across his bulk.

"I would thank you for your hospitality, but, well, swine are more cordial."

"Preferable company to you," Carrion retorted.

"Stop this childishness." Marisol huffed and frowned at both captains. "Bloody men, always vying to best one another." She shook her head as she crossed the deck to Blade.

Reaching for his hand, she pressed a familiar round object into his palm. Her eyes did not leave his and she smiled in tandem with his hiccupping heart, relieved with joy. His cameo, he knew it without looking. Ah, no more respite from his torturous condemnation. He was a beast meant to be collared and this small precious shell he squeezed tightly in his hand was his punisher.

"Forgive me."

She had so much sadness weighing down her words. How could he not? He nodded once.

"What is this?" Carrion pointed a callused finger at their joined hands. "A bit friendly, I'd say."

"No, Alain." Worry creased her brow and she quickly dropped his hand. She moved to take up position beside her captain.

Alain? So that was Carrion's real name. Coming from Marisol, it sounded so…personal.

"We're not friendly," she added.

"Not friendly? With Blade Tyburn? The debauchee of the Main?" Carrion's nostrils flared with notable disdaining mistrust. "Is that so, Tyburn?"

"In all honesty, Carrion, we are not *friendly.* I can barely stand her." The evil look she plastered on her face was laughable. He did well not to show his amusement. The line he walked couldn't have been any thinner. Should Carrion detect deceit or insult, things could get nasty.

"That is good." He cupped her chin to peer at her. "Otherwise I would feel compelled to kill you." His voice dipped to affection. "You see, I will protect my sweet at all costs."

To watch Carrion touch her, to hear him speak of her, it scored Blade, etching into his already weakened defenses. Damn it. How could she let that scab fondle her? An ache radiated from his jaw. He needed to stop grinding his teeth.

Marisol whacked away his hand, and her eyes flashed. "Just like you protected Luc?" She leaned into him and snarled. "Did you leave him behind to die on the gibbet like you left Monte, to save yourself?"

The force of Carrion's backhand felled her on all fours. The clean sound of swords scraping across metal scabbards sliced through the remnant sound of his slap to her face. Men all over the ship, his, Drake's and Carrion's alike, pointed their weapons at one another in a tense and frantic bid for the advantage. Blade angled his own cutlass at Carrion.

"Coward," she spat.

Carrion snatched at her hair, dragging her to her feet. She cried out and clawed at his fist tangled in a knot on her head.

Blade closed the gap between them, raising the tip of his sword under the rogue's jaw. Carrion's twisted grimace bearing down into him was known to send grown men cowering under their straw beds. But not Blade. Carrion could threaten him with his evil defiant stare all he wanted. There was nothing uglier than Blade's own dreadful soul.

"I won't say that the lass doesn't deserve to be punished for her brassy mouth," Blade said. "No doubt she must learn her place. But I won't stand by and watch you slap your woman around."

The fragile moment prickling over every tightly wound fighter on board shattered with booming laughter. Carrion shoved Marisol from his grip in a fit of mirth. She stumbled, falling at Blade's feet. The crew of the *Sablewing* remained poised for battle but they, too, chuckled.

Had Blade missed some joke? What was so damned funny? He didn't care to be laughed at. Not at all. Poking his blade higher, he pressed the tip into Carrion's flesh. "Did I say something that amuses you?"

The captain stopped laughing.

Blade slipped his cameo into his pocket and held out his hand to help her stand.

"Marisol is not my woman," Carrion announced.

A happy vine of surprise curled around his heart and bloomed at the knowledge that she didn't belong to the pirate. The strange feeling startled him.

"She's my daughter."

The vine sprouted thorns. It pierced with astonishing force. Carrion's daughter. It should have amused Blade as realization struck. All the signs had been there. She was a murderess, a thief, a lying witch—with a sinful body. Ah, a woman like her he could take pleasure with in a wicked game of "who's on top." Yet he was not amused. He was livid. She should have revealed to him her identity and not played him for a fool. But he was a fool, wasn't he?

He lowered his cutlass from the *Sablewing*'s captain. All others followed suit, eyeing one another for any false moves.

When he met her gaze, she looked away.

"Daughter or not, it is no way to treat the chit," he said.

"I'll deal with her as I see fit, Tyburn. She's of my blood and therefore mine to rectify her disrespect."

"I won't stand for a woman to suffer at the angry hands of a man."

"It's fine, Blade," Marisol said. Her fingers brushed along her reddening cheek. "I was out of line."

Carrion crossed his arms and tipped his chin. "It's always unwise to meddle in family affairs."

"You are in no position to threaten me." He tried to read Marisol's expression. Was that what she wanted? For Blade to leave her to her father? Leave well enough alone? Her downcast eyes said it all. He was done.

Blade waved his weapon haphazardly around. "But alas, I've grown tiresome of this encounter." He sheathed his sword. "We will be on our way."

"I should say so. You've given the quarry a smashing lead. Tell you what, old friend, let us see who can recover your lost silver first, eh?"

"You just don't know when you're beat, huh, *friend?* You won't get far with the damage your ship sustained. You'll be lucky to make it back to port."

"A useless opinion."

Blade shook his head at the captain's arrogance and glanced at Marisol. Her one shot at rejoining with her brother had come and gone in a few fleeting hours. Perched at the knees of her captain, right back to where she started days ago. He could walk away right at that moment and leave her on the *Sablewing* with her father to continue her life of vagrant piracy, wiping his hands clean of her. Be worry free of missing valuables and hurling knives. Or he could whisk her away with him, for, well, a more noble life of piracy. At least until Santo Domingo. There she could reunite with her brother and be happy, if the bastard actually sailed to the port like he was told to do.

He could help her with that—happiness. Of course that would be for his own selfish gain. Certainly she would be so grateful that he saved her from the cruel clutches of her father that she would want to thank him, properly.

"I have a proposition for you, Carrion."

"Oh?"

"The *Rissa* used a good bit of shot saving your sorry arse. As payment, I require Marisol."

She looked stunned, no doubt by his generosity. The sweet

filly. She really should close her mouth. 'Twas not attractive.

Carrion grunted. "Why would I do this?"

"Your other option is *Rissa* and *Widow Maker* finishing you and the *Sablewing* off with a round of double shot."

"Extreme measures just for a strum with my daughter."

"I have plenty of less ungovernable doxies to occupy my time with."

The ice in her piercing angry stare should have cooled the hot midday sun.

"What use would you have of her, then?"

"The lass is exceptional at pick-pocketing. I should think her an entertaining advantage in port. I could use a gallows bird like her on my crew. Once she ceases to be a profitable bawd, I'll toss her back."

Carrion rubbed his chin, an obvious ruse at contemplation. No one bargained with Carrion. His pride swelled too large for that. The man had already made up his mind. Blade had him right where he wanted him.

"Your answer, Carrion."

"Done."

"What?" Marisol sputtered, her eyes wide with disbelief. "Alain, why would you do this to me?"

"My ship, for you? I'd say I made off like a thief."

No. It was Blade who made off with the thief.

CHAPTER 11

"Don't raise your voice to me." Blade pulled her inside the companionway away from the working crew. "I doubt Carrion let your tongue wag under his command. I won't have you doing it here."

"Carrion." Marisol had been unaware of her father's brethren name. Disgusted by the sound of it, she spat, landing her mark directly on Blade's boot. Blade lifted his eyebrows, not at all pleased with her aim. "To hell with Carrion," she said, for good measure.

She reached her limit. The edges of her control began to crumble away. She'd dug herself in too deep this time. All she wanted was to have her brothers together again. A family sailing the ocean blue in search of adventure and riches. Fanciful? Perhaps. But something to dream of at night after she lay her head down.

As usual, she tangled things up, plunged herself into another bungle. This time it became clear Alain no longer planned to bail her out. She'd been problematic, at best. If not for her, Alain would not have gone after the *Gloria.* The *Sablewing* would not have been damaged. And she would not have been traded off to a pirate captain she knew damn well and good she couldn't trust herself around.

It hurt. Deep inside, she hoped that Alain loved her more, at least more than his actions showed. Hadn't she proved to him her loyalty? Hadn't she worked on an even keel with the rest of the crew, expecting nothing but fair treatment in return? Hadn't her escapades helped pad his strongbox with riches? What more could she have done?

The truth was hard to swallow. To expect to earn his love had been foolish. He showed so little of it with her mother and she wasn't certain he was even capable of the emotion. She assumed that there had to be some fiber of affection within him since he occasionally visited her mama. For what other reason would he go to her if not out of love? His visits made Mama happy. His visits made them all happy.

But this wasn't about Alain.

She gave Blade a hostile glare. "How dare you demand me of him?"

"I'm a pirate, love. It's what we do." He braced a hand on the wall behind her head. "We take what we want." His smoldering green eyes darkened as he bent his head. He had her pinned with absolute craving. She couldn't be sure if it was his desire or hers that kept her fixed in place. His lips loitered so close. "Especially if what we want holds some advantage."

His musky scent mingled with a hint of sulfur from the earlier gun battle, a deadly mixture sure to break her. She inhaled deep and slow, breathing in as much as she could of him. "You want me?"

"Aye."

The word fell like heavy velvet, warm and thick. *Curse it! I'm going down.* She lifted her mouth to meet his.

Blade pushed off the wall, away from her. "You may come in handy when I need my rum brought to me. Henri don't get about as easily as he used to."

"What?" Shock followed closely by humiliation soon became colored by anger. The bastard meant to turn her into a cabin boy.

"You can wipe that look of reprisal from your face, Marisol." He reached up with both hands and grabbed hold of the door frame above him. His relaxed posture filled the entire hatch. "What else would I have you do?"

He challenged her. Oh no. She wouldn't take the bait. Davy

Jones would have her soul before she'd admit hoping for a warmer, cozier position on his *Rissa.*

"You could put me back on Alain's ship."

"No. That wouldn't do."

"For who? You?"

"That's right. For me." He wore smug well. It infuriated her.

"Do you require my company in your bedchamber again?" There. Switch what went unsaid around and toss it back into his lap.

"Require? No. But I wouldn't turn you away should you seek *my* company."

Ooh. She clenched her fists and willed her rigid arms to not take a swing at him. "You'd like that wouldn't you?"

"By your moans as I pleasured you last night, I'd say that you'd like it, too."

"Wretch."

"Hypocrite."

She considered plugging him with her gulley knife for being right. Or, at the very least, slapping him across his conceited mug. His arresting dimples kept her from it. She struggled to not become distracted by his beautiful smile, not to become ensnared in his magnificent charm. *He wants to make you his personal valet. Remember that. Walk away, Marisol. Walk away.*

Tearing her eyes from him before she did something foolish, she headed for her cabin. His low laugh reached her when she came to her door.

"I can't figure you out," he said.

She turned to him as he closed the distance. The corridor suddenly became too narrow to accommodate them both. No telling what she would do to him in the uncomfortably confined proximity.

"You do things without thinking of consequence," he said. "You seek instant gratification."

"Don't we all?" she asked. "You said it yourself. You take what you want, when you want it."

"Aye." He leaned his back against the wall, the space still too cramped for her liking. "But my mates and I take advantage of opportunity. We're not greedy, bloodthirsty hellions like our earlier brethren. A little planning gets you much more than whimsy. Spares the innocent, too." His eyes grazed over her. "You're quite careless."

"It sounds as if you think you *do* have me figured out." She crossed her arms in protest.

"Not at all. You rectify yourself and your actions as an afterthought. You either are indeed manipulative or plain lucky to have managed this far in this dangerous line of work. My guess is that you've your brothers to thank."

The idea made him chuckle, something she didn't quite appreciate.

"What I don't understand," he continued, "is how someone as strong-willed and skilled in weaponry as you can be so…vulnerable. One instant you are battling tooth and claw for control, the next you gladly relinquish it and, forgive me for saying so, to someone who cares more for his rotten ship than his own daughter."

"Is that what you thought you were doing? Saving me? How chivalrous of you." Her petulance sounded harsh even to her own ears. Yet Blade was right on target. She could stand defiant against the most infernal cutthroat, and then submit to Alain with the snap of his sullied finger. The verity of it stung.

Why did the men in her life feel they needed to shelter her? 'Twas true, her brothers taught her how to defend herself and fight well. 'Twas equally true they coddled her. Though that made her madder than hell, she couldn't help but feel a pinch of contentment that they cared enough to shield her from what they considered too hazardous. Sometimes she felt they deliberately withheld things from her so she would always be in need of them. Now, more than ever, with the events of the last several days, she believed it to be true. "You need to be thinking of saving yourself, Blade."

His warm laugh echoed in the tight space. "I can take care of myself, I assure you."

"Alain will not tolerate being dishonored by you."

He tilted his head and studied her like an oddity. One corner of his lip twitched. "You worry for me?"

"No." She answered too quickly. The other corner of his lips twitched. She looked away. In truth, she worried far more than she should.

Alain had been known to inflict torture on people. He had at times receded into a place far from sanity, drunk on the agonizing screams of his victims. He terrified even his most hardened crew. The first time she witnessed his cruelty, he'd bound a prisoner to the mast and cut him open, bleeding him to death. He collected every last drop of the blood into a bucket and held another prisoner's head down into it until he drowned. Alain thought then, that after seeing his savagery, Marisol would beg to be returned home. She almost had. She'd become so sickened by the deaths, she hadn't recovered for several days.

She had questioned her will for independence. There had been no freedom remaining home. A woman had little hope to achieve much more than becoming a prostitute, or worse, a wife to a husband who lived by the sea, coming home once every couple of years to make another babe. Just like her mother. Marisol did not want that for herself. She wanted more. She wanted to see what lay beyond the shores of Cow Island, to experience the colorful life of a seaman, to feel the rewards of hard work. And one day, along with her brothers, she wanted to have a ship and crew to call her own. She expected the dangers of the life she longed for. A short courageous life held far more appeal to her than a long, lonely, monotonous one. But beholding such unspeakable violence by her father's hand nearly cracked her.

Luc and Monte had been there. Luc sat with her all night, rocking her and giving her comfort. Monte paced the room like a caged animal. Her dear Luc had opened her eyes to the truth of survival on the seas. Insubordination could not be tolerated, he had said. It literally meant the difference between life and death. Those captives had planned a mutiny against Alain and would have killed them, too, for being kin. And, Monte had added, the mutineers would have had their way brutally with her before they finished her off. She remembered the spark of liveliness in Monte's wild eyes, sparing her no detail.

Her brothers had been right. Understanding these dangers dulled her fragility. If she were to stay, if she truly wanted the seaman's life, she had to toughen up. It was their reality.

It wasn't frequent that Alain became crazy carrying out atrocious suffering, but it happened often enough. If death was the order, in her mind, then death should come clean and quick.

Somehow, she couldn't bear the thought of Blade and Alain...

"He will come and get me." She let out a breathy sigh. "Even if it's not me he's after." Her whisper left her mouth quiet and defeated.

"I count on it."

She glanced up at him.

"You see, Carrion is careless, too," he said. "He challenged me for the silver. 'Tis only a matter of time before we cross paths again."

"I don't understand."

"I have the advantage, dove."

She frowned, still not getting his meaning. What would she have to do with any part of his mission.

"You can go back to your father after I get that silver to Charles Windham, if you'd like. Till then, have my rum handy."

"I'll not be your..."

He shook his head and turned to leave.

"Hey. Don't you walk away. Blade?"

Hands on either side of the hatch door, he paused. The sunlight filtered through, illuminating his golden hair and highlighting all of his masculine lines. He turned his eyes on her. The brightness diluted their color and she quaked at how intense his stare had become.

"You will dine with me tonight." He looked back outside, distant, distracted. "Aye," he said, as if agreeing with himself. "I'll have Henri bring you a dress. Practical clothes are nice, but I want to see you in something that suits me." Stepping through the door, he disappeared into the sunlight.

Marisol stood alone in the companionway that no longer felt small. It felt empty. Despite the humid, still air, she shivered in the darkness with the chill left in his absence.

Her shoulders slumped and she went inside her cabin, plunking down onto the bed she'd slept on the night before. She needed to sort out the day.

All morning Blade had been aloof, not once giving away that she had shared his bed. She was left without the benefit of even a smile. Then he'd been angry with her about Alain. She'd given him back his cameo. He got what he wanted and was free of her. What else could he want? Certainly not her. He wouldn't even kiss her in the companionway.

She lay back and rested her head on the impossibly soft pillow.

Many emotions showered her—anger, guilt, apprehension, sadness, resignation, exhaustion. And what of her family? Alain bartered her away, Monte disappeared again and Luc was dead. She choked back a sob and rolled over, curling up into a ball. How would she manage to get herself out of this one? How would she make things right?

She opened her eyes at the sound of a knock. Her body ached from lying askew and it took a moment to get orientated. She had fallen asleep. For how long, she did not know.

"Lass?" Henri called from the other side of the door.

"Come in." She arched her stiff back and sat up.

Henri ambled in with a deep golden gown draped over his stubby arms. He tried with much difficulty to keep it from dragging across the planks. She rushed over to help the old man.

"Oh, it's heavy." She lifted it from him and let the dress unfold. The fabric rustled to the floor in layered satin. She gasped. "It's gorgeous."

The triangular stomacher matched the petticoat, their cream-colored arabesque design stunning against the darker gold of the gown. She had never seen a more beautiful dress. The dresses Luc would bring her from raiding forays were indeed pretty, but she rarely had occasion to wear one. She couldn't very well work her shipboard duties layered in skirts and so she had asked Luc to bring her more useful gifts, like weapons. The dress she held gleamed in the light; the patterns surely had been sewn by meticulous hands meant for a woman of nobility, someone worthy of flaunting its feminine beauty. And Blade wanted her to wear it.

"I can't imagine why Tyburn would have a dress like this. It's so lovely."

Henri shoved a pair of matching mules at her. "He keeps a supply of 'em on hand. Likes to please his lady friends in port."

She frowned and a pang of jealousy slipped. "Does he, now?" She snatched the pointy shoes from him. "And I suppose he has a lady in every port."

"Nearly."

"Of course he does." Why wouldn't he? The infamous libertine probably had *two* girls in every port along the Main. Ugh. She shouldn't care and it burned her hide that she did. Knowing what pleasures he brought with his warm touch and how he made her feel like the world had been created for only them, she didn't want to think of Blade making love to another. She didn't dare.

"Capt'n says for ye to come to his quarters when ye be done."

"Humph." She'd just as soon stay in her own cabin than go back *there,* to the same room, with his candlesticks, with his bed.

Oh, she'd be a fool not to. She wanted to put on that grand dress. She wanted to feel like an aristocratic darling for one moment in her life. She wanted to leave him speechless when she swept into his chambers. Aye. That was what she wanted.

"Food will be waitin'." Henri turned for the door.

"Be sure to have plenty of rum ready." She had no doubt he expected her to keep his cup full.

"Lass?" Henri paused on his way out. "The Capt'n, he looks at ye differently than the others." His brow pulled together and he nodded before closing the door behind him.

What do you suppose he meant by that? She huffed. Blade could look at her with those emeralds and she would never know if he desired her or pitied her. She felt like a leper in his world of dancing harlots.

Tonight, though, she would at the very least be a well-frocked leper.

* * *

Blade sprang up from his chair. "This is ridiculous." He stomped over to the windows and clasped his hands behind his back, kneading his fingers impatiently. "What is taking the lass so long?"

"Would ye like me to fetch her, Capt'n?" Henri sat at the table polishing the old broken flute he always carried with him.

"Nay. If she's not here in the next five minutes, I'll drag her to dinner myself."

In the reflection of the window, Blade watched Henri steal another sip from the rum. He smiled. Bless the old fop's soul, he would drink himself to death yet.

He looked to his own visage in the glass. There was something different about the man staring back at him. Something was missing. Tired eyes hinted to indecision. He didn't like it. It fractured his character. He always had a plan, always knew what course he would take. Whether right or wrong had never been a concern. His will he held steadfast. In his occupation, doubt could be deadly.

Though he hadn't had trouble making decisions on the spot, this day he scrutinized his every move with further thought. Since rolling out of bed, he toiled over and cursed each time he wondered if his actions had been the right one. Where was his buoyancy? Where had his confidence gone?

It went right down the hatch when you let Marisol into your bed, you idiot.

Smiling inwardly, he remembered the flare of rage in her eyes when he suggested she would be his serving girl. He preferred her fury over the profound sadness taking root. He understood the empty, soul-crushing pain of not being worthy of returned love far more than he cared to admit and he couldn't stand to see her dwell on her no-good father any longer.

He raked a hand through his hair and growled. The chit seeped under his skin. She was bold and brash enough to be a part of his world, and all the while, sustaining her need for someone, a man, to protect her. That made him crazy.

He should have never taken her.

But he had. And he kept her. Now he struggled with whether or not that had been a good idea. 'Twas true having her on board held him an advantage. Only slightly. Past experience with Carrion proved the pirate to be a fickle man. He believed Carrion would go after the silver. Before or after Blade retrieved it was the burning question. Did he care enough about his daughter to avoid attacking Blade's ship and seek the silver first? Perhaps he thought to barter for her with Blade for a higher price? Or would the captain consider her an unfortunate consequence to gaining the bounty?

The uncertainty chafed his resolve and aggravated him further.

He focused on what he did know. The *Gloria* had been boarded and stripped of her crew and cargo. Drake spotted a mystery ship in the area shortly after. The *Sugar Lady* sailed into Puerto Plata also about the same time and then set a course for Puerto Rico across the Mona Passage. Carrion's *Sablewing,* too, docked in Puerto Plata. The port suffered an assault. The mystery ship attacked the *Sablewing* then escaped to the west. The *Gloria* also headed for the deadly currents of the passage.

Five vessels sailing straight into the vicious, hacking teeth of Mona. They best make their peace for not all would make it through.

Missing silver, rogue ships and hostile enemies. The challenge couldn't be sweeter.

The eyes reflecting back at him regained their familiarity. Good. Confidence inflated within his chest again. A hearty meal with a lovely lady would top off his evening. If she ever arrived. Damn, where was she?

A brisk knock at the door and she rushed in like a crisp autumn breeze. Her beauty glittered through the mirrored image on the glass. She took his breath away, literally.

"Sorry I'm late."

Blade suppressed his smile before he sharply turned on his heel.

She flustered in her haste and gave a proper but quick curtsy.

Henri stood, slower than normal, and ripping his wide eyes from her, fumbled to pour the cups—again. By the sideways glance he cast Blade, the little man probably thought he would be admonished for the double error of ogling Marisol and helping himself to too much drink.

"See your way out, Henri." The jack sprat nodded and took his leave.

It was difficult to frown at her. She radiated in that gown. The golden color mingled with her warm skin and he wondered if the glow coming off her would burn to the touch.

"Do you find it appropriate to keep your host waiting?" he said.

Her eyes flashed with anger. "You try squeezing yourself

into this contraption, with no one to help, mind you, and see how long it takes you."

Ah, yes. There was that fire he so enjoyed to stoke. He chuckled and she lifted her chin. Her beauty would blind him as sure as the shining sun. Taking that risk, he soaked her in a moment longer before coming forward to pull out her chair. "You look exquisite, Marisol."

A faint blush crept into her cheeks and her chin dropped a degree less defensive. Brown locks were secured at the crown of her head and the remaining flowing tresses tumbled down onto her shoulders and across her back. The flat plane of the boning on her dress gave way to curves he would not soon forget. The low cut of the dress fit snug against her chest, crushing two smooth mounds of flesh to near overflow. He cursed himself for not having a bejeweled necklace to lie upon that inviting bosom. He would need to procure one soon.

"Come. Sit."

"Thank you." Her dress billowed with a flourish as she took her seat.

He ladled out a bowl of turtle soup and set it before her and then scooped himself his own bowl. "Please, eat."

Though the soup no longer steamed piping hot, it warmed his mouth, delighting his tongue with piquant spices. "'Tis good. Henri has made another fine meal."

"Mmm." She nodded. "I'd say this is the best turtle soup I've ever had. The garlic and onions, so flavorful. Is that a hint of lime I taste?"

Blade watched Marisol bring her spoon to her mouth. She flicked her tongue to catch a dribble of the soup on her lip, bringing a delicate finger up to wipe away what escaped. The innocent action sent an undercurrent of desire rippling below his belt. He shifted in his seat as she slipped her finger into her mouth.

Conversation was minimal while they ate. He found it near impossible to string intelligible words together while she sipped the broth and nibbled the meat. Midway through, she caught him staring. Their eyes locked and a grin edged up her lips.

She brought her spoon to her mouth again. Her gaze still on him, she puckered her lips and gently tipped the spoon to take in the juice.

Blade raised his eyebrows. *How tantalizing.* He swallowed his own spoonful of tangy broth, slowly dragging his tongue along the corner of his mouth, watching for her reaction. He smirked when she momentarily averted her stare downward. *Two could play at this game.*

She reached for the smaller platter of figs and plantains in the middle of the table. Plucking a purple fig from the fruit, she captured his gaze once more before she brought it to her mouth. The fig disappeared behind her plump lips and she nipped off the stem. *Glory be!*

He, too, selected a fig. Slowly he bit into the flesh and, chewing it leisurely, measured his success by the heat flushing up her neck.

Next, she picked a plantain from the tray. Peeling back the yellow and blackened skin, she flared a coy smile. If her seductive eyes burning into him from underneath those dark lashes were not enough to send him to explode like a flash pot, those lips wrapped around the banana surely would. Sweet, merciful heaven.

"Belay," he hissed. "'Tis quite enough sporting."

Marisol smiled, a wonderful smile that brimmed with pride. She had bested him. He wouldn't deny it. His rum ran dangerously low as he chased away wicked visions and hoped to numb his mischievous merrymaker, already causing him a certain amount of discomfort straining at the fabric of his trousers.

"Oh," Marisol said, "your drink." She rose from her place at the table and brought the flagon of liquor to him. "I've got to earn my keep." She winked and bent forward to fill his tankard.

The way she leaned in, the angle to which she bent, brought her chest eye-level and dangerously close. He ground off the first layer of his teeth. Damn. In another moment, he'd sweep everything off the table, throwing Marisol down on top to feast upon. He had to get her out of his cabin. Now.

"What do you say we take a stroll topside?" He stood and threw back his rum in one fast quaff.

"A fine idea. Fresh air would be nice." Setting down the flagon, she moved to the door. The spring in her step made her backside sway with exaggerated flare.

Indeed. Fresh air to cool off my carnal heat.

He grabbed her cup and finished off the liquor before following her out the hatch.

Outside the air was warm and pleasant. Blade hardly noticed. He had been too distracted with the well-deserved low whistles and gawking stares from his crew as Marisol passed by them. No man would dare make an advance on the captain's lady but he couldn't ignore the iron spears of annoyance at the attention. He rested his hand on the hilt of his sword and, with the other, guided her by her elbow to the front of the ship.

Off the starboard bow, they watched the sun dip below a vast valley of sagging clouds. The large orb's bright light stained the clouds in colorful hues of pinks and purples and violent shades of orange.

"'Tis beautiful," Marisol said.

He admired her peaceful smile, her glittering eyes. In the dying light, she was even more spectacular. "It doesn't compare to you, dove."

She turned to him. Surprise shimmered across her face like newly minted doubloons. Quickly, she looked back to the sunset. "The sky is turning so red."

Blade tore his appreciation away to the setting sun. The deeper it sank, the darker the sky blazed with fire. He took notice of the clouds. They stretched across the eastern horizon in front of them, growing fast and rolling in low.

A gust of wind scooped in from behind them, lifting her hair to skip across her face. "Mercy. Where'd that come from?" she said.

Above, Blade watched as the clouds raced in a broad arc toward the dark wall of an advancing squall line. Realization slapped him like a nasty ill-begotten bastard son.

"Hell-fire."

"What?" Marisol asked. "What is it?"

"We're heading straight..." he let out a long frustrated breath and shook his head, "...straight for a bloody hurricane."

CHAPTER 12

Blade took advantage of the winds for as long as he felt he safely could. The *Rissa* skimmed along the passage at a swift pace. But the sails began to twist with the whipping gales and the sea had grown much more wrathful. The sails had to be furled and fastened before it became too dangerous to maneuver on the yards. Everything had been battened down, all lights and the cooking fire extinguished, and everyone ordered down below.

The ocean swells reached high enough to lick away any of his men from the deck. Only he, Willie and the helmsman remained topside. They struggled to secure the wheel with rope to keep the rudder from being free to spin the *Rissa* around in the vicious water.

"Make sure you tie it tight," Blade called. He shouted but the howling wind shrieking in his ears snatched away his words. He only knew that Willie had heard him by the man's nod.

Two ropes held the wheel fixed firmly. It strained to turn one way then the other, jerking to either side that would give. Another rope had been tied to the helmsman to keep him from washing overboard while he held the wheel steady and on a somewhat easterly course, the same direction as the winds.

Blade shielded his eyes from the driving force of the rain smarting across his cheeks and peered at the masts. He'd never been much of a religious man but he wondered if it would be too late to start praying. *Please don't let those masts break.* Nay. That sounded too much like begging. Something he despised. Nevertheless, the wind wasn't his only enemy.

In the dark with the blinding horizontal rain, he couldn't see far. Flashes of blue lightning revealed black swells rising high up from the sea like abysmal cloaks. He caught glimpses of frothy, white foam cresting the mountainous waves only to be blown off and disappear into the next growing surge. The sea could easily swat the *Rissa* from her back, open up and wipe any trace of his ship and crew away in her wrath. But not tonight. He would do his best to deny her their souls.

His legs ached as he shifted his weight with the rocking ship but he checked the strength of the ropes one last time. Satisfied, Blade motioned for Willie to head below deck to relative safety. He followed Willie along a lifeline rope tied across the breadth of the ship to the hatch, about to step in after him. An ominous ripple in the fabric of the mourning wind caused Blade to pause. He looked out over the larboard side. A massive wave crashed over the side, knocking him off his feet. The force slammed Blade into the other side of the ship. Excruciating pain ripped through his shoulder. He couldn't move his arm. *Damn it.*

He sucked in a hard breath of waterlogged air at the agony. He had to get up, get off topside before another wave carried him overboard and met his death with the sea. Not yet. He wasn't ready to go with her.

Coughing, he turned over to his knees. He pushed himself up with his good arm, reached for the lifeline and staggered toward the hatch. Slipping once, he smashed his injured shoulder into the wall by the doorway. He hissed a string of profanities at the stabbing ache before stepping into the windless companionway.

Blade latched the door, muzzling the screaming wind which yelled at him from beyond like a spiteful banshee. He took a moment to ease his breathing and adjust to the darkness unburdened by rain. Salty water streamed down into his eyes and burned. He shook his head to get rid of the excess water in his hair. The throb in his shoulder compelled him to keep his arm close to his body as he worked his way down to the galley. Blade knew his ship well enough, but should he become disoriented, he'd only need to listen to the sounds of pathetic moans to find his way through the dark.

* * *

Marisol kneeled next to Sam who was doubled over a chamber pot. The mighty man had been heaving most of the night. He moaned and groaned like a wee child. The violent pitch of the ship had given poor Sam and several other men nausea. If there'd been more light, she was certain the mammoth would be green from sickness. She rubbed the plateau of his back hoping to bring him ease.

"Shh," she said. "Shh. You'll be all right."

Now that she had settled down from helping Henri snub out the lights, her own stomach grew squeamish. The lingering odor from the smothered cooking fire churned atop her queasiness. She swallowed it down.

There was nothing more to do but wait for the storm to pass.

The *Rissa* creaked and sighed as she protested the fury outside. She rose and fell, jounced and jolted as a coach might along a craggy hillside road. The terrible ride rattled Marisol's bones and nerves.

Squalls were bad enough, but hurricanes were a seaman's worst nightmare. Marisol had heard the tales from old sea dogs about vessels snapping in two during a storm, of ships bursting into flames from a carelessly lit lantern, of ballasts shifting and overturning ships, the sea claiming all on board. Only a lucky few ships survived. These stories scared Marisol much more than the superstitious yarns she kept close to her heart. They were real threats with fatal results.

In her two years of sailing with Alain, they'd encountered a few gales and rode them out in fair shape. And she had weathered more than one hurricane in her life, but only onshore. The fierce winds and raging seawater flooding past the coastline and into the portside town, into her mother's home, frightened her. As a young girl, she watched many die from a hurricane's destruction. Yet, the horrific storms were accepted as a part of life in the Caribbean. Youthful naiveté fooled her into thinking the safest place to be during a hurricane was on a ship. She knew better now. The odds weren't in their favor and the shuddering

Rissa sharpened that awareness. Worry buried itself deep within her. The feeling of helplessness bothered her most of all. She preferred far more battling for her life with a foe than struggling to survive against the deadly throes of nature.

A loud thud pulsated throughout the room and the vessel rolled to the right. She braced herself with the sudden shift. Damn. That had to be one awful wave. Fear skittered up her spine with the breath she held.

Her thoughts raced to Blade. Where was he? Was he all right? Oh dear God, what if he'd been swept away? She hadn't seen him since he ordered her below to change her clothing and report to Henri to give him a hand. He'd been so severe in his command, so unyielding; she'd flinched under his tone and followed his orders without a word. But that had been hours ago.

She glanced over at Henri huddled in the corner. He'd been nursing that bottle of rum for a good spot of time. Had it not been for her uneasy stomach, she'd wrestle him for the blasted thing. It wouldn't be much of a contest against the old man and she needed a crisp shot of courage.

Where was Blade? Did he mean to stay out there throughout the entire storm? She had to know if he was safe. Perhaps she should go check on him. She slid her gaze from the rum bottle to the door and back again to the bottle of courage. Henri let out a slow growl and pulled the bottle tight to his chest. Crazy fool.

"How about a sip of that there rum, Henri?" Sam let out a pitiable moan as she moved away from him and set her sights on the liquor.

Henri cradled the rum closer. "Doncha think about it, lass. You won't be havin' any of this."

"Come now. Just one sip." The wooden floor bit into her knees as she shuffled on them toward his corner.

"I mean it. Stay back." He arched his back as far as the curvature of the wall would allow.

Almost there. "One sip, Henri."

He'd sat up on his knees ready to protect his lifeblood. "No."

She reached out, grabbing the neck of the bottle. "Give me one sip!"

"No!" His chin jutted defiantly out at her and his grip on the bottle wouldn't loosen. They yanked it back and forth between them. Blimey. He was stronger than she first thought.

"Let go." She all but screeched the words through her clenched teeth. "I'll yank out those ribbons in your beard if you don't."

He sneered at her. "No."

The dark did not keep their eyes from locking in battle.

"By thunder, Henri, let go of the damned bottle."

"Ten thousand curses to ya, lass! Ten thousand curses!"

The galley door slammed open. A shadowy figure loomed against an inky backdrop before reeling forward.

"Blade," Marisol said.

She slackened her grip from the liquor and Henri snatched it back, hugging it. He took a quick swig, keeping his eyes on her, and then returned to wrapping both arms around it.

"Humph," she mumbled.

The ship took a quick slope and Blade spat out a curse as he caught his balance on the door jamb. He clutched at his arm. He held it oddly forward and crooked.

"Are you all right?" Clamoring to her feet, she hurried to him. Something, or someone, caught on her foot and she toppled forward, knocking him back into the jamb once more.

Blade hissed in apparent pain. "Damn, woman!"

"I'm so sorry." She righted herself and reached out for him. "Are you hurt?" Pawing her way over his wet clothes, she searched for any signs of injury. A gash, spurting blood, foreign objects sticking out of his body, anything that pointed to a wound.

He scudded down the wall away from her. "Marisol, stop."

His tone sounded irritable but she continued her examination. "Are you cut? Bleeding anywhere? I'm very good at suturing, you know."

"I said stop." He recoiled before she touched him. "I dislocated my shoulder."

"Oh, that probably hurts. Here let me help you."

"No!" His hand shot out to keep her back. Was that panic she detected? "I've got it."

"You've got it? No, no. I'll help you."

"Marisol! Stand—back."

She couldn't see his face clearly but gauging by the shadows across his mouth and his clipped words, he meant to push her down if she didn't obey him. She gave him his distance.

He stumbled back to the door and held on to the threshold for balance when the vessel took another deep dip. The ship's anguished moan had only been topped by Sam's whimper.

Biting her lower lip, she braced herself against the table behind her, more to prime herself for what Blade prepared to do than because of the shifting vessel. He rocked back and forth, aiming his shoulder at the jamb. Her body tensed. In one blink of an eye, he whacked his shoulder into the threshold with such force that she heard the crack in his arm over his roar. She cringed with his medley of profanity.

The ship had grown silent. She continued to roll with the sea and the winds kept up their howling and beatings. But no one inside the galley breathed a word. Not even the sick whined. Blade staggered to the corner Henri had wedged himself into.

"Hand it over." Salt water dripped from the sleeve of Blade's waiting hand.

Henri lifted the rum to his captain.

"Nay. The other bottle, Henri. The one you're hiding."

Without hesitation, Henri reached behind himself for an unopened bottle.

Marisol shook her head. She should've known the greedy little lunatic had more stashed.

The cork popped out under the twist of Blade's hand and he drew long and hard from the liquor. "Ah. That's better. Nothing like a tipple to wash your mind clean." He took another swig and rolled his arm around, letting the rum grease his joints. Crouching down, he plopped to the floor and propped his back against the wall next to Henri.

"Come." He invited her to join him, patting the floor as he drew his knees up.

Careful not to topple him again, she sat down beside him. Even in the stifling room, she welcomed his masculine warmth. She hadn't realized how chilled she had become. How strange. They swayed together with the rocking ship. Each time their shoulders touched the comforting warmth seeped through her, despite his cool wet clothing.

Blade handed her the rum bottle and she gleefully took it.

The heavy liquor slid down her throat with hellish heat. Oh, how good it tasted. She licked her lips and swallowed another mouthful. Another drink and it swirled within her blood to chase away her anxiety. Bending forward a hair to look past Blade, she shot Henri a satirical smirk. Henri pursed his mouth, shook his head and scooted to give her his back.

"You must be frightened," Blade said.

Couple more rounds with the liquor and she'd be afraid of nothing at all. Not even a wasp. And she hated those. "Aren't you?" She returned his rum.

"Of dying? No. The sea is my life. I am a part of her as I live and breathe. Should she no longer favor me and call me back to her womb, I shall be at peace." He let the bottle dangle by two fingers between his knees.

"Then what are you frightened of?" she asked.

"I'm not frightened of anything."

"You were angry enough when I stole your cameo." She shouldn't have brought it up. She'd gone too far and she couldn't stop herself. "Enough to be scared you'd never see it again." Her last word cracked as his face jerked around to stare through the darkness at her.

"Is there something you'd like to say?"

"No." Why would she say something so careless? It was as if she challenged his honor as a man.

The ship bucked and several metal cups fell from their secured place on a shelf. As they rolled over one another across the floor, the clanking and clattering rang loud in her ears. A lad swore and they came to an abrupt stop.

The quiet that followed compelled her to ask the question that plagued her mind. "Do you think we'll survive?"

Less harsh than before, Blade answered. "The *Rissa* is a strong ship. She'll hold. Though we're at the mercy of the storm, we're sailing with the winds into deeper waters." He placed a hand over hers and droplets trickled from his sleeve to slip between his fingers onto her own. "We'll be fine."

She tried to search his eyes. Even in the shadows, they held a ray of confidence. Beads of water dripped from the tips of his mussed hair, traveling down thin rivulets on his cheek and neck. His soaked tunic lay pasted against his broad chest and his sodden breeches cast a sheen stretched tight over his thighs. He looked positively handsome. *Oh, mercy's sake. Here we are in dire straits and I'm admiring him like a fine-crafted piece of weaponry.*

She pulled her hand from under his. "You should get out of your wet clothes."

"Not unless you get out of yours." He reached over and looped a finger through the bow closing the top of her tunic and gently tugged.

"Tyburn!"

"What? Oh, come on. The lads won't mind. Might lift their spirits. Especially Sam over there. Just listen to the poor sap moanin' and carrying on."

She glanced over at the dark lump across the room, gripping on to the chamber pot for dear life.

"He could use a beautiful naked woman to get his mind off his seasickness."

If it weren't for the flash of his teeth flanked by darkened dimples, she'd have taken him seriously, the devil.

"Well, since you put it that way." She pulled at the lace of her shirt, slowly letting it slide through the bow until it slipped free. "If it'll make the men feel better...we're all about to die anyway." She untied the laces farther, watching Blade's smile disappear.

"All right, Marisol." He stopped her from loosening her top any more.

"But you said—"

"Never mind what I said." Reaching over, he tied her tunic closed.

His fingers grazed her skin above the valley of her chest. Something inside her inflated. It started out small, unidentifiable, but then grew. Was Blade afraid she called his bluff? Was he suddenly possessive? Did he care for her enough to want to keep her moral character intact? Her stomach fluttered. Was that it? Did he care about her?

He finished making the bow and pulled it tighter than necessary.

She chuckled. "You really should get on some dry clothes."

"They'll just get wet again later."

She understood. He'd go topside to check on the helmsman and the condition of his ship.

Despite the raging storm outside and the convulsing ship, Marisol fought against exhaustion. She yawned. Tension and anxiety wound tightly in her muscles. It had been a terribly long day and the vengeful night seemed to never have an end. They may all very well perish before sunrise—the fact rebounded in her mind. The ship's continual tossing and the waves beating at the hull made it impossible to rest. Yet sleep drew at her eyelids and another yawn surfaced.

"You need sleep." Blade pulled off his tunic and wrapped his arm around her. He stretched his legs out as he pulled her close. "Lay your head on my shoulder."

Gladly. There was comfort there so near to him. In his warmth, cradled within his embrace, breathing in his brackish heat, the hurricane no longer mattered. Their impending demise evaporated. She snuggled closer and let her lids fall.

He stroked her arm. "That's right, sleep, dove. Sleep."

At some point in the early hours he must have left her. Voices carried her from the edge of a deep slumber and she became aware of the wooden planks beneath her arms where she had her head tucked. Opening her eyes, she uncurled her body and realized the ship had stilled. Footsteps hurried past in the companionway. No one remained in the galley.

The storm. It passed. We made it out alive.

She scrambled to her feet and raced to get outside. The early morning light choked against the cloudy sky and hazy sea. Gusts of wind sputtered briefly then died off in unremarkable gasps. A quick inspection of the ship revealed that she had fared well during the hurricane, just as Blade said she would. The spanker yard had twisted and broken and was significant enough to need immediate repair but any other damage to the ship she could not see. Men worked to secure the yard but many of the crew stood at the railings.

What were they all looking at? They spoke quietly amongst themselves and as she neared the side of the ship, something in the water caught her attention.

In the sea scattered across the choppy waves, debris floated by. Planks of wood, barrels, and pieces of shredded sail bobbed with the currents, bumping with muted thuds against the *Rissa*'s hull. And bodies.

Marisol sucked at her breath. Lifeless bodies of men, facedown with their arms spread out quietly gliding atop the sea like the birds in the sky, drifting on without any disparity among the wreckage.

She cupped her hands together and brought them to her mouth. Sadness consumed her. How horrible for them. They surely suffered. She fought back the tears and desperately swallowed at the lump that burned in her throat.

"Who..." Her voice mangled and she could say no more.

Loud voices thankfully prodded her to the flurry of activity on the other side of the ship's waist. She moved with the crowd and pushed her way to the front.

"Careful, lads. Don't lose him." Willie leaned way over the rail, looking straight down. "Careful, I say! You're gonna lose him."

Three men pulled at a rope and a fourth stood at the railing with a long hook ready to snag the catch. Blade waited beside Willie. With his hands resting on his hips, he paced the perimeter. He paused to watch the men's progress then returned to pacing. The man swung the hook down to capture a body.

"That's right, get him in the trousers." Willie reached over and grabbed a man's shirt collar to help haul him over the rail. Together, they heaved the body up and dropped it to the deck.

Marisol closed her eyes with the sopping wet thump the man made hitting the planks.

"It's Duncan all right, Capt'n," Willie said.

Blade took one knee beside the dead man. He swiped away the matted hair on the man's forehead. Marisol then saw the wound. A fleshy hole gaped in his brow.

"Just as I suspected," Blade said. "He's been shot. By the looks of many of those bodies out there, they all were shot."

"Aw, hell." Willie rubbed the back of his neck.

"What?" Did she hear Blade right? Shot? These men didn't drown in the hurricane?

Blade and Willie turned to her. When she moved forward, Blade rose to meet her. Willie lowered his head and stepped back so that Marisol came to stand between them. She took a closer look at the buccaneer by her feet. The wound had a distinct spherical reddening around its outer edge. He'd been very near to the gun that delivered his death.

"What's going on here?" she said.

Sorrow colored Blade's eyes, their green hue dark and cloudy. It scared her. She didn't like the troubled look he gave her. He slowly shook his head. "I'm sorry, Marisol." He placed his hand to the center of her back, a placating gesture.

Sorry? Sorry for what? Panic reared up from the depths of her soul.

"It's the *Gloria.*"

No. She refused to hear him, refused to let his words sink in and touch her mind, her soul. "You're lying." She recoiled back from him and he let his arm drop.

"I'm not, sweetheart. Duncan, here, and some of those other men down in the water belong to the *Rissa.*" He put a hand on the railing and gazed to the remnants of the broken vessel riding the wakes as they sailed past. "I sent them with your brother as a part of his crew. That wreckage is the *Gloria.* She didn't make it through the storm."

Monte. Her dear younger brother, gone. How could this be? All her searching, all her deceptions, and the lives she invariably destroyed. 'Twas for nothing.

"I just got him back." She choked back the lump clogging her throat.

"I know, dove. I know." Blade reached for her but she flung up her hands.

"Don't," she said. She didn't want him to touch her. Not that way. His frown deepened but she knew better. He wouldn't give her what she needed, not in front of his crew. He would merely mollify her and that would only cause the chasm of hurt to rupture further. That she did not need. She was alone now. Both her brothers were dead. Her father cast her out. What would become of her?

She lowered her head and stared at the body.

"But what about Duncan and the others? You said they were shot."

"Murdered, yes."

Reaction among the crew grew into an angry chorus. Blade

raised his voice over the incensed din. "Probably before the storm hit."

"How do you know?"

"'Tis obvious these men went down with the *Gloria* as she broke apart. They must have encountered trouble before the hurricane."

He glanced at Willie. "Perhaps with our mystery ship."

She hung on to her denial. "I don't understand."

"Neither do I," Blade said. "Something afoul happened on the *Gloria.* However, if there were anyone alive on the ship when the storm hit, it is doubtful there are survivors now."

Murdered. Marisol let the word sink in. It snaked around her heart, tightening like a vise. If Monte had been murdered, well, she regained a new resolve.

Vengeance.

CHAPTER 13

"You're losing her!" Marisol screeched and paced the quarter deck.

Blade found her action of alternating between frantic waving arms to keeping her hands tacked to her hips amusing. To a point. But for the past half hour, the mystery ship spotted earlier in the morning had gained considerable distance from them. Marisol's twittery distress eroded his patience.

He wanted to catch that vessel as much as Marisol. Blade needed answers. Who commanded her? What was she after? Was she to blame for the deaths of *Gloria*'s crew and why? He snarled inwardly. No quarter would be given to the bloody bastards responsible for killing his men. He'd see to it personally.

The mystery ship was smaller than his *Rissa,* making the vessel faster. With the *Rissa*'s spanker still in need of proper repair, she struggled to keep up with her enemy. They followed the same course for hours and Blade realized the other ship had not assumed a defensive plan of action. She had not tried tricky maneuvers to lose the *Rissa,* but merely kept a steady easterly route instead. Whoever captained her, taunted him. That rankled Blade and uneasiness stalked in the shadows of his good sense.

Willie joined Blade by the rail. "We've lost sight of them, Capt'n."

Marisol flung up her arms. "Bloody hell." She stormed off muttering unladylike curses and descended the ladder, probably to sulk in her cabin. A door slammed.

"Blazes." Henri grumbled, grunting from the effort of climbing the ladder with his lame leg. At the top, he paused long enough to scowl at the offending steps. He toddled over. "What's gotten into the lass? She came flyin' down the ladder an' nearly plowed me down. You go an' make her mad, Tyburn?"

"What makes you think that?"

"She was sayin' somethin' 'bout a capt'n needin' to grow some ballocks."

Willie choked on a chuckle, coughing to hide his mirth.

"Loose tongue, that girl." Blade shook his head. She had brass but he couldn't be angry. So long as she kept it to herself. Too much scoffing from her and he'd have to deal with it.

Henri retrieved the crate he kept secured near the wheel for those times he liked to reminisce about steering the ship and glory days long past. He set it down and stood on top.

"So whatcha gonna do about this problem?"

Blade wasn't so sure anymore. The hurricane changed everything. His initial plan included catching up to the *Sugar Lady* and engaging the mystery ship. He was confident his answers to the missing silver lay there. Now his confidence ran low. A ship laden with silver would be heavy. It would move slowly and would not be easy to maneuver during a storm. It very well could be at the bottom of the sea. Now there was the matter of hunting down who was to blame for massacring his men.

"We'll have to stick with the original plan. Get across Mona and sail into San Juan waters. 'Tis obvious this rogue ship is trifling with us. I'm convinced we'll happen upon them. We'll need to be prepared to engage."

Henri snorted. "I meant whatcha gonna do about the lass?"

Blade cleared his throat. He suddenly didn't like the turn of the conversation.

"Miss Castellan provides us with a bit of indemnity. Carrion is clever. He wants Windham's silver, if for no other reason than because it was under our protection. If by chance the bastard manages to find the silver before we do, he will use Marisol as an excuse to cross me. He will come for us. He can go before the brethren with a plea that I took her and he was forced to fight me to get her back. His plan is to destroy me and keep the silver. She is our pawn in his quest."

Blade couldn't suppress his smile if he wanted to. The thought of engaging Carrion and putting an end to his vagrant practices gave him spurs of excitement.

What of Marisol? She's lost so much already. Will you be able to kill her father? Will you be able to wipe her clean of Castellan men? Can you handle her hatred once you do?

His excitement wilted.

Henri eyed him carefully through slits of suspicion. "Is that all?"

Blade felt Henri's scrutiny bore into him. Just what did the little man expect him to confess? "Aye, that's all."

Henri nodded in a slow show of doubt. He turned to Willie. "You hadn't talked to 'im yet, has ya, Willie?"

Willie shrugged. "Hadn't got 'round to it."

"Hadn't gotten 'round to it? I'd say you avoidin' talkin' to 'im, ya coward."

"Maybe so," Willie said.

"Talk to me about what?" Blade said.

"Ya see," Henri began, "Marisol overheard one of the tars blame 'er brother for what happened to the men on the *Gloria.*"

Willie piped in. "She flung a knife at 'im, pinnin' 'im to the wall and threatened to gut 'im like a fish."

Blade imagined her speed and precision. He'd been duly impressed by her knife-throwing abilities. She probably scared a few years off the seaman's life.

"I had ta coax her nice like away from the fella," Willie said. "'Twasn't easy, I tell ya. Nearly lost a finger, an ear, and—" he patted his hip, "—me tobacco pouch."

That chit was a wearisome handful. Blade couldn't let her get away with physical threats to his men, not if he wanted to maintain their respect. She wouldn't like what he'd have to do. *He* didn't like what he had to do. "I'll have her weapons removed."

"Good luck to ya," Henri said.

A lookout high up the mainmast called out. He pointed off

the larboard bow.

Blade moved quickly to the other side of the ship.

Willie and Henri, with his crate in tow, followed.

Blade untied his spyglass from his belt and scanned the waters. A mass of land rose straight from the gray watery plane. He recognized the island's square shape.

The tempest blew them hundreds of miles southeast. "What do you make of it, Henri?" He handed over the telescope. "You reckon it's Monito?"

Henri braced his torso against the rail to steady himself and adjusted the view. "That be the Monito, all right. See the cliffs? No way on the island."

He sighted in on the hazy rock. The steep cliffs rose high from the ocean, black and craggy. Waves crashed against the walls in a steady rhythm.

"That storm blew us clear off course," Henri said.

"Can't complain." Willie patted Henri on his back. "We still breathin', ain't we?"

"That we are, mate. That we are."

A moment of silence hung heavy. Willie finally asked the question Blade was sure had been on all their minds.

"Do ya think Drake made it through the storm?"

"Drake's a damn good captain," Blade said. "He's at his best in rough seas. But even he is at the mercy of a hurricane."

Another moment of hush hung between them. He could only hope his friend survived the nasty tempest.

Blade scanned the sea beyond the ridge.

"Mona Island isn't far." He couldn't see it rising from the water, but it was there, shrouded by the shifting illusions of the horizon. "Willie, have the helmsman bring her around three points the starboard beam. We're going to make our way to Mona's southeast side where we can navigate the reefs."

"Aye, Capt'n." Willie left to give the orders.

"I'd wager we'll be there 'fore midday," Henri said.

Blade agreed. "We'll anchor, finish repairs and let the lads have a night of rest."

"A bit of dry ground be welcome after last night." Henri hopped off his crate. "You'd best see to that woman of yours," he said, toddling away. "'Fore she hurts someone."

Somehow, Blade didn't think seeing to Marisol would be an easy task.

He made his way to her cabin and knocked. The door swung open. By the angry bonfires blazing in her eyes, getting her knives from her would be difficult indeed.

"Can I help you?" She held nothing back in her tart tone.

"May I?" Blade nodded his head to be let in. After an irritable sigh, she stepped aside.

A smile brightened his soul as he looked around the room awash in the exotic blue fabrics. Many fine memories lay within those walls, with many fine ladies. A queer feeling crept into his heart, one of wistful lovers who soon would be forgotten. He didn't want to forget but they floated away on a wind of change he could not identify.

"Why are you here?" She didn't move from the door left open, a clear sign he had not been invited to stay.

"We need to talk."

"Talk?" Her brow lifted in what he decided was ridicule. "Shouldn't you be topside looking for the enemy ship you let slip away?"

The time had long since passed for her to end her biting words. "I understand your thirst for revenge, but you will hold sway your spiteful tongue. I will have no more of it."

"Then I suggest you take your leave for I have nothing else to offer."

Her words brought him close, irresistible like nectar to a bee. "Oh?"

She stiffened, realizing too late the delicious challenge she presented him. "That's right," she said.

"This I know to be a lie." He put his hand on the door and she pressed her back against the wall. "I can think of many things you can offer me."

He closed the door slowly enough to allow her a chance to flee. But Marisol didn't move. In fact, he didn't think she even breathed. The door latch made a soft click and her eyelids fluttered at the sound. He bent in, nearing her lips, but she turned her face away. For a fraction of a second, he paused and smiled. She wouldn't fall for that trick again. No matter, her slender neck invited him to a savory feast. The faint smell of sweet plumeria enticed him. He dragged his nose along her smooth skin, inhaling all he could of her. Wanting more, he started a trail of kisses back down her neck to the curve of her shoulder. A tiny moan escaped and her breath resumed, quickly picking up pace.

His own breathing ragged, he pulled back. "I need you to give me something."

Marisol nodded and he couldn't deny her parted lips. Swooping in, his zeal to taste her was matched by her eagerness. She laced her arms around his neck and he deepened their kiss. He pressed harder into her, their tongues mingled together in a passionate dance. The curve of her body kindled his yearning, a swelling tightening down below. He teetered on the edge of control.

"Please understand, dove." The words tumbled out between kisses, yet for what he was about to do, he could all but guarantee his plea useless.

"Hmm." She pulled him tighter.

Her tunic slipped out of her pants easily and he took special delight rubbing his hands over her dips and bends, appreciating every silky inch of her bare skin. He dared to caress one taut breast, cupping her, fondling her. Damn, he loved to feel this woman. It pained him when his other hand found what he had been searching for. One last succulent taste of her lips, one gentle squeeze more, and he removed her gulley knife from her waistband. Blade stepped away from her. Already, her warmth on his skin faded.

Surprise rimmed with outrage became softened by the tears building in her eyes.

Blade was a bastard. He'd known that all his life. It never bothered him before. In fact, being a bastard made his life easier. There never had been a need to explain or apologize for his actions. Even his paramours understood. But now, staring into those sad, brown puddles, he hated himself for it.

"I'll need the other two, as well."

The lines of her face stiffened. When she made no move to oblige him with her other daggers, he let out a heavy sigh.

"'Tis for your own good, Marisol. I cannot have you harassing my men with your weapons."

"So you leave me helpless among a ship full of pirates?"

"You're hardly helpless. And my men will not harm you. They are aware such a mistake would cost them their lives."

"I've no choice in the matter?"

"No."

Shaking her head, Marisol looked away. She blew out a disgusted huff and bent to remove the two knives strapped to her legs. Blade moved a pace away, not entirely trusting her. As angry and hurt as she was, she might try to attack him—again. With the handles facing out, she handed him her weapons.

A witch's brew of hate fermented within her glowering visage. He couldn't let her feel that way about him. He had to make her see. Her touch, her body, her kiss, that was real to him. He didn't toy with her; he reveled in all she offered, all he could take.

Longing to touch her, he reached for her face. She turned away.

"Get out." She threw open the door.

Anger sallied through him at being spurned. "Marisol."

"Out!"

No sooner had he taken a step back through the threshold, the door slammed shut. The force sent a gust of wind across his face. He returned to his quarters, slamming his own door. The room brightened with the sun outside climbing higher in the sky. A red-footed booby flew past his window. Soon, they would be anchored. He should be looking forward to an evening on the beautiful Mona.

Instead, he couldn't stop thinking about Marisol. When did she get to him? How? Her disappointment, her loathing as she glared at him, sickened him. She had a disturbing effect over him, a sure sign of weakness.

Damn that woman.

He stabbed the knives into his desk, the force embedding them deep into the wood, and stormed out of the room.

CHAPTER 14

Marisol skimmed the surface of warm water with her fingertips as she and Sam were rowed to shore. Black reefs below stretched across the ivory sea floor and looked close enough to touch, but the crystal-clear water deceived. The depth was much farther down. Still, she could see stingrays glide along the underwater landscape. Flashes of silver reflected from the sunlight as a school of fish darted around the blooming coral.

On a breeze she caught the scent of vegetation, not fragrant but fresh. She swiveled around as the longboat neared the shore. A thin strip of beach cut across the shoreline. The frosty white sand blinded her and she couldn't wait to dig her toes into the soft grains. It presented a beautiful contrast to the crowded green trees butting the boulders and the rising rocky terrain.

"I wanted to t'ank you, ma'am."

Marisol turned back around to face Sam sitting on the bench across from her. Blade had ordered the hulking giant to stay with her at all times. It was his way of giving her protection in the wake of taking her weapons. Though she hurt deep inside from what he had done, from how he took advantage of her in a weak moment, she realized Blade did what he had to do. She wouldn't have handed over her knives without a fight. But she hated him just the same.

"What are you thanking me for, Sam?"

"Yer kindness…for when I was sick." His downcast eyes did

not hide his embarrassment.

She patted his arm and smiled. “My friend needed comforting. ’Twas nothing.”

He looked upon her with a gentle smile and responded with a slight nod. Expecting no more from the man of few words, her heart filled with happiness over their amity. She liked having a friendship with him.

A rip in his trousers caught her eye. It had been crudely stitched and the thread strained against his large thigh. A rush of guilt nipped at her conscience.

“I’m sorry for stabbing you in the leg before,” she said.

Sam’s smile widened. “T’ain’t nothin’.”

The longboat slid up smoothly onto the bank. Waves rolled in, kissing the shore only to steal back to sea. Birds cast off from tree limbs and tiny crabs ducked under the cover of pitted rocks lining the beach. The crew of the *Rissa* toiled about in various activities. Some prepared holes in the sand for campfires. Others gathered timber dry enough to burn. Still others, armed with pikes and makeshift spears, waded through the shallows for supper. Marisol couldn’t help but notice Blade was nowhere in sight. Most likely, he hunkered down somewhere dulling her knives by whittling figurines of busty mermaids out of whale bone. Miscreant.

She clambered out of the boat and followed Sam to the shade of the many trees fronting a hedge of stone. “What are we to do now?”

“Wait for t’e capt’n.” Sam planted himself against a tree. Even leaning, his head nearly reached the low lying branches.

“Where is the unreasonable captain?”

“Here.”

She flinched at the sound of Blade’s detached voice, loud and hoarse. Looking around she couldn’t locate where his voice had come from. Sam offered no help. A carpet of thick vines against the rocky wall shifted and opened, revealing a cave on the other side of the leafy curtain. Blade ducked out of the darkened cavity.

Blinking her surprise, she hadn’t seen the cave there as she stood directly in front of it. It had been so well hidden; no one would ever know it was there. A perfect place to hide, or to watch. How long had Blade been observing her from the secret alcove?

"The island is riddled with caves," Blade said. Her surprise must've been plastered on her face. "Some go for miles and many are underwater."

He pulled back the vines to allow her access into the cave. "This is where we will sleep tonight."

"We?"

"Many of the men will sleep on the beach, some on the ship. But we will stay in here where you will be safe."

Safe? She had strong misgivings about that. Staying within a league of the infamous libertine proved hazardous. She wanted far away from him, where he couldn't hurt her again.

Yet, her raw heart begged for his healing touch. How did he do it? How did he cause her knees to wobble and her mouth to go dry when he came near? Until she met him, she never before lost command of her feelings for a man. With Blade, she fell prey too easily to his charms. A single kiss and she was a hopeless starry-eyed lamb. Oh, suffering catfish. When had she turned into such a milksop? She rolled her eyes and stepped through the entrance.

A lantern cast flickering lights to wink off the jagged walls. She choked as the thickness of newly spent oil pervaded the enclosed area. Above her, the ceiling reached higher than the tree canopy outside. Rounded boulders provided places to sit and dirty bottles littered the floor, a testament to prior nights spent inside the hideaway. Shadows lengthened deep beyond the range of the lantern, leaving her to ponder just how far in the earth the cavern extended. A large iguana ambled out from behind a rock and scurried into the depths of the far-reaching darkness.

Marisol moved farther into the interior. The air there pressed cool but heavy against her skin. Her lungs filled with an aroma of dampness, though she could neither see nor hear any water.

"There are many pitfalls in the caves," Blade said.

He moved in close. Her heart thudded in her chest, picking up thundering speed. Damn. She must stop swooning over him every time he came too near. She anticipated his touch, praying for it. She leaned back into him. How could she so easily respond to him? She was supposed to hate him. Yet, he made it hard. No, impossible. If only he would hold her again.

His breath tickled her ear like the wisps of dandelion fluff. "If you venture too far, you could get caught by the rising waters of the tides and drown."

She swallowed hard and whispered, "I'll stick close."

"I know you will."

Was he sincere or was that a warning? Either way, she held her tongue. His comment was not worth sparring over. Not while her emotions bubbled close to the surface.

"Damn woman. What have you done to me?"

Her skin prickled as he growled against her neck. "I don't…what do you mean?"

"I thirst to taste you. I crave to feel your body against mine. I want to take you…I can't resist you, Marisol. I try. Bloody hell, I try."

His words weaved a soothing web, tangling her logic. She didn't want him to stop talking. She needed to hear more of his shameless confessions. His sedate voice nourished her with sweet rapture. Yet the effort to understand what he said fractured her wits. Thoughts unraveled in a losing bid to piece together his meaning. Could he be sincere? Did he speak from the heart? Fear of being hurt by him again gave her the impetus she required to be cautious. But her body warred with her mind. She responded to his touch so wantonly. In an amorous trance, completely against her will, she craned her neck to further expose her skin for him to devour.

"I hate you," she said. Her hand slipped down to stroke his flexed thigh. A betrayal she could no more stop than the rising sun.

"As well you should," he replied. Blade reached around her waist and pulled her close. *Thank God.*

She let her other hand rest upon his, not wanting him to let go. *Never let go.* Her back bowed to mold into his sturdy frame. Too close was not nearly close enough.

"Especially for the indecent things I want to do to you at this very moment."

He made no attempt to veil his desire. His hard member nestled snug against her bottom. A slight shift sent a tremor of titillation to a spot rapidly coming alive.

"Give me a reason to hate you more," she said.

"I will, if you let me." His mouth hovered above the bend of her shoulder, moistening the curvature with his oath.

"I want to hate you more than anything. Please." She begged him like a common whore and she didn't care. The way Blade made her feel frayed any thread of good sense. All she knew for certain was she didn't want this effervescent feeling he stirred in her to stop. Not even for a moment. For better or worse, he was what she wanted. Nothing else mattered.

Blade shifted again, burying himself deeper into her rear and planting a kiss on her shoulder. She moaned in kind. Their bodies fashioned together in a perfect fit. His free hand caught her wrist and ended her enjoyment of caressing his leg. Steering it away from him and onto her own thigh, he snaked his fingers with hers and put his mouth to her ear.

"Are you ready for me?"

She nodded. *More than he could ever know.*

He directed her hand upward, slowly. What did he mean to do?

Their hands meandered up to the juncture between her legs. She bit her lip and cast her gaze to the dark ceiling. *Oh, by Nick's twisted tail, yes!*

Cupping her, he set smoldering fires with his lips as he rubbed their palms in circles. The coarse fabric of her trousers provided no barrier at all from the torturous pressure he placed there and instead increased the amazing sensation. She squirmed; for relief, for more, she didn't know which.

A reprieve came as he continued the guided tour of their hands away. Was she purring?

"You sound ready," Blade murmured. "But are you wet with need?"

"Yes, Blade. I'm ready. I'm ready and wet."

"I'm not entirely convinced." He unfastened the top button on her pants and moved her hand to slide under the waistband. "Persuade me. Show me you are eager for me."

In an excruciating long moment, he drew their hands down to her mound. Her fingers, his fingers, grazed through her curly, smooth tuft of hair. Primal lechery bloomed in a crazy rush and the instant he pressed her finger to her vibrating nub, the cave came to life with her carnal cry. Her legs knotted with tension. Her vision was but an echo of shadows and light. Touching herself under his power sent her swimming in a muddle of desire.

She let her head fall back to his shoulder and lolled with the tiny loops they rubbed. Her moans crested on each roll over her nubbin. Like a seagull riding a current of wind, she flew higher and higher. Higher and faster. Yes, soon she would burst through the clouds skimming the sky and reach the heavens. Higher. Higher. *Al…most…there.*

"Mmm. You are drenched." Blade removed his hand.

No, damn it!

"Don't stop, dove. Bring yourself to come off for me."

Could she? The trembling of her body prompted her to continue petting herself to abandon. Her manipulations felt so good. Blazes! How had she not known she would react to depraved manual stimulation? Her hand let go of his and she threw it up to latch into his hair.

"That's it, Marisol. A little more."

Blade nibbled the skin behind her ear, amplifying her wild need. Dipping and swirling, her fingers moved rapidly, hastily reaching for surrender. All too soon she burst into an outbreak of tremors and her legs clamped together over her hand.

His chest provided the support she needed to stay upright whilst she caught her breath.

"I'd say you are more than ready," he said, not breaking the stride of kisses across her shoulder.

Of course she was ready. What was this torment he insisted on bringing her? The steel rod pressed against her backside hinted his readiness, as well.

He found his way to her chest; he squeezed and plied each breast. Every spot he touched ignited hot and sensitive. With the all the grace of a marauding cat, he spun her to face a large boulder.

"Now is the time to stop me, dove. If you want no more of me, now is the time."

Strain sifted in his voice, as if he were afraid she would refuse him. Telling him to stop would certainly prove far more painful for her. The loss of his touch would cool her to ash. She would dissolve like cinders in the rain if he pulled away now. This was insane.

"I need you, Blade."

"And I, you."

He made quick work of her trousers and, taking her by the shoulder, bent her over the rock. Cool air blasted her buttocks, but her cheeks warmed instantly as Blade's hand pawed across each one.

"I've never seen a more beautiful arse." He stroked her as if appreciating a work of art. "I've never seen a more beautiful woman."

Her heart spurred with a smile. But how could she know he wasn't just speaking in the raptures of lust? No matter, she would believe anything he professed as long as he touched her.

His sword thudded against the sandy ground. Bottles clanked against one another as he kicked them aside to move in close behind her.

"You mustn't deny me."

"No. I will not."

His tip pressed against her and she arched her back. He found her wet spot and brushed himself bit by bit across her shuddering folds. She towered with need, need to have him. If he didn't take her soon, she would surely expire.

Oh God, hurry. "Please, Blade, no more taunting."

"I would ask the same of you, dove. You've had me caught in your eddy of temptation from the moment we met."

He grabbed her by the hips and eased himself into her. With her trousers at her ankles, access was limited and, in the tight position, he filled her completely. He slid back and forth in a measured pace, creating a friction that lit her like a slow match. His palm pressed comfortably into the small of her back, governing the tempo. The fuse of her flared body already ran dangerously low but he picked up speed. Marisol thrust back to meet him at every plunge. Bucking, rocking, she raced up to the heights to which he had brought her before.

The cave, once cooled by the dank darkness, flooded with suffocating heat emanating from their wet bodies and heated breaths. Even the boulder she grasped for support became slippery with sweat.

"Do you hate me," he ground out. "Or do you desire me?"

How...how could he not know? The words she wanted to say lodged into her throat, unable to break through her moans.

"Marisol." He drove into her harder. "Do...you...desire me?"

Marisol seized, reaching her zenith. She cried out with the waves of exquisite pleasure. The cave walls sparkled in the flickering light as her vision cleared. Blade placed a chaste kiss to the base of her neck. He began to glide in again, skimming against the gradual decrease of sensuous ripples. Already, her muscles clenched with a crescendo of exalted indulgence.

No. She had all she could take of him, at the moment anyhow.

Before he could stop her, Marisol twisted around, not near as graceful as he with her trousers at her feet, and knelt to the soft grainy floor before him. The backs of his thighs constricted under her grasp to keep him from backing away. She looked up the stratum of his firm body.

"I *desire* to show you how much I want you." Marisol wrapped a hand around his rigid shaft. "Please, do not try and stop me this time."

A rakish dimple flashed at the corner of his smile.

She took him into her mouth, all of him, slow and easy. His zesty flavor tasted warm and rich upon her lips. Blade growled low as she pulled back, withdrawing her mouth from his crown. She swept her tongue over the tip and dragged her mouth down the side of his velvety cock. His shaft jerked under the path of kisses on her way back to the top. The muscles in his thighs bunched when her lips reached the end. She flicked her tongue across his tip, stimulating him with erratic licking.

Marisol glanced up as she took him whole into her mouth again. He flung back his head and moaned, a most wonderful sound.

More than anything, she wanted to give him all the indulgence he could handle. She wanted to be the one to control his pleasure. She wanted to bring him peace and set him free. Do to him as he had done to her.

She suckled him with shallow pulls and groped his ballocks.

"Perish me," Blade hummed.

Gradually her nursing built to greedily tapping him dry. She held him tightly, stroking him as he pumped himself into her mouth. Quicker, harder she drew upon him. His rapid breathing stopped, his muscles coiled. Blade roared. Hot juice spurted into her throat, but she held fast, swallowing every drop of him until he fully relaxed.

Blade pulled her up and kissed her deep. Her thoughts scattered with his zeal. How she loved that he wasted no time taking back control. She wrapped her arms around his neck and cast adrift in desire.

He whispered into her lips. "Why did you not stop me, dove? Why?"

She didn't know how to answer. What did he expect of her now? Sharing this intimacy, sharing their bodies, how did he play this out in his mind? Did they just knock about or had they made love? She couldn't be sure. Either way, she didn't want to know. Whatever the truth, whichever way the pendulum swung, it terrified her.

"Capt'n?"

Sam's throaty tone carried in from outside the cave and Blade let out a heavy sigh of frustration.

Marisol's sigh was more out of thankfulness. She tussled with unexpected feelings again. Something was different, strange, and yet, tangible. This she knew. Her relationship with Blade, it confused her. Did she despise him? Yes. He had treated her like an unwanted chattel. Dallied with her heart and caused her untold crestfallen misery. Did she covet him? Yes. He had given her comfort when there should have been none to have. The libertine proved masterful in bestowing indulgences of the flesh. He made her feel like a woman unlike any other, had taken the time to see to *her* pleasure. He tested her strength and lingered nearby during her weaknesses. And he had trusted her with his most guarded secret. The man stirred emotions she didn't know existed.

Was she the one guilty of merely making merry with him? Was there something…more?

"Give me a moment, Sam," Blade called.

He swept a strand of hair from her face. Those green eyes cauterized her composure. Oh blast. It *was* something more.

She shook off the disturbing thought and looked away. "Um. We should get dressed."

"Too bad," he teased. "I was hoping to quench my insatiable thirst for you."

That sounded divine...and unwise. She should find the strength to sort out her feelings before she did any more damage. Courage eluded her. Standing there half-naked while the wolf licked his chops called for immediate action.

In a clumsy fashion, she tugged her pants on, stepping on the cuff and hopping in place. The drawstrings would not cooperate; her fingers must have grown to an inexplicable size for the task of fastening them into place.

Blade, however, pulled up his trousers in one sinuous movement. Damn, he handled the most awkward moments with manly poise.

"Come," he said. "There is work to be done."

Work? If the man only knew how much *work* he put her through already.

She joined him at the entrance. Blade grabbed her by the back of the neck and crushed his mouth against hers in a soulful kiss. Her head whirled with his quick capture and release.

He held open the vine door and followed her out into the humid afternoon.

Sam took one look at them and his eyes dropped to the sand. Horror tightened her chest. Did he know what she and Blade had been up to? Were her trousers on right? Maybe her face was flustered. Her fingers flew to her lips. Were they swollen from his kisses? It was then she realized Blade had left his tunic untucked. Why, he practically announced their copulation.

Blade smirked.

Rake.

"Sam. You take Miss Castellan to gather water."

He looked to Marisol, all business now. "There is no fresh water on this island," he explained. "We lost our rain barrel to the hurricane and it will take us some time to reach San Juan. Clean water is a priority. The two of you will collect the rainwater from the storm that has gathered in pools among the rocks and from large plant fronds. Anywhere you can find clean water, pour it into those jugs."

He pointed to a dozen jars tied in pairs at each end of long strands of rope.

"There are only a few more hours of daylight left. Fill as many as you can and get back before it gets dark."

She looked up the steep embankment. Did he expect them to climb up the wall like a couple of human spiders?

"There's a foot trail around the bend that will take you to the plateau at the top."

Why did he always have to be one step ahead of her?

"Watch out for holes," Blade said. "This place is teeming with iguanas and they build tunnels for nests everywhere."

Sam lumbered to the jars and slung them around his neck. He picked up the remainder and held them out for Marisol. She put the ropes around her. The jars were light and knocked together when she moved.

Blade walked toward the beach, pausing to put a hand on Sam's shoulder. "Keep her safe, mate." He then left.

Marisol let Sam lead the way. Tiny rocks shifted under her weight, making the scale up the embankment slippery. She relied on her hands in some places, digging into the loose dirt to help keep her moving in the right direction. Pebbles jabbed into her palms sending shots of pain to her wrists. Her knees banged against the jars that dragged along the ground. She chanced a glance behind her once, only once. How they planned to get down without plummeting in a landslip to certain death, she had no idea.

The top of the trail leveled out onto flat terrain. Brush and trees grew despite the rocky and arid ground. Out of breath, she licked the tangy perspiration from her upper lip. A gusty breeze shoved her from behind. She turned to meet the wind and let it cool the sweat on her brow.

"Saints." She was unprepared for what she saw.

They were high above the sea. Emblazoned across the turquoise water, the shadows of the reefs fanned out. Shades of light and dark swayed with the sun- dappled currents. The beauty of Mona's coast stole her breath.

She tried to look down, but the beach was nowhere in sight. Her head spun from the dizzying height and her vision blurred. They were much higher on this cliff than any ship's mast she had ever climbed.

"Come away from t'e edge, ma'am." Sam guided her back to the trail. "T'e rocks t'ere come loose."

"Yes, of course." The island was indeed beautiful, but she had no wish to become a permanent part of it.

They walked along taking the path deeper into the isle, collecting tiny amounts of rainwater wherever they found it. She cursed at the tedium of finding even the minutest drips of water. She began to think Blade had sent her out on the wild goose chase to torment her. The terrain varied from dry, filled with scraggly brush and cacti, to clusters of lush forests. The forests yielded the most spots for finding water. Much would be trapped in patchworks of large glossy leaves.

True to form, Sam didn't chat with Marisol. At times, he would tell her not to fall behind or to stray too far ahead, but nothing more. She tried to strike up a conversation on several accounts, hoping to ask about his captain, but she found the iguanas more talkative.

With their water jugs only half-full, Sam decided to make for the clearing ahead and then turn back to camp. Marisol couldn't be happier to hear it. The weight of her jars cramped the muscles of her neck and back. She rolled her head and rounded her shoulders to relieve the aching strain before stepping out of the copse.

The trees opened up to large flat boulders. Many contained crevices brimming with rainwater. Marisol rushed forward, leaving Sam still emerging from the forest, her excitement almost too much to bear. Get the jugs full and get back to camp. Get back to Blade. Her emotions ran amok when he was near but she had decided within a space of half-glass from scaling the island mountainside that she enjoyed his company. She yearned for nightfall and the seclusion of the cave where they would *sleep.*

A large pool glimmered at the top of a rise. Marisol scrambled up, already uncorking her jug. Her head in Blade-marinated clouds, she bent hastily to dip her jar in the cool water and jammed her arse into a barbed cactus arm. She yelped and shot up. Tears sprang from her eyes as the needles injected spikes of pain.

Sam ran to her aid. "Stop bouncin' 'round. Hold still!"

"Get them out! Get them out!" She hopped wildly in place. The hopping helped alleviate the pain, so she thought. Every move seemed to sink the thorns farther into her fleshy cheeks.

"Ya gotta hold still."

"All right, all right. Just get them out."

Sam kneeled behind her and gingerly plucked out a spine.

"Ouch!" She swatted at him.

"Miss Marisol."

"Sorry."

He plucked out another. She gritted her teeth, scrunched her nose and closed her eyes. She refused to think of Sam down there eye-level with her backside. He held on to her hip to keep her from squirming. Thank the Lord no one around would bear witness to her mortifying predicament. She wouldn't be able to handle the humiliation.

He plucked out another and then another until all were gone.

"T'ere. Done."

Marisol pried her eyes open. The pain faded and she rubbed her sore behind.

"Thank you, Sam," she said.

He stood, failing to conceal his grin. She smiled too and they shared a laugh. The kind of laugh reserved for friends.

All too soon, her laughter died. Beyond Sam's shoulder, for the first time, she noticed the outcropping of rocks overlooking the sea below. And there, anchored offshore, was a ship.

"Miss Marisol?"

A lump lodged in her chest. "Is that the *Sugar Lady*?"

CHAPTER 15

Blade paused just outside the cave door. He smiled at Marisol's melodic laughter wafting through the leafy vine door. His heart tripped at the image of her cheerful face. Turning his mug to the sky, he gazed at the stars filtering through the tree canopy swaying to the sea breeze. Puffs of the gentle wind tingled against his skin, reminding him of her soft touch.

All his anger toward her vanished the moment she stepped onshore that afternoon. Every bit determination, every bit spirit, she surveyed the beach for her enemy, for him. She was lovely and dangerous. He couldn't help himself. His attraction to her baffled him and made him mad as a March hare. The frustration eating him triggered an instinctual reaction. He seduced her.

Blade had given her a chance to stop him. It wasn't fair what he had done, to get her aroused and then give her the choice. Thankfully, she didn't turn him away. Hell, he wasn't sure he'd have been able to stop anyhow. That she readily accepted him was more than he could have hoped for. He needed to finally prove to her he truly relished every inch of her tawny skin, every word fallen from her luscious lips, every glorious moment with her.

And then the little nymph changed the course. No other doxy had ever quite made him feel the way she did. Her succulent mouth on his…

Flog me. He had shuddered like a red jack flying top mast in a tumultuous gale.

To embrace her again, that was all he wanted. Tonight, he would make things right and ask for a truce.

He pushed through the verdant opening into the cave. Marisol and Sam sat on broad boulders along the wall. The same boulders among which Blade had made love to her. Remnants of their fish supper were piled between them. Willie sat near the opposite side and passed across a flagon of rum.

"What say you, Capt'n?" said Willie.

"I've sent three men to scout out that stretch of the island. We'll know soon enough if the ship Marisol and Sam saw is the *Sugar Lady.*"

Willie stuck a pinch of tobacco under his lip. A small bulge appeared above his chin as he worked the leaves down with his tongue. "We gonna take 'em by surprise?"

"Before sunrise."

Willie nodded, satisfied with Blade's answer.

Blade leaned on the craggy wall beside Marisol. "How's your arse?"

Marisol's mouth dropped open and she looked to Sam.

"You told him?"

Sam took hasty purchase of the rum and swallowed, avoiding eye contact with her. Marisol punched him in his arm. Blade laughed at the priceless sight of the duo. His mirth bounced off the stone. The echoes intensified when Willie joined in. Her horrified expression traveled from Sam to Willie to Blade and back to Sam, serving to make Blade laugh harder. Still gulping the liquor, Sam grinned, snickered and choked on the rum.

Marisol laughed then. "Serves you right." She slapped him on the back to help ease his coughing.

"What's all this?" Henri ducked inside.

"Ah, Henri," Blade said. "Just the old tar I'd like to see." Blade motioned him in. "Play us a tune on your flute, will you. A spirited ditty perhaps."

The little man always beamed when Blade asked him to play. "I reckon I could."

Jubilant, Henri sat on a rock next to Willie. He tightened his red bows in his beard and pulled out his broken pipe, pride pumping his chest as he blew into it.

The sound filled the cavern in a merry harmony. The highs and lows of the music whistled along at the perfect tempo—not too lively, but enough to get the toes tapping.

Perfect.

Blade took off his sword and leaned it against the wall. He extended a hand to Marisol and bowed. "Would you give me the honor of a dance, dear lady?"

She squirmed in her seat, her eyebrows creased and her brown eyes clouded with fear. *She's so lovely when she's flustered.*

"Come." He said it loud enough for her ears only. "I'll teach you."

Indecision skipped across her face and she gnawed her bottom lip. Blade wiggled his fingers for her. Finally, she nodded and took his hand.

Plucking her up, he led her to the center of their very own sandy dance floor.

"Just relax and follow what I do."

Facing her, he grasped her hand and lifted it out in front of them.

"Ready?"

She flitted a timid smile.

"We'll go slowly." He pulled her close then stepped back and brought her around to switch sides. He drew her in again, closer this time. His arm fit neatly into the curve of her waist. Her tiny fingers dwarfed in his extended left hand. "Watch my feet," he said. "Side step, side step, side step."

Leading her in tight circles, she caught on quickly to the movements. He separated from her to take her one hand and faced outward. Not letting go, he said, "Spin." She made one revolution and he brought her back into his embrace to lead her in another circular whirl.

"Good. Faster now."

They picked up speed, and he urged her along into a skip. She bungled a few steps and trampled on his boot.

Her cheeks flushed a charming rosy color. "I…I'm so sorry."

"'Tis all right, dove." He winked. "Let's do it again."

Soon, Marisol had the dance down pat. Henri played his flute livelier, his stubby fingers flying over the instrument's holes. Sam and Willie kept beat by tapping their heels and clapping along. Blade spun her quicker and quicker around the cave floor. She squealed in delight, laughing, skipping, hopping and twirling. Blade's heart sung in tune with her harmonious glee. Her happiness meant his happiness.

As he spun her close, he reveled in the wafting hint of salty sun-kissed skin blended with an exotic scent of the white island flower that she wore tucked behind her ear. Dancing with her and sharing this moment wreaked rapturous havoc upon his soul.

All too soon, the song ended. Marisol collapsed into him, her laughter sweeter than any melody. How glorious to wrap his arms around her, to feel the gentle rumble of her giggles against his body.

Blade took a step back and bowed. "Thank you, my lady."

"Nay." Her chest heaved from shortness of breath. "Thank you, Captain Tyburn." Her eyes sparkled with her enjoyment. "What merriment! I should think to try dancing more often."

"Is it the dancing you find sprightly or perchance is it you cannot deny your desire for your dance partner?" A wicked thing to suggest but her allure made it difficult not to toy with her.

"Oh, the dancing, for sure."

He raised his eyebrows at the speed with which she tugged on her earlobe. Any fool could argue her sincerity. She lied like a sunken Spanish treasure fleet in the Straits of Florida.

"You give yourself far more credit than you deserve," she said.

"Duly noted." He presented her a crooked grin. "I would be honored to dance with you again, Marisol."

* * *

How could she ever say no? His persuasive dimples and spellbinding eyes made it impossible to refuse even if she had wanted to. At the moment, with the way her feelings soared, she doubted she would ever say no to him again.

Blade had taught her many new things. He had more to offer, no doubt. His company, his imminence, the trust she placed in him, it was like a strong bottle of the finest liquor. Too much of him and she could become drunk, a slobbering, moon-eyed drunk. *Hear, Hear! To a plentiful cup of Tyburn.*

Marisol curtsied to Blade. She took his extended hand and he nodded to Henri. Henri drew a swig from the rum before piping another hardy jingle. Again, Blade led her around in a whirlwind. She followed his lead easily enough, skipping on her toes in circles of gaiety.

She didn't need a few half pints of liquor, either. Not as she did a few nights ago in port. What a debacle that had been. And she was glad for her dancing disaster now as Blade held on to her.

Willie began to sing an old familiar song she had long since forgotten. Sam thumped his knee with the rhythm.

The song brought back happier memories of happier times with her brothers. Those times disappeared when Alain left Monte behind at Matanzas, and with her brothers gone forever, she had found it difficult to believe she would find happiness again. But with Blade, things were different. This bliss felt more…whole.

She could dance with him all night.

"Excuse me, Capt'n." A swarthy buccaneer stood in the cave entrance.

The music died. Willie broke off in mid-chorus. Sam stood. Blade let go of her, his smile wiped clean.

"What is it, Cromby?"

"The men, they haven't made it back," Cromby said. A look of concern creased his frown. "But there is a glow in the sky, northwest of here, over the ridge. Maybe a large fire."

Blade snatched his sword and tied it back on to his waist. The urgency of him rearming himself skittered curdling dread down Marisol's spine. Something was very wrong.

"And the *Rissa?*" Blade said. "What's the word?"

"Repairs are done, sir."

"Good. Willie, make the ship ready. Chances are we will sail sooner than planned. Sam, Henri, get the men on alert and ready for any action. Cromby, grab a few hands. We're going to see what's going on."

Blade spat out his orders in rapid fire and his crew rushed in a flurry of excitement to do what was required of them.

He turned to her and, in an instant, stood inches from her. Taking her hand, he planted a firm kiss to it. The warmth of his lips branded her skin. Intense eyes rose to meet hers. "We will dance again, dove. I promise."

The low timbre of his words, the force of his stare, melted her insides. Quite suddenly, panic reared up. She didn't want to be apart from him. The very idea constricted in her breast.

"Stay here, in the cave."

She expected him to say that, but she shook her head. "I want to come with you."

"You'll be safe here."

"I'm coming with you."

"The cave's well hidden. No need to worry."

Worry? Did he not hear her? "I said I'm coming with you."

"No, you're not. You'll stay here where it is safe."

"But—"

"That's an order."

"An order? You can't order me—"

"I can and I did." His impatience built in the hemming of his brow. "Have you forgotten that I bartered for you? You are mine to do with as I wish."

"I'm not a possession to be owned."

"I say you are." His jaw squared and grim gloom tinted his darkening eyes. "And if I have to spend you like a piece of eight to keep you safe, I will."

A snap of rage exploded within her and she swung at him. He caught her wrist before making contact. She snarled and spit in his face.

With eerie calm, he dabbed at his cheek. "This is not child's play, Marisol. You *will* stay here." He turned and left her standing in the middle of the grotto.

She called after him. "Bastard!"

Marisol sank down on a hard rock. The corked pitcher of rum lay nearby. Just what she needed to clear her mind and sulk. If it had been Alain ordering her to stay put, by now she'd be making her plan to disobey him. Perhaps she'd already be out the door. Why wasn't she doing the same now? She simmered. There wasn't much she could do but wait. The beach swarmed with his men. It would be foolish to set off on her own. If she caught up to Blade, he'd probably send her back with an escort, or two. And that was a big "if." With the dangers of the island at every turn, and those damned cacti, she couldn't possibly find her way in the dark.

"Damn him."

* * *

Half the rum was gone when she first became alerted to a noise outside. Leaves rustled like crumpled paper and the vine curtain shook. She plugged the bottle.

"Sam? Is that you?" No answer.

The leaves stirred again. Marisol reached for her knife tucked in her waistband. But she'd forgotten Blade took it. *Damn him! Twice!* Raising the flagon above her head, she moved toward the entry and steadied herself, ready to deliver a crunching blow to any unwelcome guest.

A man burst through the vines, flourishing a pistol. Impulse kicked in and she smashed the flagon over the intruder's head. The ting of the metal reverberated in her hand, causing vibrations to tickle her fingertips. The man swiveled his head and fell to his knees.

"Monte? Oh dear Lord, Monte!"

His eyes rolled around, wavering in a dizzy fog. "Ooh. Whaddya do that for?" He rubbed at the top of his head.

She helped him to his feet. "You're not dead."

Her little brother stood before her, alive and well. Maybe not *well* with the big knot growing on the crown of his head, but as sure as the sea was deep, there he stood living and breathing. She squeezed him in a hug, hardly able to believe it.

"You tryin' to suffocate me? Let go." He shrugged away from her embrace, bristling something fierce.

Monte was much like their father. He kept his hair shorter, of course, a mop of unruly curls. He had a slighter build, too. But the similarities didn't come from appearances. Rather, their likenesses emerged in their mannerisms.

He straightened his jacket and gave her the same reprimanding look Alain did every time her father had to clean up any mess she'd created. She dismissed Monte the same as she dismissed Alain—come what may.

"I thought you were dead. The hurricane. The *Gloria,* it was destroyed. How? How did you survive? How is it you are here?"

A grin slunk up one side of his mouth. "It takes more than a temperamental briny drink to take me down. I'm invincible."

Arrogant. Just like Alain. She crammed down the urge to chuckle, but her smirk gave her away.

"Don't mock me, sister."

Marisol had not heard him speak with such malice before. His icy words sent a chill surging through her blood. She read the rancor in his murky eyes and could not recall them being so dark, almost black. In the dim light, long shadows lengthened across his angular face. He was too much like Alain and his threat alarmed her.

"Of course not." She fumbled to regain poise. "It's only that you used to say you were invincible when we were children. You remember. You'd stand on ol' James Mason's fishing house with your wooden sword—" she paused, grinning, "—fighting pirates."

The spite furrowing deep in his scowl loosened. "Ironic, isn't it? But then who could blame the useless musings of a stupid boy?"

He picked up the flagon from the cave floor. "Weren't you the one pretending to be the pirates? A pirate queen, correct?" He opened the cork and pulled from the drink.

"Aye. When Luc wasn't insisting I act a governess instead."

"Phff." Monte wiped his mouth with his sleeve. "He took the joy out of it."

Luc had always played the hero. At least until Monte would sit square in the middle of the footpath and squall like a wee babe. Monte wanted to be the dashing swashbuckler. But even when Luc conceded to be the villain for their little brother, he still wielded his sticks and make-believe pistols with grace and gallantry, often over-dramatizing his defeat by Monte. He'd clutched at his chest from where Monte had inflicted his imaginary fatal wound, spun around several times, flung an arm out before collapsing to the dirt, and let his tongue hang out the side of his mouth. Monte hated it, complaining real people didn't die that way. Marisol and Luc would laugh to near hysterics till their pouting Monte would crack and join in the hilarity.

She missed those gay times betwixt them. She missed Luc. He would always be her hero.

"Those were good times," she said.

"We were ignorant. Pretending to be something we were not."

"We were children. Play acting is natural. We worked hard to help Mama keep us fed and clothed. The games made us happy."

"You forget, sister, we starved and she barely kept a stitch on our bodies." He shook his head.

Marisol struggled to understand his disappointment. Certainly, they had lived hand-to-mouth and there were times they were forced to wear clothes they had long out-grown. But Mama gave them a roof over their heads and a bed to sleep in at night. And love, plenty of love. She had no complaints and neither should he. "Look at us, Monte. We made out fine."

His demeanor changed. Boyish softness, if not for the weathered roughness, returned to his face.

"You're right." He pulled her into a hug. "More than you know."

Harried voices carried in from the beach. A call came for extinguishing the fires. The men outside were ready for their next orders.

"We need to go," Monte said.

"Go? Go where? Why would we need to go? Wait. Tyburn doesn't know you're here?" She realized he hadn't answered her earlier question. "How did you get to this island?"

He smiled as if humoring a child. "Dear sister. The storm blew us all into the middle of the Mona Passage."

Monte raised his eyebrows, indicating that his reply should be good enough for her. It wasn't. "How did you know where to find me?"

"I came when I saw the *Rissa* on the horizon. It wasn't hard to find you, watching Tyburn and his men from a nearby outcropping."

Hushing her with his hand before she spoke, he tilted his head and listened to the noises outside. "We must go."

"Why? We're safe here."

"Safe from whom?"

"Well, I...I don't know. 'Tis something amiss farther up the coast. Tyburn has gone to investigate. Moreover, the mystery ship that attacked the *Sablewing* is still out there." She gasped at a sudden awareness. "What if the mystery ship is *here?*"

"Ha. Mystery ship, you say. Wouldn't it stand to reason that your safety would be in jeopardy with Captain Tyburn as long as he has a nameless adversary prowling after his silver? He's tenacious and will insist on engaging his enemy."

"You're losing me. What is wrong with that?"

He exhaled an irritable sigh. "Damn it, Marisol. I know you think going into battle is an adventure, but it is not. It's horrific. You fear for your life. The fear controls you. You taste it, breathe it, it courses through you like venom."

His gaze shifted. He curled his lip and stared into the recesses of the cave. Pain swirled within the depths of his eyes and she suspected his nightmare at Matanzas replayed in his mind with vicious clarity. "You fight but there are too many. Weakened, you run, you hide, a wretched coward. Caught, you stare down the barrel of a gun, not ready to meet your maker. You mess your pants, lose all dignity. They laugh at you, call you worthless, weak, and should be fed on your mama's pap. If you live, they beat you like a mangy dog until you wish they would finish you off."

The horror of his suffering she could never imagine. It plagued her mind to know of his pain. Guilt beleaguered her and the anger toward Alain for not returning to rescue his youngest son devoured the tears forming in her eyes.

She touched his arm. "I'm sorry."

His eyes flitted down to her hand then up to latch on to hers. "There's no glory there for you. Would you rather die beside an egotistical rogue or come with me, your flesh and blood, to live out your destiny."

With Monte alive, Marisol had no reason to join in the folly of chasing Blade's mystery ship. What she had wanted, the reason for her reckless behavior, stood right in front of her. Vengeance over Monte's death had vanished like a raindrop in the sea as soon as he stepped through the cave door. Retaliation was worthless to her now.

Yet, she couldn't leave Blade, not without an explanation, not without a goodbye. In truth, she wasn't certain she wanted to leave Blade at all. The blush of springtime in her heart when he approached, the nest of comfort he cosseted when he held her, and her sensation of completeness when she stood beside him. These were newfound emotions and she had merely begun to welcome them.

"There's no time, Marisol. They won't let you leave. *He* won't let you leave." He held out his hand. "We must go, *now.*"

"Monte..."

"Now, Marisol. Come with me."

Her mind reeled. She had no choice. The challenge in his expression warned that she may never see him again if she dared stay. He had come for her, unlike how she failed to rescue him at Matanzas. Marisol would not forsake him again. They would be together, a broken family no more.

She took his hand.

Monte drew his pistol. He used the muzzle to pull back the vine door enough to peer out. Looking over his shoulder, she saw that most of the men were off to the far right of the beach, far enough away that she and Monte could dash out into the darkness undetected.

Breezy sea air ruffled her clothes but did little to cool the duplicity of her departure. She wished there had been another way. The budding affection for her irresistible pirate shriveled inside her racing heart. To be with her brother, she must sever ties with Blade. He would be angry, of that she had no doubt. No man tolerated defiance. She had a scar or two which proved it. But never would she fault Blade for scorning her. Their intimacy went beyond hasty trysts. He had whispered secrets only bestowed between lovers. Now, as she left his camp behind, she imagined how hurt and betrayed he would feel.

She felt sick.

Perhaps they would meet again. She could plead for his understanding. That glimmer of hope, to one day meet him again, was worth holding on to. He may yet forgive her.

At least she had been able to return his cameo. The treasured trinket kept him sound. Lucky man. She had nothing but another memory, sure to vex many sleepless nights. She sighed.

Monte pulled her along to the steep slope leading up to the plateau. In the dark, it loomed high and promised peril.

Eyeing the incline, she whispered her concern. "Isn't there another way?"

"Aye. But those men back there are blocking the passage."

The climb became more hazardous since the sun disappeared into the western ocean. Had someone greased the blasted slope with cooking fat? Without the benefit of light, Marisol made a sloppy effort to scale the unsafe path without falling. Loose earth slid from beneath each footfall. Her fingers smarted from soil and pebbles embedded deep under her fingernails. Dust swirled behind Monte's ascent, causing dirt to sting her eyes. She choked on the grime coating the inside of her throat and, in an attempt to steady herself, grabbed an unstable rock. It tumbled free, rolling and bouncing down the embankment, dislodging other rocks on its way down. She cringed as the stones bashed and cracked together on the sandy beach below.

Monte groaned. "I verily believe you to be a devil's curse. You've alerted them." He climbed faster. "Move!"

A glance back confirmed they had indeed been spotted. Sam and a lad bearing a torch ran to the base of the rising footpath. The firelight clearly displayed Sam's disappointment. He drew his pistol.

Madre de Dios, what have I done?

The weight of her actions hit her with astonishing force, rendering her certain that Blade would have her killed should she try to escape. But hadn't they gone past that? Wasn't she something more than spoils plucked from her father's ship? For God's sake, she wouldn't make a decent serving wench, anyway.

What was worse was the danger she put Monte in. "Come on, sister, before you're picked off the hillside." Pebbles nipped at her cheeks as he scuttled up the path.

She risked another quick look at Sam. Hanging by a moment, she took in a full breath of brackish air, listened to the gentle song of the waves and waited. Waited for the blast of the gun.

But Sam lowered his weapon, slowly shaking his head.

The loss of Sam's respect stung worse than any flogging.

Marisol scrambled the rest of the way to the top. Monte helped her scale the last few paces and she bent over, hands on her knees, to catch her breath in her burning chest. She filled her lungs with the fresh air rising in a mild shoot up the ridge. Beyond a peninsular part of the island, a dusky light flushed the sky. That must've been the fire Cromby spoke of and the direction Blade and his band of men traveled.

Monte peeked over the edge. "They're not following us. Dirty, chicken-hearted fools." Patting her back, he walked past, into the dark ahead. His form silhouetted against the faint orange haze. He, too, headed for the distant glow. "Let's go. We don't have much time."

"Wait." She lifted a finger, not ready to push on, but Monte ignored her request. She trotted to catch up to him. "If they're not coming for us, what's the hurry?"

"We need to get back to my ship. The crew is waiting to weigh anchor."

That didn't make sense. The *Gloria* broke up in the storm, thrashed to mere fragments of splintered planks and rags of canvas. There was nothing left of the ship he captained. "Your ship?"

"Aye. My ship."

Marisol pulled him to a stop. "You don't have a ship."

He lifted his brow but chose not to reply. She pressed on.

"How did you make it through the hurricane? Were you picked up by another vessel? Were there other survivors?" *Please let there be other survivors.* Blade would be glad to hear of news that some of his crew made it out alive.

A smile twisted the tips of Monte's lips.

Nighttime creatures chirped from the nearby grasses. Foliage from the palms and leafy trees fluttered with the wisps of wind blowing across the terrain. But his silence lingered. A harbinger of doubt scratched the walls of her perception. Not all was as it seemed. Monte skipped around her every question, being vague if not downright nasty. Whatever his reason, she didn't have a good feeling about it.

"Well? Speak me the truth."

He snorted. "All right. I left the *Gloria* before the storm. I alone." He turned and walked away.

Whoever heard of a captain leaving the ship he was in charge of during the middle of a voyage willingly? Had her brother gone daft? "I don't understand. You left your post on the *Gloria?*"

Marisol sprinted to catch up again. She stumbled on an iguana nesting hole, pitched off to the side and rolled down an embankment, coming to an abrupt stop against a scrubby bush.

"Marisol!"

Branches poked into her back. Knarls of sticks and thorny twigs scratched and pecked her arms. "Christ!" What was it about the bloody plants on this island?

Monte descended the bank. "Are you all right?"

"Yes, I'm fi—"

The ground beneath her gave way. She screamed, plunging downward. Cool air blasted her exposed flesh. Fingers of jagged stone walls clawed her face and arms, ripping at her clothes. She landed face down in a pool of water. The smack stung, knocking the wind from her lungs. Salt burned her eyes, her nose and the fresh cuts on her tender skin as she sank beneath the surface. Panicked, she flailed her arms and legs in the water for something solid. She fought hard in a battle for breath against the thumping of her heart in her windpipe. Her foot scraped the bottom but she couldn't quite stand in the turbulence. A strong undercurrent cuffed her from behind, slapping her against a wall in what felt like an alcove. The rough surface abraded her skin further. She anchored her feet on an underwater heap of rubble. Coughing, she strove to maintain her balance.

"Marisol! Marisol! Can you hear me? Marisol! Answer me!" Echoes of Monte's shouts bounced down the passage.

"Monte!"

She could see nothing at all in the cavern. But the rumble of rushing torrents droned on and by the hollow noise reverberating off the sides, she guessed the cave was small. Above, she could make out her brother's figure against the night sky.

"Help me, Monte!"

"Hold on!" He disappeared from view.

The water splashing against her chest receded, draining away at an alarming rate. The droning grew louder and the space rumbled like a thousand horses stampeding toward her. Violent water flooded into the cavity. The raging tide pushed and smashed her against the serrated wall. The flux of the maelstroms pulled and whirled, threatening to haul her off the rocks and into an underwater whirlpool. She grasped at the walls too slick to hold on to, the uneven notches worn from the incessant pounding of the surf.

"Monte!" Oh God, where was he? "Monte, hurry! The tide is coming in!"

The seawater rose to her chin. She screamed for Monte again. Still, he did not return. Fear marched in with a steady rhythmic drumming. Did he leave her to die just as he had been left at Matanzas? Did he mean to make her bear an excruciating demise as he had suffered at the hands of his father? No, she refused to believe he would do such a thing. He was her brother. He loved her. He had come for her, rescued her from what he thought was trouble. Monte wouldn't let her die here. He just wouldn't.

She bent her head back as far as it would go and stretched her neck above the water to take advantage of the small pocket of air the niche had left to offer.

Marisol sucked in a life-sustaining breath before the water engulfed her. Her chest tightened and her feet slipped, but she hung on horrendous second after second.

The water finally ebbed down to her chest, but stopped higher than it had before. She strained to see into the darkness and ran her hands along the rugged sides for handholds. There had to be a way out of there. Grooves within the wall lent her little leverage to climb upward. She was trapped. All she could do was stay afloat and not get sucked down into the underwater channel. The roar of the returning torrent built. The catacomb would turn into her burial chamber if she didn't get out soon.

The swells came and consumed her, she held on, but the tide persisted longer. Her shrinking lungs burned with the need to breathe. Panic flooded her dizzy head. *I'm going to drown.* She gave in to the spontaneous impulse to inhale. Gulping for air, she swallowed water. Her nose scraped against the ceiling of her watery coffin just as the sea once again retreated.

She coughed up water, searing her throat and nostrils, gasping for air through salty caustic saliva. The horror of nearly drowning did not recede with the tide. In moments, the tide would return.

How much more could she handle? No more. The next surge would be her last.

"Monte!" Calling out his name triggered a fit of coughing.

"Here!"

Glory be! He returned.

"Hurry, Monte! The tide!" Could she hear him over the sea's bellows?

He threw down a rope, no, a thick vine. "Grab a hold!"

She seized it and planted her feet against the wall. An herbal fragrance from crushing leaves and smaller trailing vines under her grip wafted briefly. The vine was green and should be strong, she hoped. *Please don't break.* Hand over fist, she tugged herself up and out of the water. The cave walls closed in, the oppressive air thickening with saline and heavy wheezing.

"Don't let me go," she cried.

Monte heaved and she steadied herself from spinning with her feet along craggy toeholds. Near the top, a cool breeze washed over her face. Clouds and stars came into view. Dirt crumbled from the edge, raining down into her face. One more tug. Monte grabbed her by the scruff of her shirt and hitched her out of the hole. Marisol collapsed to the ground and spat at the soil stuck to her lips.

"Damn you, Marisol."

"For a moment…" She cast an apprehensive glance to the gaping cleft. "I thought I was going to die."

"Not yet." He yanked her up by the arm. "You bloody almost ruined everything." He gnashed his teeth and stalked off. "Come on. You've wasted enough time. We've got to get back. They're waiting."

Large fronds closed behind him on the trail he followed. Marisol pushed through the jungle, keeping on his heels. He mumbled on about the trouble she always caused and how he was forever saving her arse. Her gashes whimpered for attention but she knew better than to complain. Monte would wait no more for her.

"*Who* is waiting?"

"My crew," Monte said. He stopped and plied her with a

sanctimonious smile. "On *my* ship. The *Huntress*." He placed his hand on her shoulder and bent his head to meet her eyes. "But you know her as the *Sugar Lady*."

CHAPTER 16

Flames from the burning ship licked at the inky sky. The blaze burnished the darkened inlet water, sending rippling waves of firelight stretching toward shore. Mild breezes painted the air with bitter smells of burning pitch and wood. Small explosions ripped through the hush of distance.

Blade watched a mast crumble, falling into the open mouth of the infernal flare. Such a shame to see any vessel be destroyed, especially by fire.

He took careful note of another ship floating beyond in the flickering glow. From his vantage, the ship resembled the *Sugar Lady* but for one distinct difference. She blazoned many open gun ports. He didn't recall the merchantman having them before. But he did remember how the mystery ship had flaunted her arms, the worthy adversary. Could the two ships be one and the same? It wasn't unheard of that a vessel could cloak herself as a harmless trade ship.

What piqued Blade's interest the most was how low the ship sat in the bay. A ship such as she would have a shallow draft. There was definitely something in her hold that had her weighted. He had an idea of just what cargo she carried. His silver.

Cries and moans lifted to his ears and Blade scanned the beach before him. Men, a dozen or so, crawled from the edge of the water, their bodies bloodied from swimming through the jagged reefs. Some collapsed to the sand, desperate for air. Others huddled together. Still others floundered in the water, unable to swim and unable to make the expanse from the burning ship to the shore. How terrified they must be, dead men even before drowning.

Blade motioned for his men to stay hidden but for Cromby to follow as he stepped from the copse of trees onto the beach. He closed in on the beset group and recognized some of them. He stepped beside one battered man sitting with his head hung between his knees. Crouching down, Blade studied him. Aye, he'd seen this tar before. The man made no move to his presence.

"What might you call yourself, mate?" Blade said.

The man raised his head slowly. Fatigue ringed his hollow eyes. His dead stare hovered before answering. "Ben."

"Who's your captain, Ben?"

"Capt'n Carrion."

Ben confirmed what Blade already figured. Now he needed the rest of the story.

"What happened, Ben?"

Ben looked back out at the burning ship. The *Sablewing* tipped and the fire had eaten much of the topside away. Flaming debris floated away from the wreckage. Ben's gaze traveled to the surviving men, wet, sandy and bleeding on the shore.

"We came 'pon our quarry. Thought to trap 'er 'ere in the cove. Capt'n said 'twould be easy. Just needed ta scare 'em. Make 'em surrender." Ben shook his head, still looking at his defeated shipmates. "Never 'ad a chance."

"What do you mean?"

Ben shot a disconcerted look between Blade and Cromby. "She be better gunned. We 'ad no business fightin', no 'ow. With the beatin' we took and then the storm, our ship couldn't do battle. We'd been takin' on water. Capt'n said we'd abandon 'er and take the merchant. Damn, if we didn't know the *Sugar Lady* was fitted like some bloody warship."

"So she is the *Sugar Lady*." This cinched Blade's suspicion. A very bold disguise, one which regrettably got past him. He should've recognized the deception, suspected the masquerading ship. After all, the *Sugar Lady* had been there every step of the way, from the disappearance of the silver to leading Drake into Puerto Plata and then the attack on Carrion. How could he have been so foolish?

He cursed himself for not being more alert. Ever since that woman, *his* woman, came colliding through the tavern back at Puerto Plata, his concentration had been crippled. He couldn't afford to lose focus again. The time had come to take action.

First Blade needed to get more information. "Where's Carrion?"

"Capt'n was taken pris'ner. The crew were given a choice. Turn on our capt'n or go overboard. A few scurvy dogs turned, rest of us refused. They threw lit powder flasks at us. Set the *Sablewing* to fire. Capt'n orders."

"Who is the *Lady*'s captain?"

"Don't know. Never saw 'im." Ben looked around again at his mates. "Guess not many of us made it." His voice cracked with resignation.

No captain on deck. Peculiar. Why take Carrion alive but destroy his ship, kill off his crew? Carrion, alone, brought nothing of value. And the heavily armed *Sugar Lady* disguised as a merchantman proved more than suspicious. It could mean only one thing. Trespassing pirates.

Someone had made a grave mistake. The western Caribbean waters belonged to him. That fact was known far and wide. To simply sail into his territory invited serious scrutiny. But the foolish captain of the *Sugar Lady* nailed his own coffin shut when he took his silver. There would be hell to pay.

Blade looked to Cromby, nodded and then jerked his head to the trees. Cromby trotted off to where the other men waited.

"Gather your men, Ben. If you promise allegiance to me and the *Rissa,* you can join my crew."

Color returned to Ben's face, but wariness waited in his inquisitive expression.

"We go after the *Sugar Lady.*"

A slow grin broke free, flashing Ben's crooked teeth. He nodded. "Aye, sir…Capt'n."

"Keep up." Blade stood. "I've got a score to settle and I won't wait for you."

"Huzza, mates!" Hollering to his brethren, Ben clambered to his feet. "We be *Rissa* lads now! Death is but their due and we will plunge the *Lady* forthwith to the bowels of 'ell!"

Cheers and excitement followed Blade as he left the beach. As members of the brethren, he had their loyalty now, but if Carrion made it out alive, they were sure to return to the blackguard. He didn't take such things for granted. No matter, he liked to keep his enemies close.

Time was running out. They needed to get back to the *Rissa* before the *Sugar Lady* weighed anchor. If she did escape, it would be hard to give chase in the dark. Blade could only assume her course continued to be San Juan. That was a risk he didn't want to take. He picked up his pace. They forged ahead in silence. Whispers of sworn vengeance upon the *Sugar Lady* kept the *Sablewing* lads hungry.

Soon, Blade and his men broke through the hedge of foliage along the beach. The *Rissa* sat primed for his return out in the cove. Sam rose from his roost on the driftwood log next to the lone fire. The behemoth pointed at his company to douse the flames.

"Get these men to the ship, Cromby," said Blade. "See to the wounded and garrison them for battle." Only one longboat sat on the beach, not enough room for all to make it in one trip. "Handsomely! We've not a moment to spare."

Sam met Blade at the edge of the surf. "Everyt'ing's ready, Capt'n."

"Excellent."

"Capt'n," Sam said. "T'ere's something—"

"Whaddya find, Tyburn?" Henri interrupted as he joined them. "Who be them dogs?"

"Carrion's men, what's left of them."

"They be prisoners?"

"Nay. They will fight with us."

Henri's scrunched, weathered face smoothed flat with his shock of disbelief. White lines appeared where stiff wrinkles usually overlapped.

Blade spoke before the tiny man railed him. "The *Sablewing* was what lit up the sky. Carrion has been captured." He paused to give significant magnitude to his next words. "By the *Sugar*

Lady."

"Do me ears need swabbin'?" Henri stuck a fat finger in an ear and waggled it. "Did you say the *Sugar Lady?*"

"Aye. She's well-gunned and loaded with our silver."

"I'll be damned," Henri said.

"Now you see the urgency of the matter. We must leave now."

Henri puffed his body to attention and shuffled off, barking at the three other crewmen left on the beach to finish putting out the fire and prepare for departure when the longboat returned.

"Sam, I'll need you to keep an eye on our new recruits. Supply them with weapons."

He nodded. "But Capt'n..."

Blade spun around and took deliberate strides to the hidden cave. Marisol should know her father had been seized and the *Sablewing* reduced to ashes.

She could have been on that ship. A shudder racked him with the thought, at the fate that would have befallen her had he left her in Carrion's care. 'Twas a damn good thing he negotiated for her. She had much to thank him for. Maybe he should keep a tally of her debt to him. The payout would be sweet and he looked forward to settling up with her.

Until then, he would have to break the news about what he learned. She wouldn't take it well. The poor lass had been through so much already. Losing both her brothers in the span of a few days hurt her tremendously. Word of her father and the ship she called home would not be welcomed. He wished he could ease her pain. Instead he brought her more heartache.

If she could hold on a little longer, he would bring her comfort. He would do his best to carry her weight. His shoulders were strong enough to bear her yoke of suffering as well as his own. *Just a little longer, dove.*

"Capt'n." Sam called out to him. "Capt'n, sir, wait."

Blade slowed for Sam. His massive feet kicked up tufts of sand in his hurry to catch up.

"What's on your mind, mate?"

"It's Miss Marisol, sir."

"She didn't skin you for singing about her arse, did she?" Blade chuckled, but the remorse sagging at his loyal mate's mug unnerved him.

"What is it? What has she done?" Blade turned back toward the cave and quickened his steps. "Is she hurt?"

"Nay. Capt'n, stop. She's not in t'ere."

"Well, where is she? Is she on the ship?"

Sam took a deep breath, staring at the ground. "She be…gone."

"What in the devil are you talking about?"

"Left wit t'at maggot, Castellan."

"Monte? You saw her leave with Monte?"

"Give you me Bible oat'."

Blade had no reason to doubt Sam, but there had to be a mistake. Monte should be dead. "Are you certain, man?"

"I tell ya true, t'ey went up t'e footpat'."

"Son of a—"

She deceived me again.

* * *

"Monte, please. I don't understand."

Marisol followed Monte down the ladder to the main deck. He had spoken little to her since leaving Blade's camp and the dreadful pit. On their escape, he had insisted she recount her last few days with Captain Tyburn, finding a great many humors in her tale. How odd that he took such delight in the misfortune of others.

It had taken a while for them to reach the bay where the *Sugar Lady,* or the *Huntress,* or whatever bloody name the ship went by, sat anchored. They hadn't taken the straightest path back, but rather, it seemed, took a wide berth of the inlet, breaking through the tree line to scramble over slick boulders on the far side of the beach.

Monte pulled out a longboat hidden well among the rocky coast. She had been standing right next to it and failed to see the craft. In the gloom of night, no one would have ever seen it.

They rowed to the waiting ship, and the last of a charred, dying vessel in the middle of the bay slipped below the water's surface. Log-like shadows darkened the sea close by. Marisol had shuddered and said a quick prayer for the poor souls who drowned.

Monte snorted. Taken aback by his callousness, she had questioned him. Didn't he have any sympathy? After all he'd been through, didn't he have respect for the dead? Who were those men? What ship lay on the sea bottom? In the dark, she could not read his expression. But the emptiness in the black holes of his eyes startled her.

* * *

That thieving liar. That conniving minx. I should have counted my blessings and left her to Carrion.

Blade paced his cabin and swilled his cup of wine. He prized his Madeira wine, only breaking it open for big celebrations such as the recent wedding of his best mate or the capture of a prize carrying crates of precious gems. Events worth rejoicing over. Instead, he drank to put the devil in him. Anger coursed down his throat with each swallow and spread hot through his wits.

Let the liquor wash Marisol from my mind. Deaden any fond thoughts of her.

He tipped the bottle to his cup but stopped shy of letting the wine drain. The cup held too little of the liquid. Straight from the bottle would do splendidly. After a swig, then another, he cursed her again.

It had all been a ruse. She'd led him on from the beginning. Killed his messenger. Used him as an escape. Mocked him by snatching his cameo. She must have thought herself clever. Oh, and what a good actress. The chit's performance of a desperate girl searching for her dead brother had been believable, all right. And he played the buffoon.

There were too many coincidences. The raid, the sudden appearance of Monte, the mystery ship… Thoughts reeled and he tried to add it all up. The murder of his men on the *Gloria* had him straining against a tether. A beast clawed from within him, ready to be unleashed on the person responsible.

Blade would wager his soul, blackened and worthless as it was, that Monte had some connection to the death of his crew. That the lad had been spared from the chilling doom of the *Gloria* again seemed preposterous. Monte couldn't be that lucky.

No man could be that lucky.

He moved to the window and watched the dark shape of Mona Island slip along the blue backdrop of the drowsy sky. The early rays of the sun would wake the day soon. By then, the *Rissa* would be upon her prey.

Blade chuckled. His throaty laugh soured into a sneer. Reckoning. It would be his. Monte would be given no quarter. He sensed the little bastard was trouble from the start. But Marisol believed in him. Blade saw it in the way her smile touched her face at the sight of him, when Monte patted her hand resting in the crook of his arm. He had watched them as they took a stroll on deck. They laughed together and fell silent together. They were comfortable with one another.

Perhaps they shared a rotten secret together, as well. If she had a hand in what happened to his men on board the *Gloria,* may God have mercy on her, for he'd have none.

He clenched the smooth neck of his wine bottle harder and savored more of the wine.

One thing didn't make sense. The attacks on Carrion were fruitless, wasteful of ammunition at best. Marisol wouldn't be a part of that deadly skirmish, would she? Family meant a good deal to her. It seemed uncharacteristic for her to turn on her kin.

He recalled her lackluster readiness to stay on the *Sablewing* and how she spat when she spoke her father's name. Perhaps she fostered retaliation for his abusive hand. Would that have been enough to destroy his ship and sentence his crew to death? Men whom she worked alongside?

Aye, a good actress, indeed.

Yet, it didn't change the fact when her brother Luc met his end on the gallows, she had been near inconsolable. Her grief, that had been real.

It all puzzled him.

Blade growled. Too many unanswered questions. Too many happenstances.

He brought the bottle back to his lips but stopped. The smell of the wine, sweet and rich, filled his head. Closing his eyes, he resisted another drink. He needed to be sober. A captain should not be roaring drunk before he attacks his enemy.

Blade was no fool. There would be no element of surprise.

The captain of the *Sugar Lady* knew he was coming. The sooner, the better. Under cover of darkness, the *Rissa* might be able to get close enough to prevent escape. With *Sablewing* sitting at the bottom of the bay, Blade wouldn't underestimate *Sugar Lady*'s guns, either. The *Rissa* would need to position herself to her advantage. Aye, it was all about the timing.

Shoving away from the window, he corked the wine and set it on the table. *Save the rest for a victory toast.* He shrugged into his bandolier, securing each of the six primed and loaded pistols in the brace. His sash tied at his waist proudly displayed his cutlass.

The weight of his weapons satisfied him, reminding him of the thrill of combat. The power to tip the scales of life and death with the pull of a trigger or the swipe of a sword intoxicated him more than any liquor. Power, the sheer force of it bubbling in his gut and rising to the surface, had to be contained, suppressed until ready to be wielded. An enemy deserving his judgment needed only to know death would come quick. But this morn, he couldn't be so sure. It had been a very long time since he'd felt this betrayed.

Blade knotted his scarf around his head. He felt angry and worn. Distant.

Ready to go topside, he gave his jacket a tug. A small lump in his pocket distracted him. Reaching in, he pulled out his shell cameo. He gazed upon its raised relief, its delicate features, and his demons reared up to haunt him. But instead of bludgeoning visions of the bloodied, mangled body of the young boy whose life he took, a raven-haired beauty appeared. She beckoned him, reaching for him. What did she clutch behind her back? What did she hide? A gully knife?

Bloody hell. She's even invaded my damnation.

His cameo held his thickened mire of suffering. The source of his hell made no difference.

With a disgusted grunt, he shoved the cameo back into his pocket and left his cabin.

Daylight outside approached in commanding fashion. The deep indigo of the sky waned into lighter hues of blue. In minutes, the light would crown the horizon. Crisp breezes cleansed Blade's muddied mind, rinsing away the bleary stupor of Marisol-tainted Madeira. Not that he was drunk. Not that it was of consequence. He drew in greedy breaths until his cunning tenacity returned sharper than before.

The order to clear for quarters had been given and everything not used in battle had been removed from the deck. Sand crunched under his boots. Buckets of it had been thrown on the floor to keep the men from slipping during battle. His crew stood in clusters near their posts, their dogged faces pinched with grit and their movements strained, eager for bloodshed. Carrion's lads, too, stood poised for action. He nodded in turn to each group, ready as he for a mighty good fight, and made his way to the quarterdeck.

Henri stood atop his crate next to a young helmsman at the wheel, barking commands in his unique placid way. "Watch it now as ya bring her in."

The leads-man at the ship's bow called out the water's depth. "By the mark thirteen."

The small Frenchman moved his thick hands around, steering an invisible wheel. Blade patted Henri on the back.

"How're we doing?" Blade asked.

"Damn pilot is greener than a milkmaid."

"By the deep ten," the leads-man hollered.

"Criminy, boy. You're bringing us in shallow. Not too close. Not too close, I say!"

The evidence of disappointment and frustration burrowed in the lad's frown, but he kept his eyes forward and listened to the men calling out the areas of reefs that came into view.

"We all have to start somewhere, Henri. Not everyone was born in a wheelhouse."

The helmsman cast him a glance and Blade winked.

"Well, they oughta," Henri said. "Careful! Yer too close, I tell ya! These reefs will rip *Rissa*'s belly open, ya knothead."

The vessel cleared a neck of land and a large bay opened up ahead of the bow. Mona's morning shadow blanketed the inlet. Birds took flight from the island's interior in search of a fishy meal, squawking the dawn awake.

On the other side, a lone ship crept toward the open sea. Her sails had not been fully unfurled. A twitch yanked upon Blade's smile. They would be on the vessel soon and his excitement unchained from his glum cynicism.

He nodded to the helmsman. "Let's go get our silver, lad."

In two strides, Blade stood at the quarterdeck rail overlooking the ship's waist and her crew. "We got her, boys!"

The crew erupted in cheer, taking their places ready for the oncoming battle.

"Whaddabout the lass, Capt'n?"

Blade looked back over his shoulder at Henri. His beard had been combed, the red ribbons neatly tied. His shabby vest was gone, replaced by a less tattered one. He stood tall on his crate, even as the young helmsman at his side dwarfed him. It had been a ritual for Henri to present himself dapper in the face of combat. "Gotta be well-groomed if'n today's the day I meet me maker," he would say.

Henri's usual tetchy disposition held a look of concern.

"The lass? A regrettable casualty." Blade turned away, avoiding that judgmental scowl his short mate gave him each time Henri disagreed. Better to skirt that argument altogether.

Henri grunted.

Blade closed his eyes and willed himself not to respond. Responding would only have him defending himself. But when Henri grunted again, jeering Blade's words, he lost the fight.

"Do you wish to say something, Henri?"

"Never pegged ya for a blind man."

Glancing at the helmsman who wisely kept his focus ahead, Blade tipped his head to the side, motioning for Henri to follow him out of earshot.

"And what are you implying?"

"Just that I 'member a time when ya could see things as they are."

"I don't have time for your riddles."

"Ain't givin' ya riddles, Blade," Henri said. "I've known ya fer most of yer life. Always able to put things in their proper place. Never failin' no one. 'Specially yer friends. Now this lass comes along an yer as blind and foolhardy as a live goose in the galley."

"She betrayed me…us." Blade made a monumental effort to keep his voice down.

"Did she, now?"

"Aye." He took on a defensive posture and crossed his arms. Damn.

"Can ya be certain? I know how ya really feel 'bout her, can see it in yer eyes when ya look at her. Ya fallen fer the girl right hard. An' she gone an' done the same. Are ya blisterin' the two of ya without knowin' fer sure what be goin' on? Have ya found the truth?"

"Don't question me, old man. Friends we may be, but I'm not above retiring your meddling arse at the next port. Marisol is a lying, thieving bitch. She's on that ship with her turncoat brother and our pay. I'd say that's truth enough."

"Stubborn fool."

"Likewise."

Blade left Henri to take up an authoritative stance next to the wheel. He stewed over Henri's claims that he was in love. Sure he was. He loved *all* women. Didn't he? Marisol was just another flower to be plucked. It was too bad she crossed him.

"Capt'n." Willie called him from below, drawing Blade from his thoughts.

"We're almost upon her. Your orders, sir?"

The *Rissa* gained within two boat lengths from the *Sugar Lady*. The lack of frenzied activity on the other vessel did not surprise him. While most crews would be scampering to get into defensive positions, these men had expected him. Perhaps they looked forward to a consummate match, a battle easily won.

Splendid.

"Fire a warning shot over her bow. Careful not to hit her. We don't want to sink her with our silver."

Willie gave the order to his master gunner. Four fellows prepared, loaded and rammed a gun for firing. Ready to light the slow match, they waited for a favorable shot.

Blade turned to Henri and the helmsman. "After the warning, bring her astern. We want to remain at a safe angle from behind to avoid the guns, and then swing us around. He won't have his gun ports open on the other side. We'll position ourselves to disable her rudder should he try something foolish."

"Aye, Capt'n."

The time had come. Soon he would get what was his, the silver and revenge. "It's time to pay the hangman."

* * *

Marisol stood alone on the deck of the *Sugar Lady. Or was that the Huntress?* Not one of the crewmen spoke to her as she sought out answers. Most wouldn't even cast a passing glance at her. Exhausted, she found a looped stack of rope to sit upon. It had been a long day and a longer night. Her tired body protested each movement, aching for a spot of rest. She had just closed her eyes when the gentle jerk of the ship knocked Marisol off her perch.

She caught sight of Monte and raced to him. She would get her answers, damn it.

"Monte. Tell me what's going on. I demand to know."

But he didn't stop. He descended down the ladder. "Not now, Marisol."

"Now, Monte. You've avoided me long enough. If you are the captain of this ship, why the secret? Why were you picked up in the middle of the ocean while the *Sugar Lady* sat docked in Puerto Plata? Why did you agree to sail the *Gloria?* What is going on?"

He stared at her with cold dead eyes, eyes she didn't recognize. Where had her little brother gone?

Someone above called out. "Ship ho!"

Together, she and Monte looked in the direction the man pointed.

A majestic ship curled around the rocky outcrop of land. The rousing deep gold of first light traced the fine vessel in a brass haze. A true testament to her glory.

"Blade." Marisol whispered his name under her breath. Her heart lurched and quite unexpectedly she was scared. Extreme foreboding iced her muscles. She froze to the planks, unable to move. Yet her heart raced so fast, it throbbed in her chest, beating so she felt as if she might empty her stomach into the sea. She—*they*—were in big trouble.

"Fast bugger," said Monte.

Oh God, this is bad. Bad, bad, bad. Blade has probably given the order of no quarter. How am I going to get out of this one?

"Are you coming?" Monte stood several feet away, smiling.

She hadn't noticed he had moved away.

"You'd be smart not to stand too close to the side, lest you become a popinjay to shoot."

He was right. At the speed with which *Rissa* crossed the mouth of the inlet, Blade would be in range momentarily. No way would she be what he aimed for. Moving away from the edge, she joined Monte. He seemed unaffected by the pirate ship heading their way, but the perils Blade would wreak ratcheted her nerves. She couldn't bear putting Monte in any more danger at her expense.

"It's me he's after, Monte. Put me in a longboat and I'm sure he'll spare you and your ship."

His boisterous laughter mocked her and his face crinkled up in ridicule. "Sister, dear, pitiful sister. Do you really believe he's coming just for you?"

He circled around Marisol, shaking his head. "How quickly you forget that he's been chasing the *Sugar Lady* all along hoping to cross the mystery ship, my *Huntress,* and find his silver. I'd say I pulled off a damn good hoax, eh? I led the great Captain Blade Tyburn to think there were two ships instead of just one."

The pieces still were not coming together. Marisol couldn't quite make the connection. She struggled to understand why he would go to such lengths to fool everyone, including her. Why didn't he just confide in her?

Monte laughed again. "This masquerade turned out to be more than I could have hoped for. But you're right, Marisol. Tyburn is after you." His smile disappeared and his countenance turned serious. "By now, the honorable pirate knows his silver is in this ship's cargo hold."

"What? *You* have the silver?"

"And he thinks you are behind stealing it."

The blow of his statement pelted her like a swarm of yellow-jackets. *Sink me! He* is *after me.*

A deafening boom shook the suddenly thick air. A cannonball plunked into the sea in front of the *Huntress,* and a spray of water rose high over the bow.

She was as good as dead.

CHAPTER 17

"Have all hands prepare for attack, Grimshaw."

Assessing his enemy, Monte gave his orders to a burly fellow, wild-eyed and thick of beard. Ripe for warfare—and a good lathering with lye soap—he stepped in front of Marisol, expecting her to step out of his way. She arched her eyebrow, daring him to make her move. The brute growled low and brusquely jostled Marisol aside to bark out the command.

That well-known flush of exhilaration perforated through her. She mustn't smile. She would settle on the satisfaction of her nimble fingers. The coarse handle of Grimshaw's gully knife warmed in her hand and she quickly slid it under her waistband at her back, fluffing her tunic out to conceal it. Armed again, she relaxed, but only a degree.

"I'd ration you a pistol and ask you to join in the fun," Monte said, returning his regard to her, "but I suppose you'd prefer to stay neutral. Wouldn't want to fight against the man who keeps you as his pet, would you?"

"What's wrong with you? Why does your tongue speak with such spite?" This side of Monte troubled her. He acted as he did as a young man when Marie, the girl he had been smitten on, took a liking to Luc. And then again when Alain passed him over and made Luc his first mate. Envy drove Monte's nastiness. It hadn't mattered that Luc turned down Marie's advances and tried to get her interested in his little brother. Or that Luc, the eldest son of Alain and the most probable choice, suggested to their father that Monte deserved the position because Monte wanted it more and had worked very hard to be Alain's right-hand man. Monte still spat out the hateful lines.

He ignored Marisol's questions. "Honestly, it's a sad pity. You used to beg Alain to fight in close combat. Now's your chance to go up against the oh-so formidable Blade Tyburn."

"Are you insane? You intend to engage Tyburn?"

"Bless me, if it doesn't tickle my fancy." He cast a ghastly smirk.

"That's suicide."

"For most, I would agree. But I'm not most. I'm smarter." He granted himself a self-satisfied nod.

"You've not the experience of seasoned men, Monte. Tyburn has been doing this since you were in nurse strings." She tossed a glance to the approaching *Rissa.* Damn! Blade drew close. Maybe she should jump overboard.

"I've learned to listen to the brotherhood winds." Monte moved to the gunwale, casually watching his enemy. "I've heard the fears from the coastal peoples willing to give whatever goods they could to stave off raiding parties, and I thought, why not me. Why shouldn't I take what is my due?"

"But we did that. On the *Sablewing.*"

He spun around, eyes alight in acrimony. "And just where was the *Sablewing,* Marisol? Answer me that."

She turned away. "You know better than to ask me that."

"No matter," he said. "There's some advantage to being a pirate's son. Since Matanzas, I worked up the ranks quickly. I gathered me a crew of cutthroats and hell hounds, handpicked from the cesspools of Port Royal. Made off with a merchantman and raided a few seaside towns in a space of months. Then I met Charles Windham. The fool had no idea who I was. It wasn't long before I learned of the *Gloria* and of Tyburn's escort."

"So you meant to stir up trouble." No surprise. 'Twas what Monte did best.

He shrugged. "I saw a chance I couldn't let pass. I hatched out a plan. Me and a few mates signed on to Windham's crew. The lads had thought I had windmills in my head. Perhaps I had.

But my crazy designs were quite simple. Take the silver."

"A fool's crusade."

"Perhaps not. I know a fat cull in San Juan who'd pay generously for Windham's wealth. While I'm at it, I'd undermine the brethren's golden prince. Why do the spineless brethren bow to Tyburn and let him monopolize the Caribbean? He's no king. He's a crowing mutton-monger."

She couldn't blame him for capitalizing on his circumstances. Marisol would have done the same. But she would think twice about challenging Blade.

"Tyburn is more dangerous than you perceive him to be. He's legendary."

"Among virgins and whores."

Marisol bristled under his evident implication.

"The rest are dawcocks telling tales over yarn twisting." He chuckled dismissively. "I've confirmed it by outwitting him, taking his silver and keeping it right underneath his nose. If he's legendary, then I'm immortal for taking him down."

"You've not defeated him."

"Yet."

"Your arrogance is staggering. So much like Alain."

"Ha! Alain. I'm nothing like that worthless piece of shit."

Monte snapped his fingers. Grimshaw reappeared and went to the hatch door. He whistled through the opening and within moments two men emerged, heaving a prisoner between them.

The man hung at the shoulders, his head down and his boots dragging behind him. Blood matted his hair in long stalks and soaked through his soiled tunic. Dark bruises had formed along his bound wrists. They hustled him across the deck. For a brief instant, he lifted his battered face.

"Alain!"

Monte grabbed Marisol before she could reach her father. He was so badly beaten, she hardly recognized him. Swelling sealed his eyes in splotches of blues and greens, and blood caked his crooked nose and split lips. It jarred her to see him that way. The fiendish pirate had been reduced to rubble.

"You did this? But why?"

"He needed to learn what it's like to be on the other side of torture."

"Alain never tortured you. You were treated just as any other crewman on the *Sablewing.*" Though Alain could dole out the punishment, he didn't treat anyone on board unjustly.

"Torture can be more than flesh deep, sister."

His lips scarcely moved as he snarled out the words. "String him up!" Monte said.

Towing Alain to the main mast, Grimshaw threaded the mast rope through those wrapped around Alain's bindings. Grimshaw put his entire bulk into hauling the rope down. A gruesome dolor exploded from Alain's twisted mouth when his arms yanked upward and the rope lifted him off the planks some thirty feet. He thrashed his legs about, screeching under the stretch of his weight, his face distorting with the pain.

Marisol struggled against Monte's hold. "Let him down!"

"No, I don't think I will. He'll protect my ship from having her mast blown apart by Tyburn. Then again, Tyburn might decide the bastard's not worth it. Either way, I'm content with him floundering up there."

"Do you harbor that much hate for him?"

"Is there any other feeling I should have?"

"Monte, I know this is about Matanzas but you've got to understand. Matanzas was a mistake. Alain had no way of knowing soldiers were marching in from the inland when we attacked."

Marisol had not been allowed to join in the sacking of Matanzas. She never saw the pillage and plundering of any raid other than what she could witness from the ship's stern. She only knew that she missed out on the adventure. Or that was what she thought.

From an alcove hidden in the back of her mind, a string of words, Blade's words, paraded out. *My mates and I take advantage of opportunity. We're not greedy, bloodthirsty hellions.*

Was it possible to be a person of fortune without sacking the innocent? Was it indeed more honorable to rob riches from the pompous gluttons dotting the Caribbean Isles? Intriguing. Her view of piracy had been all wrong.

Her mother was right. Desperate men would seek desperate fortunes. She made no excuses for her husband, the roving adventurer. But she made it understood no easy riches, no sparkling jewels, no fine drink, full gullet or bawdy ladybird was reason to prey upon the innocent and lay waste to the lives of good people. Alain was also right. Don't presume decency would protect the righteous and see to happiness. The world was unjust. Strike first and enjoy the spoils, for the guarantee of tomorrow was a lie. Marisol never imagined there could be a betwixt and between.

"They weren't soldiers," Monte said. "They were mercenaries."

She remembered the large company of men rushing out to strike against *Sablewing*'s marauders. Her gut had clutched into a vicious, burning knot. Men fought, men died. Many were able to retreat before the band of militia flanked around the remaining pirates, trapping them on the wharf. Monte had not escaped. Marisol, on no account, would forget the look of terror that congealed on Monte's face. Even at her safe distance on shipboard, she could see her brother's petrified expression. He was being left behind, to die.

As the *Sablewing* set sail away from Matanzas, a brawl broke out. Shots were fired, several men went down. Marisol never knew for sure if Monte had been among those who had died that night, but deep inside she knew he survived. Her guilt for not convincing Alain to rescue Monte had been monstrous. Just as her guilt was now.

"If there had been a way to save you, Monte..." She trailed off. In spite of her remorse, the fact remained. "You must know we all would've been hung. Turning back had been too dangerous. Even Luc said—"

"Bah! Luc was no better a man than Alain." He shoved her away. "It was almost too easy disposing of that prick."

The air rushed from her lungs. Quite by surprise, a sinister chill skittered up her spine. "What do you mean?"

Annoyed, he huffed. "Must I break it down for you?" He rolled his head back in mockery. "Oh, very well. Tyburn is upon us so I'll be brief."

His nonchalant attitude belied just how close Tyburn drew. And though she could almost reach out and touch the *Rissa*'s gun ports, Monte had her full attention.

"Once I heard the *Sablewing* was docked in Puerto Plata, I couldn't believe my luck. I had the silver, I had Tyburn by the nose with my ruse, and then you, Luc and Alain dropped into my lap like a gift from Neptune." Monte paced back and forth in front of Marisol, his back to his oncoming enemy. "I staged the raid, made sure to have a few of my men stir up Luc and others from the *Sablewing* with rumors of the invasion. The men following Luc said they found him in the mercantile shop buying a pair of amber hair sticks."

He reached inside his jacket and pulled out the hair sticks for her to see. The entire length of each stick gleamed of glossed wood, tapering down into pointy tips. Filigreed gold encased perfect round amber stones.

"Luc always did pamper you with ridiculous gifts."

Marisol reached for them, so lovely, so feminine.

"Ah, ah, ah. You can't have them. They're much too sharp." He replaced the hair sticks in his coat.

"You were supposed to be caught during the riot, too," he continued. "With that itch of yours to become a bona fide pirate and your unfailing knack for getting into trouble, you should have been up on that gallows tree with Luc. Instead, you got tangled up with Tyburn."

Dumbstruck by his loathing, paralyzed by his cold stare, the pain growing inside her grieved her more than believing she had lost him. Her little brother, whom she loved deeply, whom she desperately searched for, wanted her dead. It couldn't be.

"Ah, dare and be damned, I got to see Luc hang. Had a good view of that, I did. What a jolly good time that was."

Alain roared from his suspended crucifixion. "You fucking bastard!"

Monte pivoted, drawing his flintlock pistol, and fired at Alain. The bullet tore through his father's arm, missing his head by mere inches. His weight pulled at the rupture and blood poured from the splitting gash.

Alain's agonizing howls sparked an inferno of rage in Marisol. Monte wasn't her brother. He was a monster. Cut from the same cloth as their father, he took his cruelty further by killing and torturing his own family.

"Shut the hell up, old man!" Monte drew another pistol and

shot at Alain again, ripping a hole in his thigh near his knee.

Little raced through her mind other than to get Alain down and end his awful thrashing. She snatched the knife at the small of her back. With a determination of the knife's size and a quick eye, she flung the dagger, embedding the blade into the rope just above where it had been tied off at the mast. It sliced through much of the cord and the final hempen threads holding together the rope unraveled and ripped under the pressure. Alain fell the distance. The crack of bones ruptured over the thud of his body crumpling to the wooden planks.

Monte's astonishment at her audacity shifted to infuriation. His lips curled back as his gaze scraped over Grimshaw, then Marisol. Grimshaw patted around his waistband before settling on Marisol in disbelief. She smugly grinned. Monte tossed his spent pistols to his foul subordinate and planted a murderous foot forward.

"You bitch!" He raised his hand to her.

Marisol cringed, awaiting the stinging blow. Did he hold as much hate in his heart for her as he did Alain? Would he beat her as he did their father? Would she survive? Aye, she would. And she would fight back. She would fight him until she could fight no more. For Luc.

"Montenegro Castellan!"

Blade's booming voice resonated across the ship in a burst of feral aggression.

Marisol peeled her eyes open. The *Rissa* sailed a stone's throw away alongside the *Huntress.* Her captain, ferocious and mighty, had a boot anchored in a rung of the mast's rope tackle. Holding on with one fisted hand, he pointed his cutlass at Monte. Her knees quaked under Blade's sheer domination, ruling over all and sundry.

Monte lowered his open palm and wheeled around to face the sea king. Risking Grimshaw's nasty clutches, Marisol raced over to where Alain lay heaped.

"Alain." She cradled his head in her lap. The sharp stench of sweat stole her breath. "Alain," she said again.

The pit of her stomach curdled at the sight of his eyes once they fluttered open. No white shone under his swollen lids, only redness blended with animosity and retribution.

"Papa."

"Ma chérie." His mouth crept into a nefarious smile. "Do you—" He coughed and wetted his dry lips. "Do you want to make your *père* proud?"

His words scraped across her soul. Pride interlaced with love, something she yearned for from Alain. She knew what toll she'd have to pay to gain her father's hollow pride. But…would there be love?

"Now's your chance. Kill your brother, *ma chérie.*"

Strike down Monte?

"You must kill him before he kills you," he continued. "He *will* kill you."

She looked over to where Monte stood. The Castellan men often reveled in the sins of humanity. Greed, gluttony, wrath, vanity and lust—these vices ran deep and without regret in their veins. Even Luc had not been immune to the lure of overindulgence. But as Marisol watched Monte, watched how he casually took his reloaded pistols from Grimshaw, plucking them back into his brace, watched as he disregarded Blade's demands for surrender, a dawning of disgust, of pity shed new light upon him. Monte surpassed these sins.

"Don't be foolish, Monte," Blade called. "You'll not survive."

"Your bloody threats don't scare me," Monte said.

"They're not intended to. 'Tis just a courtesy."

"Ha! Here's paltry invention. Save your gentlemanly propriety and let us square away, shall we?"

"My pleasure." Blade addressed his men. "Up to the shrouds, swabs! Grapnels, ready!"

Men on the *Rissa* swung barbed grappling hooks in deadly circles waiting for the command to board. Others climbed the ropes like spiders bursting from an egg sac. Marisol recognized some of the fellows and they weren't *Rissa* lads. Alain chuckled. They were the tars from the *Sablewing,* men she deemed fine and trusty bawcock friends.

Monte turned to Grimshaw and gave him a subtle nod. Grimshaw trotted to the hatch and disappeared inside, only to reappear again. He towed a chain over his shoulder, tugging it as he pulled it along. Shackled to the other end were Drake,

Valeryn and two other *Widow Maker* men. They were unmarred but that fact made decidedly little difference by the wrath shining in their eyes. Annihilation roiled off Drake like volcanic ash from a mountainside. Marisol prayed the irons held.

"Found several longboats floating helplessly in the oggin after the storm," Monte said. "I figured plucking out the captain and a few of his chaps might come in handy. Course, I left the others to the mercy of Mona's Passage."

Marisol bit her lower lip at Blade's deadpan expression.

Alain chuckled low in her lap. "Boy learned to strategize," he wheezed. "This could get interesting."

Had Monte gone mad? Challenging Blade, capturing Drake, killing pirates at his discretion…the whole bloody Caribbean brethren would hunt him down and skin him with barnacles. And what about her? Blade must think she had a part in this. They would never make it out alive.

"You want me, Tyburn? You want your silver? Then come on over and take it." He threw up his arm in invitation. "But I give you fair warning." Monte snapped his fingers and five men bearing long arms filed in front of Drake and the manacled men. "Board my ship and these men die."

"Warning received." Blade acknowledged him with a crooked smile. His dimples nicked deep and Marisol winced. That grin sent wayward desire sparking through her that quickly fizzled. Double-edged, that smile meant he had become the predator. A predator out for blood.

"Hey, princock," Drake called out to Monte. "Don't you know when a boy plays a man's game, he gets hurt?"

"Big words from a lout who's a pig in the slaughterhouse."

"Ah, so we agree that you are a swine farmer." Drake and his men laughed.

If it weren't for the seriousness of the situation, Marisol would gag on the male conceit wafting through the air.

"Shut your yap, cur." Monte's face flushed red and his jaw tightened.

Drake's pleasant demeanor vanished. "Why don't ya make me, ya little upstart?"

"Gladly." Monte raised a finger for his gunmen to take aim.

"No!" Marisol dropped Alain's head onto the floorboards.

The thunk and groan didn't slow her from scrambling to her feet.

Too late. The wheels were already set into motion. Drake and his men spread out and rushed forward. With the chain threaded tight between them, they knocked down the armed buccaneers.

In the same instant, Blade made the call to his own fighters. "Grapnels on!"

Grappling hooks flurried through the air, snagging anything solid. Pirates poured over onto the *Huntress*. Monte's men met their attackers head-on.

Battle cries rang in Marisol's ears. So loud, so thrilling. Iron clashed with iron and the metallic strikes melded with curses and barbaric yelling. Her fingers twitched and stretched much like the pianist she had once seen exercising his fingers before a performance. She wanted badly to join in the melee, to pick up a weapon and to fight. But she had no idea which side to take up the scrap with, Blade or Monte. She loved them both. Both wanted her dead.

Above it all, a gloriously energetic tune coasted over the chaos, whipping the men into a zealous frenzy. Marisol pinpointed the source of the music through the pockets of battling pirates. Henri stood on the poop deck of the *Rissa* playing his broken flute. Too old to fight, piping out ditties of confidence made him seem taller.

A blur of dark flesh streaked before her. Sam barreled across the deck to the chained prisoners. While the other men held down and scuffled with the *Huntress* crew who would have shot them, Drake held out his manacles over a crate. Sam's mighty swing of his boarding axe shattered the pin, releasing Drake's iron cuffs. The chain slipped through the rest of the cuffs and soon Valeryn and the other men were free. They used the shackles as impromptu flails, whirling them overhead and pummeling their enemies.

The space all around Marisol strangled with the putrid odor of sweat and blood. Early morning rays of sun warmed the decks and further heated the stench. Combat waged and rivals fell as both sides engaged their foe. She itched to join in the havoc bursting in swarms on every inch of the ship. A pirate, one of Monte's she believed, stumbled away from a fray and tripped at her feet. He jumped up facing her and her instinct flared. She delivered a single pop to his snout. The blow mashed him around and he fell flat. A giddy pulsation of excitement snapped through her. She must fight, someone, anyone.

"Well done, *ma chérie.*" Alain had managed to pull his lame lower body to the main mast and prop himself against it. "Now keep your eye on your biggest threat."

Which one?

Marisol turned in time to see Blade swing the gulf between the ships. He landed on the deck with the same grace he showed while dancing with her in the island cave. He planted himself majestically before Monte. One hand held his cutlass out, and the other beckoned Monte to join him in battle.

Monte raised his sword to the challenge. A haughty smirk crossed his face and he nodded to Blade.

Their first strike resounded in a deafening hellish crash. Together, Blade and Monte thrust and parried. The sword fight waged in a ballet of precise movements and flashes of shiny steel blades. Marisol's skin crawled with each sharp clink of the razor edges. One missed block or parry could lead to a fatal blow for either her brother or her lover.

Marisol was quick to notice the men's different combat styles.

They were worthy opponents. Blade stood with his feet at shoulder width and he moved keeping his legs apart. Monte shuffled a great deal, swift with his movements. Blade never stretched his arms out and instead extended his weapon toward his adversary. Monte used his weapon like a tool, very aware of what his sword was designed for, light and nimble in strokes. Yet Blade was able to read Monte's actions. When Monte moved in, Blade launched advancing strikes, keeping parries close to his body so that he stretched less when counter thrusting.

Too many times, Monte had skipped out on lessons with Luc. Luc had mastered sword fighting with his beloved cutlass, Simone. He knew all the secrets to walking away from a fight alive. He knew how to assess the situation, his enemy and his surroundings. Maintaining a distance on the balance of his sword and his foes, being calm, having a strong defense, finding the weakness and even using trickery by pretending to be unskilled made him an extraordinary swordsman.

Marisol learned all she could from Luc, realizing that all rivals have a pattern and it was wise to use that knowledge to her advantage. Her little brother scoffed at Luc's training and because of it missed some of the most important elements to winning.

It became obvious to her now. Blade had found the flow of the battle. He controlled it. And he would decide its outcome.

Fear for her brother registered deep within her. The little boy he had once been racing up the path to their house holding a string of fish bigger than himself, his smile bursting with pride, played in her mind. The image struck a chord. "My God, he's going to kill Monte."

"God willing."

She spun around to Alain. He had ripped his pant leg and used a scrap of the material as a tourniquet above his wound to staunch the bleeding. "How can you say that? He's your son."

Even as she said it, the sad truth sank in her gut. Monte was gone. He was far from being that little boy on Cow Island, and farther from a son or brother.

"That bastard's no son of mine."

Ben, a mate from the *Sablewing,* fell wearied to his knees before Alain. "Capt'n. Can ya move?"

"Nay, lad. This here arm's numb. Least it ain't my shooting arm. Damn near shot off my leg, too, the Judas. And I think I broke something, thanks to Marisol."

Ben scanned his captain's wounds then sent Marisol a hard glance. "Be anything I can do fer ya, Capt'n?"

"Your pistol, boy."

Ben handed Alain a pistol and disappeared into the fracas.

She needed a weapon of her own. Her safety depended on it. Who was friend and who was foe? Only a fool would wait to find out. As a pair of men brawled past, she reached out for one of the buccaneer's pistols hanging from his waist. She ducked just in time, away from the downward swing of a cutlass blade. Filching a pistol or knife from someone else might leave her missing a limb at best. There had to be another way.

Fallen men may still be armed. She spied several unlucky fellows across the deck. All were too far away and too dangerous to get to.

Belaying pins used as clubs would do little in fending off any attackers wielding a firearm or sword. If she angled close enough to a pair of fighting men, she could whack one of them in the head, but probably not without getting severely injured herself.

Grimshaw's knife.

The gully still protruded from the mast. Grabbing its handle, she pulled with all her might. It didn't budge. Not even a little. Deep the blade had been buried. *Damn!* She wiggled it up and down to loosen the grip of the wooden mast, up and down splitting through the grain. *Come…on.*

The timber freed its clamp on the dagger, and Marisol lurched backward from the sudden release. She nearly lost her equilibrium, bumping into another set of fighting pirates. She hopped around and crouched into a defensive position, but the tars paid her no mind and kept on trading vicious punches in turn to one another's marred faces.

Beyond the combatants, Blade and Monte continued their impressive swordfight, a graceful performance of give and take. Sweat ran in rivulets down their faces and soaked through their tunics. The clashes of blades rang as solid as at the beginning of the spar, but Monte had clearly begun to tire.

Blade influenced the fight and Monte's footwork and parries had lost precision, becoming sloppier.

Monte overextended a thrust, leaving his side wide open for Blade to make a fatal strike. Monte twirled back, but Blade's cutlass slit through his shirt.

Marisol gasped.

At first it appeared the sword's edge altogether missed. Monte stumbled away and inspected a ghastly wound across his ribs. "Son of a—"

Blood seeped down the torn cloth of his shirt, but the gash was not life-threatening.

Blade raised his sword, his muscles bulging with the strength to finish the job, his eyes flared with victory. Monte put distance between them, stopping within a few feet of Marisol.

"Kill him, Marisol."

She closed her eyes at Alain's gruff demand. Never was it

wise to stare into the eyes of a wild beastie. That only served to provoke him further. True to her nature, and always when not in her best interest, she would rebel against him.

"No," she said. "I will not kill my brother."

"You will. Kill him before I kill you."

Marisol faced her father and a chilling terror seized in her chest.

Alain trained his pistol on her.

CHAPTER 18

Tendrils of hair wisped across her face from the mockery of a serene breeze. The noise from the ensuing battle was muffled in the vacuum of her devastation. That which Marisol had kept sealed and buried all those years ruptured free, annihilating her ill-conceived perceptions. Alain held not a single thread of love for his daughter. This she knew. Why had it come as a surprise? The valley of her despair widened. But being overcome by this revelation would weaken her chance of survival.

Alain held the gun propped in his lap.

Must relax. Must unclench my fists, regain control.

"You care so little of me that you would see me dead should I not do your bidding?" Call it a challenge, call it a bluff, she would bide her time. Look for an opening, something to reverse her fortune.

"What good are you to me if you refuse?"

"I'm your daughter."

He shrugged. "I've others, be assured."

"Bastard." The barb stung, but she counseled herself to hold her tongue further. She'd only hurt herself.

"Come now. I'm much more than that." He afforded himself a quick laugh. "I'd kill the bastard myself, I would. But he's too fucking far for me to bury one in his skull with one shot. You must kill him."

"Shoot me if you must, but I won't kill Monte for you." *Use your knife. Incapacitate him. Get the gun. Do something!*

"Brave, chit," he said, "but very stupid. He means to destroy us. I might be joining Luc soon and I no longer will be your safeguard..." he took in a deep breath, struggling against his slurred words, "...your guardian. Better you die by my hand than what the devil has in store for you."

Clanging swords, grunts, hollering, pops from pistols, the wall of riotous clamor smashed into her. In the mayhem of Alain's statement and her labyrinth of severed emotions, confusion took root. A dull ache seated in the frown of her brow. Guardian? Luc, Blade, Monte, Alain. Who was there to protect her from but the very people she cared for?

Alain cocked his chin. "He's weakening."

Marisol glanced over her shoulder. 'Twas true, Monte foundered in keeping his torso forward, making it harder for his body to twist away from blocks. Blade kept him on point, the tip of his sword eye-level.

"Could be a trick to fool Tyburn. Take him, Marisol. Take him now. Use your gift of marksmanship. Put your gully in his back before I put a plug in your head."

More time. She needed more time to figure out what to do. Why must she choose between her father and her brother? *Could* she choose? She didn't want to kill either of them. Marisol twirled the dagger in her grip, trading the coarse handle for the cool blade, readying herself to make an accurate mark, though she had not yet decided what that mark would be.

She turned to face her father. Alain leveled his pistol. Steady now, he took aim at her heart. Would she be faster than the pull of a trigger? Her fingers tightened on the blade.

Alain blew out a tattered sigh. He shifted the gun away and fired, but the pistol did not ignite. He had removed the flint, letting the gun tumble to the floorboards from the fingers of his useless hand. "My daughter, loyal and bold, I will grant it."

Dumbfounded, Marisol warred with his words. Did he have a sliver of compassion after all?

Within the moment, Drake appeared, kicking away Alain's gun and landing a solid downward punch into his blighted nose. The force of the blow left Alain unconscious, slumping against the pole, fresh blood oozing down his whiskered cheek.

Drake politely, but ever-so slightly, bowed to Marisol before ebbing back into the sea of combat.

Where'd the pistol go? She frantically searched the planks for the weapon. *There.* Among shuffling feet, the gun slid across the coarse floor. She had to get to it before someone reached down and snatched it. Flicking her knife back, she stooped beside Alain to find the flint. She patted through his filthy clothing until she discovered it under his thigh. The truth struck her hard. He really had removed the flint. What did that mean? No time to entertain herself with ridiculous false hopes.

She darted to where the pistol lay and reached down to grab it. A callused heel bumped the weapon, sending it skating past her. She wheezed on the dust swirling up from the sandy floorboards. The grit jabbed her palms and dug through the knees of her breeches as she crawled for the gun.

Almost...got...it.

Keen metal poked at the tender skin of her neck. Marisol froze, not risking a move sure to decapitate her.

"Stand down, Tyburn, or I'll tear her weasand open." Monte panted in short, exhaustive breaths. He had indeed grown tired. Blade had eroded his youthful strength during their combat.

From the outer edges of her vision, Blade stood with his sword ready to deliver judgment. He lowered his weapon only marginally.

The point of a sword pressed firmly under her jaw, threatening to slice into her throat.

"Let go of the knife, sister."

She tried to push down her terrible reluctance to let go of her dagger. She wouldn't be able to seduce her way out of this one with empty promises. It worked before. But this time, her brother was the enemy. A flick of her hip and an inviting smile would not serve as a distraction aimed at escape.

The devil's own rotten luck left her stripped of any means of defense. Her fingers, one by one, uncurled from the handle. Prodded by the sword, she leaned back on her knees and Monte kicked the dagger away.

"On your feet."

Rising slowly, her eyes locked with Blade's. Their charming

brilliance had clouded with something dark and foreign she couldn't identify. He looked straight through her. Blindness perhaps? Impartial to destroying the Castellan line?

Monte grasped her wrist, jerking it up behind her back, and pulled her in front of him. The wide part of the sword's blade, before the cross guard, tucked into the delicate flesh of her neck.

"What makes you think that I care if you cut open one of your own?"

Her heart sighed heavily, as heavy as Blade's abrasive tone. Monte had spoken true—Blade did believe she aided Monte in stealing the silver.

"I suppose there's a chance that you don't," Monte countered. "I thought since you've already bedded her, and being the gentleman you are, you would do the chivalrous thing and try to save the lady."

"How predictable. Only a coward would shield himself with a woman."

Monte's lips snarled at the insult. "A dangerous thing to say."

Blade continued, unfazed by Monte's growing friction. "'Tis true I'm a gentleman, but your theory is weak."

"Oh?" Monte said.

"You and I both know Marisol is no lady." His sword still at a deadly angle, Blade let his gaze drift to her. "She's a troublesome shrew."

A knife to her heart would hurt less. She really had lost Blade. To never feel his tender caress, taste his wicked kiss, to lie in his warmth or hear the beating of his heart, to be denied requited love, *his* love, nothing, not even eternal burning in hell could ever be worse.

"So, Captain *Castellan,* your traitorous pawn is worthless."

"Ah," Monte smirked, "but you should know, Tyburn, Marisol had nothing to do with taking the *Gloria.* Nor did she know about me and my plans. She cannot claim the merry vindication of putting a bullet in your tarry mariners' brains. No. My dear sister, for once, is a victim."

Marisol studied Blade. Was the man made of granite? No sign of compassion. No sign that Monte's declaration chiseled away at his stony heart.

Monte's grip tightened.

"It makes little difference to me," Blade said. "Lying roguelings are best left to their own kind."

"Tsk. I had hoped you'd give me a reason to kill her. Damn the luck." Caustic sarcasm spewed from him like the cackle of a raven.

He rested his temple against her head. To the casual observer, his simple action would seem like a loving gesture. "I thought to leave you in the cavern to drown, Marisol. You don't know how close I came in doing so. Walking away would have been easy."

He spoke as if recalling a fanciful dream. 'Twas anything but a dream.

"But then all my plotting would have been wasted. That, my dear sister, would be a damned pity. I'd miss the thrill of watching this grand moment. This very moment when you breathe your last breath."

He leaned in close to her ear. "Are you scared, Marisol?"

Terrified. She stared straight ahead. Stared at the man she had betrayed, the man who now spurned her. No one. She had no one left. Cheating death time and again had all been for naught. The path to the river Styx's shore would be revealed by the hand of her brother. 'Twas good she kept that silver piece. She would be able to pay the ferryman.

Marisol mustered up her nerve. If she were to die, she would die without showing fear. "I am more scared for you, Monte, than for myself. What will be left of you once you kill me?"

"Don't worry. I'll tell Mama the truth. You and Luc perished because you listed in the service of Alain and the devil." He leaned his cheek in closer. "Well then, I never cared for keeping rubbish about. Time to die, sister."

He drew the cutlass edge across her skin slowly, filleting her neck with a small notch. Marisol whimpered at the smarting pain. Squeezing her eyes tight, she blinked away the tears brought on by the tremendous sting. She couldn't die this way. Not by the hand of her little brother. There was so much more to see and experience. An entire ocean waited for Marisol, beckoning her to ride the trade winds, to visit distant shores. And there was love to be conquered. And hope. Hope that she might win back Blade's affection. Her heart pounded in her ears. The air she labored to suck in parched her dry lips. Warm liquid trailed down her neck, reaching beyond to the basin of her chest. *Please, I don't want to die.*

Blade remained granite still. Would he not save her?

Maybe she wouldn't *need* saving.

* * *

The pleading, whirlpool of panic in Marisol's wide eyes laid siege to the wall of defense that surrounded Blade's soul. The first tear of blood on her slender neck obliterated everything he had ever held against her. His anger, his misguided revenge, drained from him as her blood spilled. In that moment, with her life about to be pinched away, he realized what a terrible mistake he had made. He understood what his fiery dove meant to him. Not fully, but enough to want to explore all the possibilities with her. No way in bloody hell that wretch would take her from him.

Menacing pleasure swaggered across Monte's features at his handiwork before he turned to watch Blade's reaction. Blade couldn't let him think he'd been affected. When he first met Monte, back in Puerto Plata, Blade briefly caught Monte's fear of him. Knowing the fool had been frightened of him meant Monte could be defeated. Blade would sniff out that weakness and use it against him.

He wouldn't let the little arse believe he'd care if he slaughtered his sister. He must remain indifferent to outsmart him. But the pain registering in Marisol at his cold façade gripped him with excruciating force. Threads of remaining calm and control snapped wildly apart. He must act fast.

Speed would be useless for what lethal foolishness came next.

She struggled to free herself from Monte's hold.

"Marisol, no!" Horrified, Blade charged forward, his sword brandished overhead.

From the corner of his eye, a glint of metal arced toward him. He deflected the downward blow of a cutlass, twisting it up and around. The boxy buccaneer that mistreated Drake and strung up Carrion swung his weapon around to Blade's waist.

Blade twisted with a small step back, leaving the brute slicing the air and exposing his unprotected side. With an upward thrust, Blade sliced through his attacker's back and flank. The man roared and fell to his knees. Instead of putting his sword through him, Blade smashed the hilt into the man's skull. The barbarous toad fell over, landing facedown and motionless.

Marisol!

She snatched an object from Monte's jacket, so quick he'd hardly seen her in the act. Was that…hair sticks?

"Rot off!" she screamed.

In a blink, she impaled Monte in his gut, leaving the small spears pierced within him. Shock bolted across his face but the moment sputtered out, replaced by crazed wrath. His bellow thundered as he plunged his cutlass toward Marisol's body.

Blade propelled himself to block the mortal blow, deflecting Monte's weapon with his own. He swung the sword up, the metal sliding against metal and grinding out a grisly sound. Shoving him back, Blade pivoted around, his back to his foe, and rammed his blade deep into Monte's chest. A hard yank and his sword slid free of flesh.

Monte dropped his sword and looked down. Blood bloomed from his fatal wound. His wide-eyed stare swept up, his eyes settling on Marisol. She stepped forward, her trembling fingers stretching out for him.

A ravine of sadness for her cratered within Blade. He wanted to draw her into his embrace and stroke away her hurt. So much hurt. But he thought she would shy away from his compassion, revolted by the sight of Monte's life dripping from the end of his sword. He brought death upon her brother. She would despise him with every particle of her being. Nay, holding her would be impossible. 'Twas between Marisol and Monte, now. And she needed to walk with Monte in his final moments on her own.

"Monte," she whispered.

Wet rasps escaped his parted lips. "I…I hate you."

Crumpling to the floorboards, his last breath expelled, slow and cumbersome.

Marisol did not move. Her expression, neither forlorn nor horror-struck, was unreadable to Blade as she stared at Monte's dead body. The red streaks along her neck had dried. Blade internally sighed with relief. The cut had been superficial though would likely scar.

Monte's poisonous words chanted in his mind. How betrayed and injured she must feel to hear such excessive bitterness from a brother she dearly loved. Especially after all that she went through to find him. Blade wished he had the power to bring Monte back. Not to have him live again. Nay. He wanted to plunge his sword through Monte's rotten heart over and over again for hurting his dove.

To hell with it. If she refused him, he would understand. But she needed someone now, someone who cared. The dampness of her arm stuck to his palm. "Marisol."

She said nothing. That worried him, but she did not recoil from his touch.

"Marisol, my sweet. It's over. You're safe." He leaned around, taking in her face. Glassy eyes, murky and distant, did not blink. Had she slipped into lunacy? He knew that place well. Empty, chaotic and so very lonely, madness was a colorless prison in the backdrop of the mind and was not easily escaped. Her absent gaze trailed down to the hair sticks still protruding from Monte's stomach. Slowly, she squatted down and he let her slip from his grasp. She wrapped her fingers around the amber tips and slid the sticks free. Wiping them on her trousers she stood and turned to face Blade.

"Bloody bastard, he was," she said.

Marisol stepped into Blade and allowed him to encircle his arms around her. She had no tears, but the rise and fall of her chest against him came in staccato breaths. He could offer her no healing words, for there were none to give. Yet he prayed that she found the solace she needed in the kisses he planted on her head.

Minutes passed. The fighting around them slowed and the raucity faded. Blade's men overcame the *Sugar Lady*'s truculent buccaneers. Blade led Marisol back to the *Rissa* and away from the aftereffects of carnage. She gave one final forlorn glance over her shoulder at Monte's body before crossing to his ship. Blade pulled her into another reassuring hug.

"Marisol, you must know that I am not sorry for taking your brother's life." He needed her to hear the truth. She would be insulted by any mask he pretended to wear.

"I know."

She pulled back. Sorrow scored her features. Defenseless, her palpable grief hurt him, physically hurt him.

"I wish I could say that it is all right," she said. "I can't. Not at this moment. I…I need time to come to terms with what Monte has done. To sort out my feelings."

Guilt from executing Monte lingered, but only on her behalf, nothing more. "I understand." He ran the tip of his thumb gently across the many cuts upon her face. Did Monte do that to her, too? May the bugger rot in hell. Blade embraced her again. Selfishly he held her before she returned to her senses and despised him for his role in her misery.

"We've run 'em down, Capt'n." Willie ambled over to the edge where the ships butted together with a bit of a spring in his step and a rascally twinkle in his spirit. "You've got yer treasure back, too."

"I sure did." His embrace tightened around her supple shoulders. The apples of her cheeks rose against him in a smile. He smiled, too.

"Would ya like someone to take a look at that fer ya, Capt'n?"

"At what?"

Willie pointed to Blade's arm. "At yer wound there."

Marisol pulled back. "You're hurt!" Alarm blotted out the despair in her brown eyes.

Blade glanced down. Bright red stained his ripped sleeve. He hooked his finger into the tear. *Hmm. Hadn't noticed before.* Stinging slithered up his arm. "'Tis merely a flesh wound."

"Rubbish. You're losing a lot of blood." Her concern touched his heart. Like the morning sun's rays breaking through the dense branches of a crowded forest, faint light chased away the nightmarish dread of Marisol's resentment. She must not hate him as much as he feared.

"Nothing a dressing couldn't stop."

"Let me see for myself." She pulled his shirt free from his trousers, unlaced it and pushed it down over his shoulders, exposing his chest and arms for a clearer look.

"I know you can't resist my body, love, but here? In front of the men? Randy little spitfire, aren't you?" Blade fully expected her to pop him for his teasing. He hadn't been prepared for her radiant smirk, impish in the way one side of her smile beamed higher than the other.

"I wouldn't want to embarrass you, Tyburn." She waggled the hair sticks at him, like a schoolteacher would to a naughty student. "What would your men think—" she fanned the sticks out across the ship's decks toward his crew, "—to see their mighty libertine captain toppled from his satiric throne by his mere rum wench?"

Blade caught her, gathering her to him and, laughing, dipped her down. His hand cupped in the smooth arch of her back. A part of the feminine body he had always adored. "I think they'll bow down to her in adoration and throw roses at her feet."

He smothered her chuckle in a hard, sensual kiss.

Setting her right he said, "That's the third time I have saved you. I'd say you owe me much."

Her eyebrows rose bit by bit. "I'll repay your heroic deeds, dear sir, by not haunting you for the rest of your life."

The very idea of not spending another magnificent night with his raven-haired bonny would be a curse in itself.

"Deal."

* * *

Under a waning moon, the firelight flickering from the camps on Mona's magical beach glimmered in glowing spheres. From the *Rissa,* Blade saw shadowy figures wander in and out of the mystic light. Jovial music, clanking tankards and hearty laughter carried to his ears across the breaking surf.

The men worked hard this day. The battle won, the enemy and mutineers captured and imprisoned in the *Sugar Lady*'s hold, the silver transferred to the *Rissa* for safekeeping…aye, his men deserved a night of revelry.

For all the good fortune that shone on him, Blade's bones creaked of weariness. It had been a difficult journey, but it was Marisol he worried for.

Another brother gone, forevermore.

Proper burials were given to Monte and the other dead under

a copse of island trees. As captain, and with no man of cloth available, Blade recited a few words for the departed. Marisol stood, a solemn effigy, next to her grousing father. Her lips pressed tight with each smarting slur Carrion hurled. It took all Blade's strength to keep from planting his fist into Carrion's flapping clam, shutting him up for good. When the first stone had been placed over the grave, Blade personally clapped irons on to Carrion and had him returned to the *Sugar Lady*'s bilge to ferment with the other captives. Marisol voiced no objection. Riddled by betrayal, he doubted she'd have anything to say.

She had spent much of the day in her cabin and had been equally quiet at dinner. He had apologized to her for the suffering he had caused her in slaying Monte, hoping she would see he had no other choice. "His life was a tragedy" was all she had said. Though her smile had been sad, Blade knew she'd eventually be all right.

As he closed his eyes, a delectable scent of honey and cream enveloped him. It spread through him like a misty dream and he opened his eyes to find her leaning on the rail beside him.

"You smell delicious."

"I found scented soap in the chest of drawers in my room and sponged with it. I hope you don't mind," Marisol said.

"Not if you don't mind becoming dessert."

"Incorrigible."

"Aye." *Good. A smile.* She had no inkling how he feared the rays of her radiant smile might engulf him, burn him and cauterize him like a hot iron.

They shared their silence together, listening to the breezy din of the shore amusement.

"What will you do with the prisoners?"

Her question broke the peaceful contentment he had curled himself in. Yet she had a right to know what he planned as Carrion's fate. He turned to lean his arm on the railing, to drink in her profile in the moonlight, to watch for approval.

"Drake will turn over the mutineers and the *Sugar Lady*'s crew to the authorities in Puerto Plata, declaring he caught the rioters. Your father will be set free at port with the understanding he immediately sails out of my waters and finds new dogs with which to lie."

Her shoulders dropped noticeably and she turned to face him, nodding. She had been pleased with him for allowing Carrion's release instead of bringing him before a counsel of the brotherhood for sentencing. There, the brethren would surely have him executed for treason.

"His men that wish to carry on with him are free to go, as well," he added. "Or they may sign on with Drake."

"And the *Sugar Lady?* Will Captain Drake have her?"

"Aye. Until he finds a worthy ship to call his own."

"The silver?"

A sharp mind, she had, wanting all the details. An essential quality for a woman who desired to be a wily buccaneer. "We sail to Santo Domingo and deliver the silver to Charles Windham as planned."

"Why not keep it for yourself? You can claim the silver went down with the *Gloria* during the hurricane. Split it amongst yourselves. After all you've endured to get it back, you deserve it. It's yours."

The moonlight disappeared under a passing cloud. She looked up and as the luminous light reemerged, Blade wondered if the brightness in her eyes could have been due to the prospect of bearing so many riches.

"Tempting, love. But unwise."

She glanced back to him, curiosity in her expression.

"Not all prizes come from a ship's cargo hold," he explained. "A little trust and valuable, advantageous information can guarantee a man's wealth. Instant gratification lasts only until the pocket is empty. A day or two, at most. My men and I will be well compensated for this voyage. Not only in coin but in the steady quarries."

She grew quiet again, distant, perhaps contemplating his uncharacteristic pirating strategy.

"That would take great patience," she said. "Many aren't blessed with that virtue. Especially pirates who risk everything with each voyage."

"When a man retires from the *Rissa,* he is quite wealthy and will likely live the rest of his days comfortably."

She gazed back to the festivities on the beach. "You're an odd sort of pirate, Captain Blade Tyburn."

"One who still claims entitlement to a beautiful serving wench."

Her mouth popped open. "You can't be serious?"

"You weren't much for keeping my cups full." He frowned and pretended to ponder that. "However, I'm not ready to end your indenture."

"And just what would you have me to do?" She leaned in close, her shoulder touching his, and slipped him a coy smirk.

"Say you will travel with me to Santo Domingo." Standing upright, surprise flowered across her face.

"I'd like that."

"Good. It is settled then." He twisted around and leaned his back against the rail. A trace of honey wafted on a passing breeze. His mouth watered and suddenly he thirsted to taste her skin. "Would you care to join me in my cabin for a glass of Madeira wine? It is an excellent wine to go with…dessert."

"I am feeling a little parched."

His heart pranced at her wicked wink. Taking her hand he led her to his sanctuary.

In the warm glow of candlelight, her hair glistened like ebony glass and her eyes of the clearest amber flickered with desire. A desire that blistered him to his core.

He undressed her with deliberate care, not wanting to miss one inch of her already moist olive skin. Taking her into his bed, he explored her body in relishing kisses. To each of his gingered touches, Marisol responded with sighing moans and searing sweeps of her lips. But it was her tiny gasp as he eased inside her he treasured. She locked eyes with him, a sweet, yet wanton smile gracing her open mouth. Only when he slowly pulled out did she exhale.

He could get carried away by her sounds, her touch. Oh God, her touch. Warm hands wandered down his back and settled on his arse, sending explosive currents of need coursing through him. She squeezed, pulling him down and lifting her hips to meet him. He immediately obliged, entering her again. This time he would make love to her. Slow, easy, passionate love.

Inch by inch, Marisol matched him. Their ethereal shadows danced on the cabin walls with the movement of perfect harmony. He tasted her tangy neck, lapped the hollow of her throat, suckled each drawn nipple. His mouth on her skin was more delectable than the smoothest Madeira wine.

She ran a hand through his hair and seized the back of his neck. Delicious pain shot across his back as her fingernails dug into his flesh. Marisol was nearly there. He plunged deeper, faster to push her over the edge. Her legs slung around his waist and she threw her head back into his pillow, a scream catching in her throat.

Watching her excited him all the more. And in squeezing him tight, she increased the friction. He pumped once, twice, and he too seized, spilling over and joining her in ecstasy.

Nothing, by land nor by sea, had prepared him for Marisol.

Blade had fought against the foreign feeling of love, having never really experienced it. He had misunderstood what love really meant. It wasn't lying down with a woman, exchanging heat and passion. It was much more than that. It was sharing his essence with someone, trusting her, breathing her in as if she were the very lifeblood that kept a man alive.

Marisol was that woman. And he intended to never let her go.

* * *

Tucked within his arm, bonded against his damp, naked flesh, her body tingled under the lazy circles his fingertips drew along her hip. The ecstasy they created together left Marisol in a swoon of serenity. A master he had been at bringing her pleasure again and again, but when he relinquished control to her, the empowerment of becoming his equal shone new light on her connection with him. She licked her lips, still tasting his earthy salt on her tongue.

The hole left behind by all she had lost, Blade replenished, filling her heart to the brim with a unique, special kind of love. The fresh emotion scared her. Aye, the pirate indeed struck terror into her, and she decided she liked the fear—a lot.

Staring at the flames stretching from the candelabra wicks, she prayed the dream would never end. Marisol rolled her head up and pecked a kiss on his chin. He hummed in appreciation.

"I have something for you, dove."

"Again? Don't you ever grow tired?"

He laughed. "Not with you, my sweet."

She eyed his perfect backside as he left the bed. She should be ashamed to stare, but by the heavens, she was not. He removed something from the top drawer of his desk and she sat up as he returned to sit on the edge of the mattress.

"Marisol, you have taught me more about myself than I could have ever discovered on my own."

Perplexed, she shook her head. "I don't under—"

"Shh. No words."

He slipped his fingers over her hand and gently turned her palm upward. For a brief moment, the rough pad of his thumb rubbed across her inner sensitive skin. She became rapt in his eyes that held her steadfast, unnerved by their vulnerability.

Blade closed her fingers over a small round object. A knot embedded in her throat and she struggled to swallow it down.

"This cameo has been an emblem of my damnation."

Afraid she would burst if she lingered in his stare, trapped by his words, she tore her eyes away and looked to the cameo gracing her palm.

"Because of my sins," he continued, "I deemed myself unworthy, a bloody scoundrel, not fit for life's greatest joys." He cupped her chin and forced her to meet his gaze. "But you, you came along, and well, I realized I was wrong. Thank you, my love. Take from me my cameo again, for I no longer need it."

Marisol tasted her own tears as he placed a tender kiss to her lips.

She may have been the thief, but he had stolen her heart.

EPILOGUE

"How is she, brother?" Drake clasped Blade on the shoulder, giving him a good squeeze.

Having his friend close by for support lessened Blade's anxiety. "I don't know. They won't let me see her."

He glared at his other *friends*, Sam, Henri and Willie gathered around the table in the corner of the inn.

A blood-curdling scream erupted from behind Marisol's bedchamber door. He rushed for the knob, but Sam, as huge as he was, shifted his bulk quicker than possible to block his entry. Growling, Blade slammed his fist into the wall, rattling the pictures that hung there.

"Ho, ho there, mate," Drake said. "Take it easy."

His knuckles smarted and already had begun to turn pink. Blade exhaled a disgusted sigh. "Henri took away my weapons," he complained.

"Had to." Henri scowled, and then snorted. "'Bout lost his head. Boy don't know his place."

Blade narrowed his eyes on the jack sprat. "I wouldn't have hurt the old hag."

Willie chuckled. "Shoulda seen the fright he gave the midwife when she crowed 'bout him interferin'. Thought Capt'n meant to send 'er 'ome to 'er maker."

Drake's laughter bounced throughout the room, bringing on

a fit from Blade's men.

Blade couldn't help but be infected by the good humor. "Ha! The woman turned whiter than Henri's wrinkled arse."

The men united in the mirth.

"Hold yer tongue, Tyburn." But Henri, too, laughed.

"It's hard to believe, Blade," Drake said. "Soon, you're going to be a papa."

A papa.

Incredible buoyancy swelled within him. His pride soared higher than any bird on heaven's wind could reach, even beyond the stars themselves. Something he never imagined, never thought being a father would appeal to him.

But now, he wanted nothing more than a family, with Marisol as his wife. And what a beautiful bride she had made. Standing on the bluff overlooking the glittering sea at sunrise, the breeze whipped at the lacy hem of her white gown. A garland of small red roses crowned her head and embellished her fragrant bouquet. The blossoming petals of the flowers harmonized with the large red ruby, his gift to her, perched upon her breast. Her gift for Blade came on a whisper in his ear after exchanging vows. He could still feel the tickle of her breath upon his earlobe as she murmured she was with his child.

Marisol believed in the power of family, how important it was to have them by your side. And Blade *had* a family, his best mates and brethren. They were always there, at his back. His family fought and died for each other, mourned and celebrated together, lived like brothers. Aye, stronger than blood, they were.

But with Marisol and the life they created together growing in her womb, family, one to call his own, was the crown jewel of life.

Another scream shrieked from beyond the door. He ran a hand through his hair and paced the length of the room. "Damn it. I should be in there with her."

"Come," Drake said. "Ease your mind. Sit with me and tell me of this grand ship you are building."

Ah yes, talking of his flagship would alleviate the helplessness churning in his gut and scratching at his mind. He took a chair at the table, swung it around and sat, leaning on the chair's ladder back. "The shipwright I commissioned to build the

Iridian has a fine reputation."

Golden rays of sun had never shined brighter than the smile on her face the day Blade told her of his plans to build Marisol her own ship. He'd wager hours had passed before she let him come up for air and emerge from their bedchamber. Grinning inwardly, he should think to build his love a fleet.

"The shipwright says she'll be ready to make a maiden voyage in time for our trip to Jamaica to visit old friends. Three masts, she'll have. No less than forty guns. Very much like the *Rissa*."

Drake nodded. "She's an extraordinary vessel and ideal to use as a model for the *Iridian*."

"None other like 'er," Henri said. The other men agreed.

Bittersweet memories aboard the majestic ship showered upon him. *Rissa* had been his home for many years. He grew very fond of her. The decision to hand her over to Captain Thayer Drake had been a difficult one.

"You will take good care of her?" Though he trusted Drake, Blade needed to hear the reassurance that his *Rissa* would continue to journey across the ocean as the most magnificent and formidable vessel on the sea.

"As her captain," Drake said, "I will be duty-bound and honored to make sure *Rissa* remains the pearl of the Caribbean."

"Which direction will you point her bow?"

"Westerly. To Florida. I've followed up on an unscrupulous fellow our former industrious employer, Charles Windham, had suggested needed eradicating. 'Tis good evidence of sordid amassing of money and influencing of the innocent. And, too, with the trade route skirting the reefs around the islands, there's bound to be riches strewn along the sea bottoms."

"Salvaging." Blade consented in a smirk. "A lucrative business."

"Sounds inerestin'." Henri scratched his beard. "Ain't never crossed me mind takin' what's already belongin' to the sea."

"You men are welcome to join me." Drake paused and looked to Blade. "If your captain will have it."

Blade smiled and acquiesced.

"Will there be rum?" Henri asked.

Drake chuckled. "Enough to soak your deadlights and

witness a flock of moons."

"Blimey!" Henri slapped his thigh. "Count me in."

A spine-chilling scream longer, more excruciating than before, splintered the conversation. Everyone in the room froze; their expressions reflected how Blade felt. Terrified. He shot from his chair, panic crushed his lungs. *What is happening to her? Is she all right? What was that horrid woman doing to her? Dear God, I've got to save her!*

He flew to the door, ready to plow over Sam and kick the bloody thing down. Then he heard it. A divine sound halted him in place, his hands gripping Sam's shoulder. A babe's cries, *his* babe's cries. Relief, joyous sweet relief, washed over him. He chuckled once. The others broke into relaxed grins. Blade inhaled a deep, long awaited breath and fell into a spasm of nervous, merry laughter.

His friends gathered around him, bearing hearty hugs and congratulations. But in his bizarre haze, he could not feel the vigorous slaps on his back or hear the well wishes. Nay. Only the overwhelming sense of love and pride invaded his soul.

I'm a papa.

* * *

Marisol could not control her body's tremors ushered in by exhaustion and soreness.

Mrs. Barton dabbed a cool, wet cloth to her damp forehead. "Breathe easy, milady. You did fine. The babe is a right healthy one. Easy now, milady. Easy now. Good."

Her calming voice soothed like a magical salve, guiding her into repose. The sweet lady tended carefully to her, making her comfortable and dressing her to present to her husband. Old Mrs. Edmonds cleaned and swaddled her babe, quieting the child's cries as she hummed an ancient lullaby. The woman displayed a sharp contrast to the tart, crusty termagant exchanging threats with Blade as he tried to bully his way in during Marisol's delivery.

Her eyes crinkled with her kind smile as she handed Marisol the tiny bundle. "A baby girl, milady."

Marisol gasped, overcome by the precious child. Tears

flowed freely, wetting her cheeks, warm and salty on her lips. She choked on the sheer love wedged in her throat.

"She's perfect."

Mrs. Barton swiped her own tears from her face. "Are you ready to receive him, milady?"

"Oh yes, please. Show him in."

Marisol had to giggle as Mrs. Edmonds opened the door and Blade nearly fell on top of her. The old lady harrumphed, hewing a fierce look upon him. He straightened his back and cracked his knuckles. The two glared at one another as he skirted along past her. Once at a safe distance, Blade rushed to Marisol's bedside.

His eyes held wells of concern. "How do you feel, dove?"

All she could muster was a smile. She watched Blade as his gaze landed to the babe in her arms. She offered her to him. "Your daughter."

His lips parted open in awe, and then the dimples, his handsome dimples made their grand appearance. He lowered himself to sit on the bed and, with a tender touch only a new father could have, Blade gathered up his child for the first time.

"She's got your blonde hair and green eyes."

"She's so . . . beautiful. Just like you."

Blade stared at their infant as though she was the most priceless treasure under the noble moon and regal stars. And, to Marisol and her captain, indeed she was.

He bent down and pressed a long, devoted kiss to her brow. "I love you, Marisol."

"And I love you, Tyburn." She put a hand on his knee and gripped tight.

"Make room, you old fool."

At the door, four men jostled to get a peek inside. Henri shoved Drake aside. "Blast ya!"

"Sam, ya big beast," Willie wailed. "Get off me toes!"

"Shush. You'll scare t'e babe," Sam scolded.

The spectacle unfolded into quite an amusing sight. Who would have thought fearsome pirates could have so soft a heart?

Mrs. Edmonds trained a plea on Marisol, but Marisol grinned and nodded. "Let them in, Mrs. Edmonds."

The midwife frowned. "Of course, milady." She rolled her eyes and gave the motley bunch of buccaneers a stern warning.

"If any of you dolts causes that child to cry, I'll have you all gelded. Mark me, lads."

"Yes, ma'am." They all agreed together, perhaps a bit uneasy at Mrs. Edmonds' caveat.

Each man bowed their heads and they entered the room. And each man Marisol found adorable. Willie straightened his jacket and flattened down his hair with a bit of spit in his palm. Drake removed his hat and offered a gentleman's bow. Sam wore a lopsided grin, blushing. And Henri, dear Henri, reached up to tighten the tiny red ribbons decorating his wiry beard.

Blade affectionately shook his head. Seeing his good friends gathered around him made Marisol beam with delight. The men "oohed" and "aahed" over the babe deep in slumber. Blade's happiness and pride etched across his charming face. It had been a wonderful moment for him. For Marisol, she wouldn't have wanted it any other way. Even the midwives standing silently in the corner were swept up in the emotional mood.

He stood with their peaceful child, gently rocking her. "Fellas, it is with great joy that I present to you my daughter, Lucilla."

Blade peered down at Marisol, brightness bespangling in his eyes, and waited. An unexpected tear stole down her cheek. She smiled at the beautiful name he'd given their daughter.

Smitten, Blade whispered, "Lucilla, my little light."

WANT MORE?

Not ready to trim the sails and head for shore just yet? Stay the course with more from the **Romancing The Pirate** series.

Bring Me the Horizon

Blood And Treasure

Beneath the Water's Edge

A Kiss in the Wind

The Siren's Song

Mutiny of the Heart

To find out about other books by Jennifer Bray-Weber or to be alerted to new releases, sign up for her quarterly newsletter at www.jbrayweber.com.

ABOUT THE AUTHOR

Jennifer Bray-Weber has always wished for real life to mimic fantastical tales of adventure, especially those of the high seas. Holding two degrees, one in music and video business, the other in liberal arts, she continued her higher education, that is, until a professor challenged her to further express her creative talents and write a novel. Never one to back down from a dare, her passion led her to write stories of pirates and becoming an award-winning, multi-published author of steamy historical romance. Aside from writing, reading or researching, she enjoys the beach, traveling, loud music, shopping, fishing, tattoos, scrapbooking, and horses.

Though she hopes to one day live out her life as an island goddess somewhere in the Caribbean, Jennifer currently lives in her native state of Texas with her husband and two daughters.

For more information on Jennifer and her upcoming releases, please visit her website at www.jbrayweber.com.

Made in the USA
Monee, IL
01 December 2021